# THE BISHOP'S SECRET

# THE BISHOP'S SECRET

### A.E. Nielsen

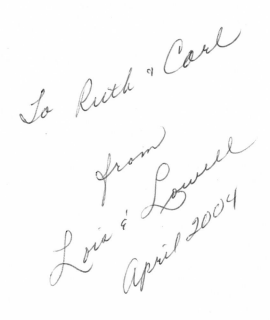

To Ruth & Carl

from

Lois & Lowell

April 2004

iUniverse, Inc.

New York  Lincoln  Shanghai

# The Bishop's Secret

iUniverse, Inc.

For information address:
iUniverse, Inc.
2021 Pine Lake Road, Suite 100
Lincoln, NE 68512
www.iuniverse.com

This is a work of fiction. Other than those well-known places and events referred to for purposes incidental to the plot, all names, places, characters, and incidents are either the product of the author's imagination or are used fictitiously, and any resemblance to actual events, locales, or persons, living or dead, is entirely coincidental. While I have attempted to write with accuracy about the history and conditions in Liberia, and use real place names in most instances, the reader is urged to learn more by using the resources available.

ISBN: 0-595-28802-2 (pbk)
ISBN: 0-595-65872-5 (cloth)

Printed in the United States of America

# ACKNOWLEDGEMENTS

Working on the staffs of Lutheran bishops Robert Miller, Stanley Olson and the late Carl W. Segerhammar provided extensive exposure and valuable experience without which I could not have written this novel. Supporters of the Lutheran Church in Liberia provided valuable information about the African setting, and stimulation to advocate for peace and justice.

The excellent Santa Barbara Adult Education classes and the related "Write and Critique" groups taught me the basics of novel writing and helped me hone the text. The Santa Barbara, Los Angeles and San Diego Writers Conferences deepened my understanding of the process, from idea to publication.

Many friends and family members read early drafts, gave me helpful suggestions, and promised to buy copies. Steven Bender, golf mate and imagicsoftware.com guru, provided the cover design and computer consultation. The staff at iUniverse.com helped me find my way from manuscript to published novel, and stimulated me to start the next book.

My wife, Marylin, to whom I am especially grateful, patiently watched my struggles, and gave me encouragement to publish—now. To each and all, I thank you for helping to make this possible.

# PREFACE

Keeping secrets about sex makes trouble for anyone, especially clergy. Living with deception drains our energy and cheats our loved ones. Whether we live by a set of internal values or respond to cultural pressures, living as a person of complete integrity calls for more than most of us can muster.

Living daily with clergy and their families taught me about the temptations, failures, triumphs, and coping mechanisms used to survive in a culture of constant scrutiny. For all of us, clergy or laity, believer or non-believer, there is more than enough challenge to go around. Looking at ourselves with honesty reveals both the gifts and flaws shared by every human, Lutheran or not.

The persons depicted in this novel are representative of some, but not all Lutheran Christians. Because of my background in the Evangelical Lutheran Church in America, I have drawn on the procedures and issues most familiar to me, but no inference should be made about how that particular church body carries out its ministries.

Over 65,000,000 persons claim to be "Lutheran" worldwide, with churches in Africa growing the most rapidly, especially in Madagascar, Namibia and Nigeria. We are a fascinating mixture of pious fundamentalists and radical liberals, and everything in between. We claim allegiance to scripture and many of Martin Luther's theological teachings, but we interpret them through different lenses. So, we sometimes behave like cousins with the same last name but little else in common.

Some of us drink beer; some of us drink fine wines. Many of us drink coffee; some of us drink nothing stronger than milk or water. A few of us even look and act like the residents of Garrison Keillor's Lake Woebegone.

Lutherans permit clergy to be married, value education and social services, and call ourselves "evangelical," meaning we proclaim the good news about God's gracious love and invite others to share in it. We are "liturgical" like Episcopalians and Roman Catholics, but many congregations offer free form worship with bands instead of organs.

Our authority structure lives somewhere between centralized and dispersed, and we claim to live in tension between law and gospel. As Trinitarian (traditionally naming God as Father, Son and Holy Spirit) Christians, we tend to emphasize the *persona* of Jesus the Christ, but don't ignore Creator and Sustaining Spirit. We cooperate with other faith communions, but have boundaries about when and where.

While some have called for a reorganization of Lutherans, the "Lutheran Church—North America" exists nowhere but in the author's imagination. The year 2000 was chosen for a "reorganization" simply because it fit the structure of the book.

This novel will challenge those who believe there are easy and simple answers to life's complex questions, and give glimpses of ways we can help one another along life's way. I do not intend to preach at anyone in this book, but to entertain, inform, and stimulate conversation. Resources and questions for discussion at the back of the book are offered to those ends. I welcome dialogue through my web site: www.aenielsen.com.

# PROLOGUE

▼

## MAY 1989 MONROVIA, LIBERIA

Jonathan Larsen and Margrethe Christiansen arrived for the opening curtain, still wondering what magic the night held for them. For a month, they'd held back their growing feelings for one another, but felt drawn into a sea of passion when the orchestra played the overture to Puccini's opera, *Turandot*. If Calaf answered Turandot's riddles correctly, she must marry him; if not, he'd lose his head. Unless Margrethe and Jonathan consummated their love, they'd ignite.

"What is born each night and dies at dawn?" Princess Turandot sang.

Prince Calaf's answer to the operatic riddle matched Jonathan's desire: "Hope is born each night and dies at dawn."

Princess Turandot looked upset, but continued her questioning. "What flickers red and warm like a flame, yet is not fire?"

Margrethe seemed pleased when Jonathan whispered in her ear, "The warmth in my heart, and the touch of your hand."

Calaf sang, "Blood flickers red but is not fire." The subjects murmured, having heard two right answers. No one had ever correctly answered both.

Turandot appeared as nervous as Jonathan felt, with one riddle to go. If Calaf answered it correctly, he would live, and the princess had no choice but to marry him. "What is like ice but burns?"

Jonathan decided to risk another whisper. "Me in a freezer thinking of you in my arms." Margrethe smiled and squeezed his hand, but put a finger to his lips.

On stage, silence hung like a bank of storm clouds. Calaf paused, then raised his head, smiled with triumph, and declared, "Turandot!" The subjects rejoiced over the right answers, but Turandot froze with fear at the thought of marrying Calaf.

As Margrethe and Jonathan listened to the music, love hung in the glance between them, knowing they shouldn't share it. Yet, desire drew their hands together in a way that felt as sexual as lying skin to skin. Their penetrating gaze shut out the opening notes of the magnificent aria, *"Nessun Dorma,"* "no sleeping."

The soaring final phrase, *"Vincero, Vincero, Vincero,"* "I will win, win, win," declared Calaf's confidence about conquering Turandot's fear and hatred of men. Margrethe's firm squeeze of Jonathan's hand and gentle kiss on his cheek aroused confidence in him, too.

When Calaf finally forced a kiss on the icy Princess, they watched her melt into his arms, then lead him to her father, the emperor, where she introduced Calaf as *"Amor."* The majestic ending lifted Margrethe and Jonathan off their seats with the audience, wanting to sing along. *"Vincero!"* From the day they met, something mysterious had connected them with a force beyond their comprehension, beyond resistance.

When they arrived at Margrethe's apartment after the opera, they couldn't speak. Their pent up feelings exploded in deep kisses and passionate embraces, alternating with tender touches and nervous glances.

"We shouldn't be doing this," Margrethe whispered.

"I know," Jonathan sighed, but he didn't stop.

Boundaries and questions and craziness wove their way into the wonder of what was happening—what they wanted to happen—what they feared would happen. Danger and opportunity combined to give them the exciting signal of urgency.

Their clothing and moral values fluttered to the floor, all barriers discarded, leaving nothing between them but their love. Throughout the night, wrapped in one another's bodies and twisted sheets, they played out the ritual of arousal. The organic union of their souls sent music soaring in every bone and muscle. *Nessun dorma, amor, vincero.*

Their lovemaking drove them to exhaustion; still, they awakened one another in the night for more. They floated on feathery clouds of delight, yet cringed before the thundering approach of Jonathan's departure.

The next morning, as Margrethe drove Jonathan to the airport, the humid air seemed light in comparison to the heaviness of their feelings about parting. She stepped back from their farewell embrace, tears streaming down her cheeks. "We can never speak again. You must go back to your wife and the church, and I must care for children at the hospital. Just because we're soul mates doesn't mean we can be life mates."

Jonathan walked toward the plane, turned, and said, "Hide me somewhere in the corner of your heart, and always keep our love alive." He knew Margrethe was right, though—he could never tell anyone of their love without threatening his marriage and career as a pastor.

# CHAPTER 1

▼

## MARCH 2002 ANAHEIM HILLS, CALIFORNIA

About the time the California Angels played their home opener, I started thinking about the bishop riddle. How can one flawed leader guide a bunch of independent thinkers to a lofty goal? Mike Scioscia tried it as manager of the Angels. Could I do it in the Southern California-Hawaii Diocese? I'd wondered about it—on and off—since I turned fourteen.

Phones ring all the time in a pastor's office. Shirlee, my secretary, said we ought to wear wireless headsets just so we'd have time to go to the bathroom. So, I didn't think anything about it when a call interrupted my reverie about home runs and bishops.

"This is Pastor Larsen." Someone said they wanted me to interview for bishop. I went into a kind of stupor, jotted a few words on my note pad, and hung up. The aroma of jasmine seeped in the open window like an anesthetic. In my dream state, I saw a tall, handsome man bow his head to receive a symbol of the revered office. A gold pectoral cross on a heavy matching chain slid over his head, onto his neck. A far-off voice intoned, "Bishop Larsen, you are commissioned to serve God and humanity from henceforth."

My secretary tapped on the door, bringing me back to reality. "She said she was calling for the nominating committee. I assume it's for bishop, not for governor."

I felt a wave of guilt. Shirlee looked like she'd lost her husband. "Yes, they want me to interview," I said.

"Alright then, I guess I'll look into retiring." She spun around and left my office.

"Wait." I followed her. "I haven't decided to do it, and even if I do…"

"They want you. You'll do it. Now go tell Kim."

I never argued with Shirlee. I'd tried a few times and lost. "Okay, call me at home if you need me."

As I pulled in the drive, the garage door opener refused to work—one more thing needing attention. When my father-in-law offered, no, insisted on helping us buy this "four bedroom terra cotta ranch with red tile roof and ocean view in the best hilltop subdivision," I wasn't convinced—too elitist for my taste. Nine years later, motors stopped running, windows refused to open, and the air conditioner demanded replacement. Even great looking houses had flaws, just like humans.

I changed clothes and wandered barefoot through my small vegetable garden toward the back corner of our lot. Over the cinder block wall, I could see a green and gold canyon dotted with eucalyptus and chaparral—a tranquil scene. Dressed in my favorite baggy shorts and red Angels' tee shirt, I didn't feel much like a potential bishop, nor did I feel at peace.

Much as I loved the rhythms of ministry, from preaching and singing the liturgy at worship to visiting the homebound, I needed time and space to get away alone, a place to keep in balance. So, when we'd moved to our home, I'd staked out a private spot behind the garage and set up an aluminum-framed chaise under a shady and messy Monterrey pine. I'd christened the hideaway, "Sacred Space."

The opportunity to interview excited me, but what pumped dread through my system involved an old deception. I'd planted a secret seed deep in the darkness of my soul thirteen years earlier. The bright light of exposure as a bishop's candidate might cause the seed to sprout, leaving me with an ugly plant to explain to my wife and church authorities. That's why I shivered, even on a warm March day in Orange County, California.

The aging chaise groaned when I sat down. I did too. I raised my chest and shoulders, took a deep cleansing breath, and blew out as much tension as possible. I hoped for a breeze and inspiration from God.

No time. When I heard Kim's Miata purr into our driveway, I knew she'd be slipping through the gate within seconds. I met her on the patio, where she warmed my heart with a kiss, as always.

"Hey, you're home early." She dropped into a chair. My wife could have been an actress. Flying down the freeway in her sporty red convertible, top down, wearing designer sunglasses and flowing scarf, heads turned to see if she might be Meg Ryan. A typical southern Californian with Danish heritage, her brilliant blue eyes and pug nose highlighted an oval face. Short natural blonde hair surrounded the one thing she complained about in her appearance: small ears; not tiny, but smaller than she wanted to show anyone. Bright, expressive, and self-confident, she'd chosen to be a teacher, because she wanted to be of use to society, and figured a man studying to become a pastor wouldn't marry an actress. I did, eighteen years ago.

She usually left school at four. I rarely made it home before six. That day seemed different, in more ways than clocks or calendars could calculate. Her comment about my early homecoming begged the question, "Why?"

I felt a lump growing in my throat. "They want me to interview for bishop."

Of the dozens of possible candidates, they recommended five or six to the convention. I felt honored. Not every diocese would interview a person of color. Like Kim, my heritage came from Danes, except for my Liberian grandmother. My cocoa colored skin left no doubt about the African genes.

Kim jumped out of the chair and wound her arms around my neck. "It's about time. You'll do it, won't you?" She'd made no secret of her enthusiasm when they asked me to run years before, but I'd been in Liberia on sabbatical, and the time didn't seem right.

I always probed every choice, taking much too long for her. "I might, but…"

"No 'buts'. You're tall dark and handsome and I'm short blonde and beautiful. What more could they want?" She hopped on decisions and expected fast answers.

"I have some concerns." She looked flushed, and not as interested as I thought she would be. "Are you okay?"

"Yes. Not really. I left school early because I don't feel too well. I think I've got spring fever." She laughed.

I moved to her and put my arms around her. "You go lie down. I'll make some dinner."

"I want to know why you're concerned about interviewing."

"It'll wait." The jangling phone interrupted our embrace.

When the ringing stopped, we heard the answering machine pick it up, and then a voice I didn't want to hear. "Jonathan, this is Peter Bloch. Call me right away."

We stood in silence, holding one another, until Kim said, "I'll go lie down. Call Pete."

\*     \*     \*     \*

Pete knew. Thirteen years ago, I'd needed a confidant. If I remembered, he did. Pete never forgot anything.

When I called, his voice sounded harsh, as always. "I hear you got asked to interview."

"Word gets around."

"I think we ought to talk. In person."

"What about?" I knew all too well.

"About the interview. We're the two most likely to get elected—unless Beverly Davidson gathers her chicks and scratches out a win." He laughed with his characteristic cackle, loud and grating. Pete didn't like the idea of ordaining women.

"You still don't get it, do you?"

"Get what? I'm joking. I know we're stuck with women pastors. Doesn't mean we can't kid about it."

I didn't feel like kidding. "How's Wanda?" Kim and I liked her a lot, but we hadn't seen either of them except at conventions since our move from San Diego to Anaheim Hills nine years ago.

"She's fine." Nothing more. He moved on to his agenda. "I want you to meet me for lunch in San Clemente tomorrow."

Talking with Pete made me feel edgy. I didn't appreciate his superior attitude toward women, and almost everyone else for that matter. He never asked people, he told them what to do. He had cut his teeth on church politics, having grown up as a bishop's son, but sometimes, it seemed like he flunked Basic Human Sensitivity 101.

During the time Pete and I had both served congregations in San Diego, we'd developed a relationship around three things: tennis, global mission, and Charger football. He'd spent time as a missionary in Japan, while I'd focused on Liberia. Tailgating and rooting for the Chargers gave us an excuse to act like friends. He played tennis like a war game.

When I confided in him back then, after a couple of beers I didn't need, his reaction troubled me. "The world might not notice, but the church makes a big deal out of things like that. If it ever gets out..." We hadn't discussed it again, and I didn't want to open the topic on the phone. I felt like Pete had me in handcuffs, dangling a key that looked like a giant cross. I agreed to lunch.

       ✱        ✱        ✱        ✱

Kim and I ate breakfast early to give us time to talk before we left for the day. I poured us each another cup of coffee before we walked out onto the patio. She said she felt fine, so I didn't ask her if she planned to see the doctor, figuring she'd tell me when she wanted me to know more. She always did, but I couldn't help but wonder.

She inhaled and looked out over the canyon. "I love spring." It gave her an excuse to plant pansies in the front yard. Blooming plants and an interview for bishop seemed to fit the season.

Kim jumped in where we'd left off before we fell asleep. "If you're worried about all the traveling and long hours, forget it. I can adjust to it in the region, uh, synod…What do we call it now?"

"Diocese."

"Yeah, that. Why diocese again?" I'd explained it more than once, and didn't feel like an excursion into the history of Lutheran reorganization, but she stared at me, waiting for an answer.

"We didn't want to confuse the other Lutherans who call them synods or districts. We decided to use the Catholic and Episcopal terminology. They've used 'diocese' for a long time."

"Okay, bishop of the diocese not the synod, not the district, but the diocese…" Her singsong voice made me smile. She turned serious. "And now they've asked you to run for bishop and you have some concerns about me and how I'll handle it."

"Yeah. Well, I'm sure you'd adjust, but…"

"But what?"

"But everybody has some things in their past they don't want uncovered." I hated glittering generalities, but I didn't feel ready to get specific.

"Sure we do. So what's the big deal?"

"Bishops sit under a bigger microscope than pastors. So do their wives. You want to live with constant exposure?"

"Why are you asking this now? You've wanted to be a bishop ever since I can remember. Your Dad's wanted it for you since we were confirmed. I've wanted it since you got ordained. I still wish you had run the first time."

"Yes, but…"

"Then just do it." She headed for the kitchen, spilling coffee on the way. "Time to leave for school."

I followed her for my usual good-bye kiss. "We'll talk more tonight?"

"Sure," she said, "but I think you know what you've got to do."

*     *     *     *

On the way to meet Pete for lunch, I drove past the tennis club where Kim and I played now and then at sunrise. I thought about the San Diego days when I played in a church league, often against Pete. He played tennis like he spoke his mind: bold, precise and predictable. Thinning red hair, athletic build, and wearing his years well, I admired his stature if not his attitudes.

The restaurant sat on a cliff overlooking the Pacific Ocean, not far from what had been Richard Nixon's estate. Pete and I joined a dozen or so other diners gathered for the day's special, fresh sea bass. The aroma of garlic insinuated its way into the room. Blue linen tablecloths matched the sail covers on boats anchored in the marina. Under other circumstances, I'd have enjoyed the setting.

"You're a bright young man, Jon, and could make a pretty good bishop someday, but I'm going to give you a list of reasons not to run." I hated lists—and lectures. He reminded me of my dad: always right, and ready to hit me on the nose with a rule. "One, you hate conflict. Two, you don't like being away from Kim, and I hear you're hoping to adopt a child. Worse, you're too liberal, and fourth, for good measure, you're too damn good looking." He cackled.

My niece called me a "hot guy." She'd heard her Aunt Michelle describe Sidney Portier as "hot," and decided I looked like him after she'd watched an old movie. My black curly hair showed a little gray at the temples and my blue eyes surprised people, but I liked the compliment. "Well, what you say may be accurate, Pete..."

"Peter."

"Okay—Peter." I wondered when he'd started using his formal name. Maybe when he'd been asked to be a candidate for bishop? "I know some would prefer not to vote for a person with Liberian ancestry."

"Yes, but being black—well, sort of—doesn't disqualify you, even if it does bother some people. I don't think folks in the diocese see you as African American, though. Growing up in the Danish capital of California didn't exactly give you first hand connection to black power."

True, I'd grown up in the mostly white small town of Solvang, and suffered less discrimination than many others. I cherished my Danish and Liberian heritage, and contrary to his opinion, I knew my skin color served as a symbol for many of our African American members, and to others whose skin didn't classify as white. "California hasn't had a person of color as bishop in years."

"I'd forgotten about him, but he was black, and you're..." He trailed off before using the cookie term I'd jumped him about years before.

"You were telling me why I shouldn't interview."

"Yes, I was. You're more a mystic than a scholar. Along with Martin Luther, you're always talking about your great Danish hero, Grundtvig."

"N.F.S. Grundtvig, Bishop of Copenhagen, writer of hymns and founder of folk schools, died 1872." I never let him forget that good theology didn't end with Luther's death.

"As I recall, he's the one who said he was human first, and Christian second, and got in trouble with the authorities." He had a sarcastic way of describing things.

"Among other things. He also taught us to live with joyful gusto, and to sing and dance to express our faith. You might try it sometime." I couldn't resist. Peter treated religious rituals like dusty relics needing protection.

"Even if some people still can't handle their racism, I think we're more ready for you than for Beverly as bishop."

"Racism and sexism live in all of us. The more we deny it, the more power it has over us. You think Bev can't win?"

"Yes, but good a pastor as she is, she doesn't stand a chance against..."

"Against you?"

"Did I say that?"

"You've been running ever since the church reorganized." I smiled as I spoke, but meant it.

"Not true. I just do my job. And we don't 'run' for bishop, we 'respond to the call.'"

"Whatever, Pete—uh—Peter. You're a good pastor and a solid scholar. You'll probably be elected. But, we still haven't talked about the biggest reason we're here today." The sea bass did flip-flops in my stomach, and my fork danced in my fingers. I didn't want to hear what he'd say, but I knew if I didn't bring it up, I'd leave worse off than when I came.

"You deceived the church." He smirked as he said it, and then stood up.

"Yes, and you know what about." He didn't know I hadn't told Kim everything about what happened in Liberia.

He smiled his "gotcha" smile, stood beside me, and put his hand on my shoulder. I felt patronized. "You lied to the church by withholding information. If you tell the committee and they want to nominate you anyway, then you'll still have to face the convention. If I were you, I wouldn't even think of running. If you do, remember, you can't hide forever."

Lunch over, conversation complete, Peter waved his white napkin in front of my face like a signal I should surrender. He strode off, leaving the check for me to pay.

When the rumor river first flowed with my name for bishop, I knew I wanted the office. Leadership came naturally: preaching and teaching, too. I kept up with most of the latest research, though Peter was right about my being more mystic than scholar. I found most doctrines too limiting for the Cosmic God. I preferred probing and embracing the awesome mysteries to boxing up and protecting them. I dreamt of leading the diocese in a spirituality of compassion, exposing issues like hunger and AIDS to the healing light. But, Peter Bloch held the power to destroy my dream.

# CHAPTER 2

▼

Driving up the "slow and go" freeway intensified my frustration with Peter. When I reached my office, I tried to re-focus on the congregation.

"Shirlee?" My secretary had stepped out. I sat down and stared at the telephone. Yesterday afternoon, I'd heard a voice on the other end of the line invite me to open a door to uncertainty. I re-read my notes from the conversation: "Nominee for bishop—Interview Saturday 10 a.m.—Diocesan office."

I remember feeling fear, excitement, and confusion. At the bottom of the pad, among some doodles, I'd written, "I'll be there." A day later, I wondered if I could go through with it.

I loved parish ministry, and had settled into a comfortable pattern. Maybe too comfortable. After the first six months of convincing the mostly white conservative congregation I didn't plan to change their skin color or their politics, we began to grow. They liked my enthusiasm and energy. We went from stagnant to stimulating.

When I sat in my cozy office looking out at the green hills, I felt like I'd been sculpted into a work of art. I looked long and hard at the blooming tulip tree outside my open window, and closed my eyes for a few seconds to rehearse the years at Lutheran Church of Anaheim Hills.

Shirlee didn't let me get lost in space for long when she stormed in from wherever she'd gone. I'd left her hanging the day before. "They're going to take you away from us, aren't they?"

"Well, no, they're just asking to interview me. Besides, everybody's talking about Peter Bloch for bishop."

"You'll win, and then you'll leave us and this congregation'll go to hell in a hand basket. Who's Peter Bloch? And you're saying 'well' a lot again."

"Well—uh—sorry." I moved my still athletic body out of the leather chair, held out my arms and used my most persuasive voice. "Shirlee, don't look at me like that. You know I can't stand it when you're upset. You're supposed to take care of me and keep me happy."

"Don't try to schmooze me." She sounded more sad than mad. She looked like Lily Tomlin and matched her age. I towered over her by at least a foot, but she'd become larger than life in our years of working together.

"Okay, so what's the worst that can happen? I go interview—they like me— the convention votes—Peter gets elected—I'm relieved—and—you get to boss me around for another ten years."

"Who bosses whom here?" She pointed at the wall. "Look around you. You got me to line up your thousand books alphabetically by author, you made me hang seascapes and dream catchers on your wall, and you convinced me to order a brand new leather chair for you just last month. I do whatever you ask."

"Of course you do, and I ask only what you've already told me." She humphed and started away. "Why are you so upset?"

"You're going to leave all this?" She had a point. Shirlee brought sweet-smelling flowers every day and organized the messes on my desk whenever I left for five minutes. She knew my habits and covered my failings. I didn't like the thought of working without her. She started to dab at her eyes, almost knocking off her glasses. "You can't take Kim away from us."

"Oh well, so much for my ego." When push came to shove, she might allow me to go, but let me take away the children's choir director, and there'd be hell to pay. My wife loved the kids, and their parents raved about Kim.

I knew I'd get no work done that afternoon. "I'm not taking anybody away from anywhere. I'm going home to think about this some more." I picked up my cell phone from the desk. "Call me if there's an emergency. And pray for me."

"Yeah, I'll pray all right, but not the way you think." Shirlee had once said, "Prayer is what you do when you can't get your own way."

*     *     *     *

I wanted some time to reflect before Kim came home. The Sacred Space invited me to lay back and meditate, inhaling the spirit of God.

"Remember your creator in the days of your youth, before the days of trouble come..." The memory verse from my confirmation class wiggled its way into awareness. My Danish Lutheran dad had insisted I use the quote from scripture to remind me, as he said then, "to avoid hubris and appreciate the wonder of God." I didn't know hubris from anything at age fourteen, and God seemed like a complete mystery, so the verse hadn't meant much at the time.

Getting confirmed required eighty Wednesday night classes during seventh and eighth grades, plus a week at summer camp. The church ritual signaled my agreement to take responsibility for developing the faith my parents had passed along since my baptism as an infant. The family ritual included a party, with gifts and guests. I liked the camp and party, and lived through the rest, informative as it had been.

About once a month, my parents invited the pastor and his wife for dinner after worship, and on Confirmation Sunday, they had invited the bishop and his wife, too. That's when I'd first learned my father's dream for me.

Dad had cleared his throat. I'd been staring at the Danish apple cake smothered in whipped cream and topped with dollops of current jelly, fantasizing about its first bite. I used my fork to push mashed potatoes and pieces of roast pork around on my plate. While I appreciated the Danish specialties my mother always made, I preferred pizza.

I'd swallowed a bite of creamed peas when Dad's dream punctured my own about savoring the cake. He'd looked at the honored guest and announced, "I hope Jonathan will grow up to be bishop some day."

I couldn't believe what I'd heard, and almost choked. My older sister snorted and my younger one's eyes locked on mine. I had thought about astronaut or forest ranger, but bishop? I looked down at my dark hands sticking out of my white shirt. Cocoa colored skin and fuzzy black hair on a gangly frame didn't fit my image of a Lutheran pastor, let alone a bishop.

My grandmother had jumped into the conversation, as if she wanted the bishop to know what a religious family I came from. "You know, Bishop, my momma gave birth to me in Liberia out in the lush jungle. She died and the Lutheran missionaries plucked me up from the village and took me to the orphanage. Saved my life, they did." I'd hoped she'd keep the bishop's attention on her, not on me. Sure enough, she'd kept telling the story I'd heard a dozen times.

"When I grew up, a handsome Danish missionary came and taught us the Bible and, well, we fell in love and got married, moved to America, and had Rebecca." Mom always fiddled with her hair when Grammom included her in the story. "My late husband, rest his soul, got a job as administrator at the retirement home."

I'd hoped the bishop had forgotten my father's comment by now, but Dad interrupted Grammom. "Jonathan can say the books of the Bible from memory faster than the pastor." Pastor Jensen flushed and shook his head. Dad had set up the contest one day after class, and I'd won a coke.

On that day of confirmation so long ago, I had slid down in my chair a little, wishing I could evaporate. I felt okay about Dad's pride, even for a little thing like a decent memory and glib tongue, but I didn't want to be put on the spot. Mom had rescued me when she offered the bishop some apple cake.

"I'd love some. It looks sinfully delicious." We'd all laughed.

I didn't hear any more about the bishop idea for a long time. However, Dad had kept me humble with the memory verse about "remembering my youth and getting ready for days of trouble," and with his constant demands that I make him proud and "do the right thing."

If I were to do the right thing about interviewing for bishop, I'd need to own up to something I'd put behind me, and face the "days of trouble" that threatened my marriage and career.

Bishops answer to a high authority demanding "no secrets." Nominating committees had a way of asking leading questions. Much as I yearned to be considered, I didn't want to open the place in my heart where I'd planted the secret. When I made the decision thirteen years ago, it seemed right. I thought then I'd be better off by getting counseling than confessing. I didn't want to hurt Kim and risk losing her. My other big mistake involved telling Peter Bloch.

My cell phone startled me. "It's Henry. I want to stop by for a few minutes on my way home."

Two years ago, the Southern California-Hawaii Diocese had called Henry Madison to serve as interim bishop while the new church worked out the kinks.

After years of uncomfortable debates, the Lutheran Church had reorganized for the new millennium by agreeing to disagree about sexuality and authority issues, among other things.

Henry and I had become well acquainted when he and his wife had settled in Anaheim, and joined our congregation. He'd told me at the time he chose Anaheim because he could walk to Edison Field to watch the Angels, and his grandchildren could get to Disneyland and Knott's Berry Farm without driving on freeways. Coming out of retirement to serve as bishop cut into his time at the ballpark.

I walked and talked my way to the patio. "Sure, come on by. I'm pondering."

"I thought you would be. I knew the committee called you yesterday. Be there shortly."

\*          \*          \*          \*

Kim came through the gate as I clicked off. She gave me the usual kiss hello and we sat down. "Henry's stopping by," I said. "Wants to talk about the nomination, I guess. How're you feeling?"

"Better than yesterday. I'm fine. Don't worry about me. I'm still wondering, though, why you need to bring up junk from the past?"

"If I don't, I'll violate my most basic value." I tried to keep my voice calm, but my stomach churned.

"There's something you want more than being bishop?"

"There's something I want to be, whether or not I'm bishop, but especially if I'm elected."

"What?"

I hesitated. "Transparent." I didn't know where the word came from; somewhere in the murky mush of my brain. As soon as the word came out of my mouth, though, I knew it was the right one, even if I couldn't define it with precision. Up until now, I'd been able to skim along, not worrying about my deception, but transparency demanded action.

"Transparent? You want to be Mr. Cellophane Man? So people can see right through you like you're not even there?

"No, but 'Cellophane Man' is a great song." I hummed a bar, but she didn't smile.

"Do you want to be transparent like the emperor's new clothes?"

"No, transparent like in 'nothing to hide.' It's something I learned from Grammmom, mostly from watching her. Wherever she went, people saw the same person: no deception. People said they always knew she'd be straight with them. She'd say, 'I am who I am.' We should have put that on her grave stone." The words poured out of me as if a muse were dictating. "That's what I want; that kind of transparency."

Kim shook her head as if she still didn't understand, when the doorbell rang. She held out her hands like she wanted me to get it.

"Probably Henry," I said, more sure than ever about needing—but not wanting—to confess to both of them.

*     *     *     *

I walked around the side of the house, where small rocks on the path pressed against my bare feet, reminding me of penitents walking over hot coals. I found a smiling Bishop Henry Madison standing at the front door, dressed in his clerical suit. "Hey, Henry, come around back."

Henry stooped when he walked, partly from arthritis, and partly from the burden of his office. I envied his silver hair, and wondered how long it would take me to develop worry lines like his across the forehead.

Kim hugged Henry. "I'm putting cookies in the oven." She disappeared into the kitchen, leaving us to talk alone. He started before I had a chance to say a word.

"Jon, I want you to accept nomination for bishop. The church doesn't allow sitting bishops to publicly endorse candidates, but nobody can tell me not to encourage you in private. You're the best candidate for the office."

I loved hearing him say that—down to the calluses on my feet. I needed his affirmation, and wanted to hear his reasons, but something else demanded attention. "Thanks, Henry, but I've got some reservations."

"Don't tell me about them, Jon. We've all got them. If the church just chose leaders who had no reservations, demagogues'd lead us." He took a deep breath. "You're the most balanced guy I know. You're smart but not stuffy. You're passionate without being radical. And, you're a great visual symbol for our diversity in the diocese."

I liked his reasons, but the old secret gnawed a hole in my satisfaction. "Thank you, but there's something I should have told you before. It's a matter of integrity."

"Don't tell me any more. You can tell the nominating committee whatever you must when they interview you."

I could imagine headlines on the web site announcing to the entire diocese that a bishop's candidate confessed to deceiving the church about a thirteen year-old secret. Most of them would yawn. The rest would demand to know all the spicy details. Kim would…I didn't want think about it.

"By the way, Jon, I know you and Peter Bloch are old tennis buddies from San Diego days, so he probably called and told you he's already accepted nomination."

"Yes, he did."

"Beverly Davidson accepted, too. She's a great candidate, and we've elected some good women bishops across the country. As for Peter, he's smart, experienced, biblically solid, and says, 'Yes, but...' much too often."

"I just assumed Peter would be elected. His experience and age..."

Henry held up his hand and turned to go. "Never assume, Jon. You know what that does."

We walked toward the kitchen door. "What's it like, Henry, serving as bishop? From what I've seen of your schedule, I don't know why anybody would want the job."

"You've got to want it for the right reasons. There's plenty not to like. You get to work fifteen hours a day, six or seven days a week, drive 3,000 miles a month, and sit in airports for hours." He sighed again.

"I know the traveling must be tough. I'm more curious about how you're received. Some pastors I meet with don't have much good to say about headquarters and bishops, even though they all seem to like you personally."

"Pastors and church members have an ambivalent relationship with their bishop. They respect the position, but have reservations about the authority of the office. They want their bishop to be a source of support, and a disciplinarian—preferably against others."

I laughed. On his way through the house, Kim pressed two giant chocolate chip cookies and a napkin into his hand. "Something for the road," she smiled, "and pick up some flowers for Priscilla on the way home. Women like that." Kim organized everyone, including the two of us.

So much for transparency. Even Henry didn't want to know.

# CHAPTER 3

▼

I headed outside to pull some radishes for dinner. About the time I picked up a plastic bucket, I heard three dings. Our neighbors, Andrea and Brent Goldman, had mounted a brass ship's bell near our fence so we'd know when they planned to peek over.

"We just picked up some fresh clams. Come on over for a glass of wine. Watch the Angels play somebody—they're on the East coast somewhere."

About once a week, we'd get together, swap stories about living in Orange County, and watch sports or play pinochle. I'd transferred my loyalty from San Diego to Anaheim, but neither team had been doing much to hold my interest since the Padres lost the World Series to the Yankees in 1998.

I sipped the gold Sauvignon Blanc and scooped another clamshell clean. "Want to be a sounding board for us?"

Kim glared at me. Did she mean to watch my diet or shut my mouth about "junk from the past" as she'd called it?

"Sure, what's up?" Andrea always took the lead. Some might call her a "femnazi" because she stood up for the poor and oppressed and made sure power people heard from her, but her arguments always come from compassion.

Kim blurted the news before I could do my usual "background, introduction, main point" presentation. "Jon's been asked to run for bishop."

"No shit!" Their expletives erupted simultaneously. We laughed, knowing they tried hard never to use that kind of language around their kids or us. Their reaction moved us from bishop talk to baseball, until the clamshells sat there empty.

"Mike Scioscia's the man. He'll get the Angels into the series this year," I said.

"Yeah, and Gene Autrey will ride back from heaven on Champion, too." Brent didn't share my optimism. I'd admired Scioscia as the Dodger's catcher in the nineteen eighties and early nineties, and he'd made a credible start as the Angel's manger the last two seasons. I wondered if I'd be a credible bishop.

Andrea and Brent had moved into their house a year after we bought ours. Ten years ago, they'd been known as DINKS: double income with no kids. Now, they had three, a boy and two girls. Andrea tele-commuted for her software company job, and Brent worked a straight forty-hour week doing IRS audits. She looked like a young Bette Midler and he resembled a tall Billy Crystal.

I counted Brent as a good confidant when I needed to hear a non-church perspective. As a sometimes-practicing Reform Jew, he provided a sympathetic ear and an understanding heart. Andrea kept us sharp with her "spiritual agnostic" questions.

"Did you get a zap from the committee this month?" Kim asked. We lived in a neighborhood where the homeowner's association officers toured on the first Saturday of each month, calling themselves the "Home Beautification Award Committee." They also passed out "zaps" for lawns cut too seldom or for weeds peeking out of the pebbled path to the side gate. The four of us represented the lone holdouts against hiring a gardener.

"Nope, you?" Andrea had little time for the committee, and neither did Kim.

"Just the usual wave and sicky sweet smile when they walked by. Haven't been zapped since the rains stopped." Kim twirled the last sip of wine in her glass.

I wanted to get back to the bishop topic. "I'm not too concerned about the length of my lawn, but I am uneasy about all the scrutiny we'd get if I interview for bishop. Kim thinks I worry too much."

"You do," Andrea said. "Every time you come over, you're worried about something. Then you go and take care of it and everything turns out okay. Remember when you worried about your "solidarity with the suffering" sermon—including the families of those who'd piloted the planes—after nine-eleven? That worked, didn't it?"

"And your idea for a panel with a Palestinian Christian and a radical Jew like me on it? Your congregation loved it." Brent had done a remarkable job outlining the various Israeli positions.

"He's just worried about some old failures or something. I told him there isn't anything people can't deal with when you give everyone a chance to have their say."

The Goldman kids started asking about dinner, so we got up to leave. Andrea gave me a hug. "What could a nice guy like you have to hide, anyway?"

My drive to be transparent failed its second test, but Kim deserved to hear it one on one anyway.

*       *       *       *

Kim popped some leftovers in the microwave, and we rehashed the interview debate one more time. She kept pressing me about why I felt so reluctant to interview.

"They're asking me to be transparent."

"No, they're not. They're asking you to be their leader. Leaders aren't perfect. And they sure don't go around talking about the past." She seemed so upset, I couldn't tell her what really bothered me. I gave up and watched the rest of the Angels game. They lost.

"Could be another bad year for our team," I moaned. She nodded, but said nothing.

We brushed our teeth in silence, undressed, put our dirty clothes in the hamper, and she started doing her usual make up removal process. I turned down the bedspread and crawled into bed.

Glowing from treating her face to a massage, Kim stood framed in the bathroom door, backlit from the bright lights over the mirror. Her hair sparkled, and an aura surrounded her nude body. Facing me with her arms outstretched, she held a seldom-used flannel nightgown in front of her, as if deciding whether or not to wear it. I wanted her to drop it and come join her body with mine. Instead, she slipped into it and turned out the lights.

For the first time in years, we violated our promise never to go to bed without resolving our differences. Silence ruled. I prayed for strength to see our way through the gloom, reached out, and found her rigid. I didn't sleep much that night.

*       *       *       *

I got up early, determined to find a way through my dilemma. Henry hadn't helped much. Neither had the neighbors. But then, I hadn't let them. I hoped to find some light from my spiritual mentor. When I arrived, Brother David asked me the same question as always: "Who are you today?"

"I'm a child of God, embraced by love, called to serve, speaking the truth in love." Our little ritual, like all rituals, sometimes seemed empty. Most times, though, the simple repetition connected us to the deep places beyond words, transforming the mundane into an encounter with the Divine and each other.

"You look like somebody in a hurry to be someone else."

"Well, I am." I didn't understand how he saw through to my heart so quickly, but he almost always hit the mark. "They've asked me to interview for bishop. And, the front running candidate knows I've deceived the church authorities."

"That would be Peter Bloch." As an Anglican, Brother David didn't know all the area clergy, but he'd led retreats for many of us, and Peter had a reputation beyond Lutheran circles. "He'd want you to tell the committee, I imagine."

"He as much as told me to withdraw. Said my secret was more than the church could handle."

"You want to tell the committee, but you don't want to hurt Kim, and you're wondering if Peter is right."

Kim and I had put our debate on hold during breakfast. She'd wanted some space, so I'd called Brother David for an appointment. I'd visited him several times a year for the last fifteen years, first in San Diego, and then in Malibu when he transferred. He and Peter—no one else—knew what happened during my sabbatical in Liberia.

Brother David looked like Ichabod Crane: tall, skinny, sparse hair, protruding ears and large nose. The dark brown robe flopped on his bony body like strips of cloth on a scarecrow. When he spoke with his gentle bass and offered a firm handshake, though, any apprehension about appearance evaporated.

Even the room where we met carried a feeling of gentleness, decorated in soft earth tones with Navajo blankets on the walls, and deep pile carpeting for our bare feet. The first time I came, he had told me going bare-foot signaled respect for "place." He'd called it "holy ground." Dad had never said those words, but I caught the same idea from him in his gardens.

From Brother David's window, we could see the sun glistening on Pacific breakers, with tiny surfing figures waiting to catch a ride.

"You've never told Kim or your parents about what happened in Liberia?"

"No. I started to tell Kim and Bishop Madison, but something stopped me. I'd never tell Dad. For years, he's had a dream that I'd be bishop, and he's taught me to always do the right thing. His weak heart couldn't stand it."

"How about your mother?"

"She'd cry. Then she'd hug me and tell me to work it out. Mom's always been the one I could talk to, but I know it would upset her. She loves Kim like her own daughters and would feel terrible if I hurt her."

"Have you considered turning down the interview?"

"Well, yes. I don't want Kim and everyone else to get hurt. Or for the diocese to get into a big argument over whether a thirteen-year-old deception should be enough to kill my candidacy."

"Would it?"

"Maybe. Some people, maybe most, could ignore it, but with the heat generated lately in the Catholic Church about cover-ups, I think revealing a deception could be explosive. Why would they trust someone who violated his covenant with the church?"

"Did you make a covenant to confess every sin, or to live a life worthy of your calling?"

"You know what I mean. If somebody decided to tell…"

"Peter's bound by confidentiality. So am I. So why are you thinking of revealing something that might upset so many people?" Brother David spoke in a gentle voice, but he pierced my soul. I didn't want him to offer anything but transparency.

"I can't believe you'd suggest duplicity."

"Was I? Our choices aren't always between good and evil. Sometimes, no matter what we choose, it's a compromise of one value or another. You have to decide what values are the most important. Sometimes you have to rely on God's grace."

One of the problems with God's grace is how to keep from making it "cheap." For me, keeping a creative tension between "doing the right thing" and "anything goes" made life anything but comfortable. "What about 'cover-up'?"

"The Catholics have discovered how hard it is to balance judgment and acceptance. A religious professional must be held to a high standard, especially with children. Sexual abuse with altar boys is not merely immoral, it's a crime. Such things must not be covered up."

"Well, what about where a crime isn't committed, what then?"

"As people of faith, we feel bound by moral as well as civil law. When a repentant priest confesses to breaking a moral law, the bishop offers forgiveness and, as they say, 'time for amendment of life.' You've repented. Years have passed with no contact. What more do you want to do?"

"Kim says to forget about junk from the past."

"But she doesn't know you were unfaithful, and you feel a need to confess, even if it hurts everyone. Why? Fear of being found out later? Fear of letting down your father?"

"Of course I'm afraid. And, I value transparency above almost everything else."

"Revelation of misdeeds, especially old ones where no victim comes forward, can be more about your need to dump your dirt than living up to a moral standard."

"I came here hoping for a simple answer. Instead you give me…"

"Reality? You'll find your way through this, Jon, but not with easy answers."

I wondered, as I drove away, how I'd fit under the bishop's mantle. Sometimes, I'd fought with the church over its codes and covenants, and sometimes I'd defended them, even helped write some. Sometimes, church regulations overpowered grace and love. Where does one draw the line? I wanted it to be okay for a leader to have vulnerabilities, but religious authorities have a long history of crucifying vulnerable leaders.

I stopped at two hospitals on the way back to the office, checking on my church treasurer's wife and another older woman, both fighting cancer. Bringing a word of hope and a non-anxious presence to the sick and dying gave me overwhelming satisfaction. I didn't see how anything could give a bishop such feelings. Maybe I'd withdraw. After all, if I refused to interview, I'd have no need to confess. Or would I?

# CHAPTER 4

▼

I stopped at the store to pick up steaks and a bottle of Merlot, hoping a barbeque would warm Kim to my irresistible drive for transparency.

While I waited for her to come home, I wandered in the back yard. The rows of new lettuce made me salivate for a bowlful, with cream and sugar on top—one of my favorites from childhood.

Dad taught me about generous sowing of seeds and about thinning and weeding, "So the healthy ones have room to grow." I thought about him every time I preached on the parable of the soils. As bishop, I'd have access to thousands of souls who hungered for a word of compassion and a challenge to sow the seeds of love without regard for the condition of the soil.

Time stood still while I listened for some kind of message from God about confessing. I didn't have long to wait. Kim whooshed into the back yard like an angel, brushing my cheek with a kiss. "What have you decided—and where's the wine—and candles?" My energy disappeared on the canyon breeze and reality took over.

"I haven't set the table yet, but dinner's ready. And I'm leaning toward saying no."

"So, got three good reasons?"

We talked while I poured the wine and she set the table. "Sure. One, I'm positive they'll elect Peter, so there's no point. Second, I don't want to take votes away from Beverly."

"And third?"

"I'd rather not get into an election while we're qualifying for adoption." We'd applied three years earlier, going through all the hoops. The final qualification interview scheduled for mid-summer didn't guarantee a child, simply that we'd be "on the list."

"Let's come back to number three later. You're better than Beverly, and especially Pete. I've seen the twinkle in your eyes when you talk about your vision for the diocese." She paused as if waiting for me to wake up the genie dozing on the table. "And, you've got a fourth reason you're not saying because you know it upsets me."

"Yeah, that too."

I wondered if she'd known for a long time and already forgiven me. Wishful thinking. She didn't hold things back. She would have demanded we go to counseling. If I told her now, either she'd leave me, or we'd need months to work it through. Either way, I couldn't accept the nomination. It wouldn't be right.

Good as the steak and wine tasted, I'd lost my appetite. "It's just all the things I've messed up along the way in my life."

"Like what?"

I knew my decision not to hurt her involved more rationalization than virtue, but maybe Brother David had been right. Telling her and the church about something so long past seemed more like dumping than cleansing. But deception didn't belong in a bishop's baggage, and if I wanted to lead the church to transparency, how could I not come clean?

"Well, sometimes I've had doubts about whether or not I belong in the ministry."

"You're not going to run for bishop because you've had doubts?"

"Doubts, and not always living up to the vows I took to be a model of the godly life."

"For gosh sakes, Jon, your reasons are ridiculous. Nobody's perfect and everybody has doubts. Either you're scared to run, or you're not telling me everything."

A band tightened around my chest. "Let's drop it, okay? I'm scared, yeah, and I don't want to drag us through the pokes and probes of running for bishop."

"You're so damn stubborn." She smiled when she said it.

"Maybe so, but transparency comes before…"

"Me?" She followed me when I headed for the trashcan with my half eaten dinner, and asked, "Are you giving up?"

"Kim, I can't interview. I'm sorry it ever came up." She moved closer.

"Why can't you just tell them you made mistakes long ago but you're perfect now?"

I felt seduced by her smile. "Wouldn't that be just great?"

"You are 'just great,' Jon, and you don't have to interview. But if you don't, you'll always regret it." Her arms slid around my neck and her body pressed hope into mine.

"So how do I tell them without telling them?"

"You'll think of something." Her kiss finished off the discussion and took me to a space where I almost believed her.

"I'll try."

She put her finger to my lips, looking serious. "I went to the doctor on the way home from school."

I felt a twinge. "Why? Oh, from your spring fever episode the other day?"

"Remember I told you I missed my period last time?"

"Yeah, but you're always irregular." Then it hit me. "You aren't *pregnant*?"

She took a deep breath, turned up the corners of her mouth and whispered, "A little bit."

"My God, Kim, how?"

She fell into my arms, tears flowing. "The doctor said it sometimes happens when you stop worrying so much." We'd faced the last miscarriage when we were twenty-nine; the first one three years before.

"Your news makes mine look like nothing. Pregnant! My God!"

"The doctor says I'll need to be careful—even then, it could be dangerous— but they know more now." I felt her uncertainty. We'd talked often about the risks involved.

I kissed her moist cheeks, scared and thrilled at the same time. "We'll do whatever the doctor says."

"Thank you Jon. I want this baby."

"Me too, Kitten, me too."

*     *     *     *

We repeated the usual nighttime rituals of brushing, hamper, and hanging, just as we had so many nights before. However, this time Kim didn't hold up a night-gown or anything else. She stood in the same doorway, but turned out the bath-room lights and instead, carried a candle in each hand. Her body shimmered as she walked toward me and said, "I'm thinking it's time we say thanks to God by making love."

She set one candle on my side of the bed, pausing long enough to bend down for a light kiss, brushing her breasts against my lips. I wanted to reach out and pull her on top of me, but she moved around the bed to her side.

Tennis and teaching kept Kim in great shape, and her sensuality bubbled over whenever she felt the "mommy urge." The first two times she'd gotten pregnant, she'd said, "I want my flat tummy to get huge." It didn't happen, but we knew what we wanted, even if the doctor said the odds were terrible.

She slipped into bed beside me, her warm moistness pressed against my thigh. I'd been so intent on the visual image of a beautiful woman carrying candles, I hadn't noticed the music. Barbara Streisand's voice from the stereo built to a climax, "There's a place for us, a time and place for us…" I caressed her back and bottom, our bodies locked together, and she whispered, "Remember our first time in this house?"

"Oh yeah—toasting with champagne in paper cups 'cuz we couldn't find the glasses—moving boxes everywhere—stretched out on the carpet—no curtains—our neighbors could have enjoyed a drive-by exhibition."

"Love me like you did that night. I want this to be another new start for us."

Any thoughts of transparency and the bishop's office evaporated in the mists of passion.

\*        \*        \*        \*

Early the next morning, I carried my coffee mug and the newspaper to the Sacred Space, settled into the chaise, and read the international summary: "Armed conflict between Liberian government forces and rebels broke out yesterday near Grbanga."

The small West African country of my ancestors became a republic in 1847, modeled after the government of the United States. In 1817, the white American Colonization Society had attempted, not always for altruistic motives, to send emancipated slaves "back home." Early colonies failed, but between 1822 and 1867, more than 13,000 emigrants settled there. They became known as "Americo-Liberians" and held most of the political offices in the new government.

I had visited Phebe Hospital, twelve miles from Grbanga. The summer of 1989 came as close to tranquility as they'd know for many years to come. On Christmas Eve, violence had exploded. An article in the Lutheran Church magazine had carried a story from one of the trainees at the medical center.

"From behind a huge tree, I watched shouting soldiers shoot everyone in sight. Those who could, ran. An older couple helped some of my class mates dodge between huts, and led them toward the jungle. The older woman stumbled and fell, and the man with her stopped, telling the young ones to hurry along. I wanted to help the older couple but my legs wouldn't move. The gunfire got closer and the man lay down, covering his wife to protect her. I watched in horror as a soldier shot them both in the head and then charged into the jungle after the young women. I ran the other way, and managed to escape."

The older couple, Benjamin and Edith Christiansen, had taught me African history in my junior year of college. I'd known them before that from letters, because Ben and my grandmother had been raised by a Danish missionary, "Grandma Christiansen," and had grown up like brother and sister. I'd spent hours hearing about the Lutheran Church in Liberia, and how many orphans Grandma Christiansen had saved. Years later, Ben invited me to spend a month of my sabbatical in Liberia. Less than a year after my return from that transforming experience, I'd read the story of their death.

That day's news and the smell of eucalyptus from the canyon opened a niche in my heart. My fingers and toes began to tingle, like anesthesia numbing my body, and then I seemed to be floating, looking down at myself.

*"Welcome to Liberia." A vision of ebony beauty in a white nurse's uniform exuded the aroma of orange trees in bloom. "My name is Margrethe." She pronounced it slowly and I rolled it around inside my mouth: Mar-gray'-teh. An adrenaline rush added an edge to my sense of belonging to the exotic land of my mother's ancestors. "I'm looking forward to helping you appreciate our beautiful country." Her lilting voice and moist handshake sent quivers through my hand and arm, directly to my heart.*

As fast as the experience intruded, it began to dissipate, leaving me limp and perspiring as if I'd traveled thousands of miles into heat, humidity, and mystical connections. Margrethe's stunning image lingered in the haze of a cherished memory, then dissolved. Nine hours earlier, Kim and I had become one flesh in passionate lovemaking. Now, this. Intense feelings for both women collided with my dreams of becoming bishop and a faithful husband.

Thirteen years ago, after spending a month of my sabbatical with Margrethe as my companion and guide, we'd promised never to contact one another. The committee's phone call and discussions with Kim had delivered Margrethe Christiansen out of the distant mist of a tearful farewell into the eye watering sunshine of right here, right now.

What causes a buried, maybe even repressed, memory of intense love to erupt in vivid color and sound? Scientists talk about stimulation of the right temporal lobe of the brain: the angular gyrus. On the spiritual level, mystics have often talked about visions and encounters. I'd never experienced either. Maybe Margrethe's reappearance amounted to nothing more than a flash of memory like all of us get now and then. No answers satisfied me. Even if I knew the cause, the sudden experience needed more than an explanation.

I stared into the brightening sky, where the feathery cumulus sometimes soothed my restlessness. As a child, I loved watching the clouds, especially the puffy white ones, while I lay on my back. I felt sure God would send me a message that morning, but the clouds looked like whipped egg whites, full of fluff with no answers to my dilemma. The memory flash of Margrethe could mean anything. Naked reality said if I didn't tell Kim and the committee about my secret, I'd violate the their trust. If I did, I'd violate Margrethe's and unleash powerful and painful forces in my marriage and career.

I jerked when my cell phone beeped. No caller I.D., just a text message.

DON'T EVEN
THINK
ABOUT IT

My hand started shaking when I put down the phone. Don't even think about what? Interviewing? Telling? Who's trying to scare me? Or tease me? Peter? He wouldn't, would he? Then who? Surely God wouldn't send messages by cell phone.

I resisted mentioning the call to Kim. It might be a practical joke. The timing, though…As for the vivid memory? Well…I thought making Kim's favorite food for breakfast might help me relax. Besides, after last night's revelation, she'd be eating for two.

*Aebleskivver*, made from pancake dough with some secret Danish additives, took a lot of work, including cooking them in a special cast iron pan with half moons—much more complicated than flipping flapjacks. She loved dipping those little round delicacies in powdered sugar, while I liked raspberry jelly or maple syrup. Mixing and baking helped my mood, and a couple of "samples" made me ready to tell her my news.

I'd decided to re-bury the secret, and concentrate on helping her get through the pregnancy. After all my pondering, I concluded a confession wouldn't help anyone but me. "I'll interview," I said and kissed her hard.

"Great! You'll do a super job. Now all we have to worry about is keeping this baby."

# CHAPTER 5

▼

Driving to the diocesan office for the interview gave me a half hour to rehearse one more time, my answer to the big question: "Is there anything else we should know?" I'd worked out my response in the garden before I left, using the tune of an old chant my ancestors sang while they hacked at the weeds in Liberian cotton fields. My hoe had pierced the ground, severing weed stalks from their roots: "Speak the truth in love, thud, speak the truth in love, thud…"

I'd worked out a risky solution. Margrethe had never revealed our affair, and neither Brother David nor Peter had reported my deception. So, I'd accept nomination and count on Peter's commitment to confidentiality. Peter would win the election, although Kim said she'd feel "super disappointed" if he did, and I'd go on serving in Anaheim Hills. I stopped worrying about someone digging around to unearth my secret, and agreed to interview to make everyone happy—except Peter, whom I didn't call. Part of me still wanted to confess, of course, because that's what transparency demanded.

I drove a little faster than usual, keeping my eye on the mirror. I flipped on the radio to check traffic on KNX—AM and caught the last few seconds of another report from Africa. "The Liberians United for Reconciliation and Democracy over ran Phebe Hospital, forcing evacuation of staff and patients to a nearby Roman Catholic hospital. Violence continues to escalate between government forces and the L.U.R.D."

The Lutheran Church in Liberia founded Phebe Hospital and School of Nursing decades ago, and continued to support the institutions. The floating sensation crept over me again, and I drove on automatic pilot.

*We walked along a dirt path near Phebe Hospital. "I trained here as a teenager. My parents taught at the Leadership Training Center over there, and see that house? I grew up there."*

*"Was it hard—growing up with all the sickness and death next door?"*

*"I loved it." Her voice caught, and she brushed her eye with the back of her hand. I touched her shoulder, wanting to know more, but she turned and started walking toward the hospital. "It's been destroyed and rebuilt more than once because of revolutions."*

*"Will Liberia ever be at peace?"*

*"Not in my lifetime."*

I emerged from my mystical visit with Margrethe just in time to see the exit sign. No peace for her or Liberia, and not much for me, either.

Locating our diocesan headquarters between the Crystal Cathedral and Disneyland gave Californians a geographical fix when asking directions, even though some suggested re-naming the diocese, "The Entertainment Capital of Lutheranism."

I'd planned to arrive earlier, but got delayed by one of those unexpected phone calls pastors often get just as they go out the door. "Could you come to the hospital, Pastor? The doctors say she won't last the night." The young treasurer of my congregation struggled with the words.

I'd promised to come by at lunchtime, said some reassuring words, and hung up. I wondered if the nominating committee understood how hard it would be to give up parish ministry for what they called "wider" ministry. I also wondered if they'd accept my answer to their "big" question.

\*         \*         \*         \*

I walked into the diocesan conference room a few minutes before 10:30, greeted by a dozen pairs of curious eyes. Monet prints on the wall, new since I'd been there last, lent the illusion of a spring flower garden to the otherwise dull ivory walls. A sturdy table assembled in an octagon, surrounded by swivel chairs, sat in the middle of the room.

Everyone else wore casual clothes in honor of the pleasant Saturday morning. I felt overdressed in my gray suit and white clergy shirt, so I took off my coat and tossed it on one of the chairs, and moved toward the large silver coffee pot. "I don't believe we've met, but anyone who has the good taste to bring Krispy Kremes is worth knowing."

She smiled and extended her slender brown hand, dark eyes glistening. "I'm Isabel Guitierrez from Mission San Pedro in east Los Angeles. I have heard many good things about you."

"Gracias." I hesitated, and then passed up a succulent raspberry-filled concoction in favor of an empty napkin with my black coffee. A jelly blob on my chest would be distracting, not to mention a waste of delicious calories.

Several other committee members introduced themselves, including Rebecca Disterhoff from St. Michael's in San Diego. Her ample figure suggested she might live across the street from the Clairemont outlet for these unique doughnuts, but I stifled my urge to make such a crack.

Ellen Olson moved toward me with a broad smile and a firm handshake. My single contact with her had been the thirty-second phone call that upset my secretary and sent me into a dizzying attempt to decide whether or not to show up for the interview. She looked like she'd be at home in a corporate boardroom: gray slacks, pink blouse, and dark blue blazer. After leading us in prayer, she asked the first question. "Tell us about the congregations you've served. What difference did they make in their communities?"

"My internship in Los Angeles—near USC—helped me see how important a non-anxious presence can be when everything else is chaotic. The inner city thrived on alcohol and drugs, which meant shootings—muggings—robberies. The congregation offered a safe place to confess, to hang out, to see something bigger than the neighborhood."

"Your biography says you went to San Jose as an assistant pastor after seminary. Was that inner city, too?"

"No, but a changing community. What had been a large congregation was losing members to the sprawl of the Silicon Valley, and the empty houses filled up with renters from Central America and Mexico. I'd honed my college Spanish in Los Angeles, so I started visiting the neighbors. Walked around. Listened. Two things happened. We started a Sunday noon worship service in Spanish, with a potluck afterward. That led to classes for new moms. *La Leche* helped us."

"What's *La Leche?*"

"It's an international organization for mother to mother support of breast feeding. A San Jose chapter got us some materials and a leader. A dozen young moms showed up with their babies at the first class."

I looked around the room, feeling relaxed talking about my history. I noticed one man who looked familiar, but I couldn't place him. His scowl seemed out of place compared to everyone else.

"You went to Our Redeemer in San Diego next." Ellen kept us moving.

"Yes, that's where I wore out three pair of shoes calling on homes in a new subdivision."

"Did you find any prospects?"

"Not many. But the neighbors got to know me, and I learned a lot about what ruled their lives: big mortgages, job stress, unemployment, raising kids who wanted everything..."

"What wonderful thing did you dream up for them?" The scowling semi-familiar gentleman had an edge in his voice. My mental range finder put him on the same committee on which I'd once served. Which one?

"What would you have done?" I asked. His face turned pink. I smiled.

"We're here to ask the questions, not you." He glared at Ellen Olson.

She held up one hand and said, "I seem to remember something about small groups."

"Yes, we organized a dozen face to face groups of six to eight people to get acquainted, study a topic, play together, and take on a service project."

"Play together? Is that what you think church is about?" Mr. Scowl leaned on the table, and looked at me like my dad had when I'd broken a window hitting tennis balls against the side of the garage. Then I remembered. He served on the constitution committee and wanted everything nailed down with no wiggle room. We'd debated several points. I remembered his name, too.

"'Play' maybe isn't a good word for you, Mr. Magnusson. Maybe 'creative activity' or 'art' or 'singing' fits better?" He leaned back as if to say he'd let it pass, but I knew he'd be back at me about something else.

"You've done some volunteer work with community agencies in Orange County since you got here, is that right?" I felt like they already knew the answers to my questions by the way they asked, but went along with the program.

"Yes, I'm on the board for a Postpartum Depression Support agency, and I'm winding up a term on the Spiritual Care Committee of the local hospital. I umpire tennis matches now and then at my wife's school, and I've done a little coaching with a couple of kids at the tennis club in our neighborhood."

I noticed Mr. Magnusson left the room when I mentioned tennis. Maybe the coffee affected him like it did me. Maybe he wanted to make a point about who held the power in the room.

The questions moved to my involvement on diocesan committees, including the Long Range Planning Task Force. I talked about the challenge our Covenants Committee faced when we wrote the policy for Professional Sexual Misconduct. We'd tried to balance our concern for victims and the accused and their families. "It's not easy to fit forgiveness and justice together."

Mr. Magnusson returned in time to hear my answer. His question sounded less harsh than before. "You know the bishop is responsible for convening a Review Panel when there's an accusation, then?"

"Yes, I helped write the language of that section." When I wrote it, I didn't think much about my own case coming up some day. The thought of being grilled about Liberia somehow caused my already complaining bladder to twinge.

"Have you ever been accused of sexual misconduct?" His tone returned to his earlier strident one. I shook my head.

"Let's stay with our agenda, Mr. Magnusson, please?" Ellen Olson gave him the kind of look my mother had sometimes used with authority when one of us children said something inappropriate.

"What do you know about the office of bishop?" The smiling plump lady from San Diego asked a question I'd expected at the beginning.

"I know it's demanding. I've been Bishop Madison's pastor these past two years, and we've become friends. He hasn't shared confidences, but he's told lots of stories about the kinds of things a bishop is expected to do, and all the travel involved. The motor home helped." A pastor dying of cancer had donated a well-equipped vehicle plus a fund to pay for insurance and gas for two years.

"Will you want to use it if you're elected?"

"Yes, it makes sense. The tricky part will be getting the pontoons on it for the ride to Hawaii." Mr. Magnusson didn't crack a smile.

We talked about the present staff, the financial challenge, and starting new congregations, then got to the issue of inclusiveness. "All races—everyone—rich or poor—gay and straight—is a child of God," I said. "If we're going to be effective, we need to use the language of the neighborhood whenever possible, both in speech and style of music. We need to help people think globally, and keep strong connections with churches in other lands. We learn from one another when we share our cultures like pieces of a mosaic." I felt myself floating again, looking down on Phebe Hospital.

*"You're descended from Liberians, but you aren't a Liberian, Jon." When the plane brought me from America, I'd looked out the window at the jungles and rivers, and something swirled inside, joining yearnings from childhood. My mind grasped some of the history, but my new feelings bordered on elation over an unexplainable connection. "Knowing how to make palm butter doesn't make me a Liberian any more than baking aebleskivver makes you a Dane, Jonathan. Singing the music and doing the dances give us a hint about what makes us who we are, but not until we join in the suffering, do we truly connect. Even then..."*

"Tell us about your leadership style." A female voice similar to Margrethe's brought me back to the interview table.

"I like the term, 'servant leader,'" I said, still thinking about the suffering servants at Phebe Hospital. To escape the memories, I focused on explaining. "Leaders are neither superior nor subservient. No matter what style we use, it involves loving the people. To get jobs done, I use one of four basic styles, depending on the readiness and willingness of the group. For example, new groups need more instruction and persuasion. Experienced groups need more participation and delegation, until they get lethargic. Then some persuasion helps get them back on track."

So far so good. They hadn't delved into my theology or asked the dreaded all-purpose question yet, so I turned Isabel down at the break when she again offered a doughnut. My stomach didn't need any fuel for indigestion. When she persisted, I offered to split one with her, so she lifted a glazed delicacy with a napkin, severed it into two pieces like a surgeon opening the cavity for heart surgery, and placed it in my waiting hand.

I savored the sweetness, crushing the flaky wonder with my tongue against the roof of my mouth. My expression must have impressed Isabel, because she said, "You love Krispy Kremes, do you not?"

When we all returned, Ellen asked Rebecca to begin the questioning. "Pastor Jon, your ancestry is of interest to the committee. I believe you wrote in your documents that your mother was born in Solvang to a Liberian mother and a Danish missionary father, is that correct?"

"Yes, that's true."

"Your father's parents were born in Denmark, and your parents live at the Solvang Lutheran Home. We understand they worked there for some time, as did their parents, is that correct?" Rebecca's mouth fought a smile.

"That's correct."

"Then can you tell us, Pastor Jon, is it your intention to spend your time in Solvang visiting your aging parents or filling up on Danish pastry?"

The committee broke up laughing. They had cooked up this little tension reliever during the break when they saw me share the Krispy Kreme with Isabel. I joined their laughter, although it didn't seem as funny to me as to them.

Pasting on a serious face, I answered, "I grew up in Solvang, as you all know. I worked in one of the bakeries during high school. They paid me minimum wage plus all the day-old pastry I could eat. To this day, bear claws make me a little nauseous." Even Mr. Magnusson laughed. "I can say without hesitation that my allegiance in Solvang is strictly to my bi-racial parents, and here, to the local franchise of Krispy Kremes."

We all laughed again. "I'm glad we can talk about ancestry. I'm proud of my heritage. I believe this diocese, with all its diversity of languages and countries of origin, deserves a visible symbol in a leadership position. Competence comes first, but we all know that white males have dominated church leadership for centuries. I will always be an advocate for inclusivity and diversity among the staff of the diocese."

The committee answered with applause, surprising me. Several more questions followed about my attitude toward keeping the present staff in place, completing the strategic plan for the next three years, and whether or not I ever consulted a spiritual mentor. I answered each of them affirmatively, and told them about Brother David.

When they asked about my continuing education since seminary, I knew the sabbatical couldn't be avoided any longer. "I spent a month at the Graduate Theological Union in Berkeley studying Martin Luther's theology of the cross, and a month in Liberia learning about the history of missions by American Lutherans. The third month, I wrote about my experiences there, and adjusted to some new insights about my Liberian ancestry."

They seemed satisfied. I could have told about the weekends Kim and I spent exploring San Francisco from Coit Tower to Ghirardelli Square. Or the great seafood at Spenger's and tasty dark beer at Larry Blake's in Berkeley. Or our tense parting when I left for Liberia, and the strain between us when I came back. Or about falling in love with Margrethe. But I didn't, and they didn't ask.

After covering some practical details, we came to "it:" "Is there anything in the past that, should it come to light, would be an embarrassment to you or the church?" Mr. Magnusson the Scowler sat at attention like a snake ready to strike.

My answer drifted out into the room as if I hadn't a care in the world, but my insides rumbled like a river at flood stage. "All of us would be embarrassed if our entire life were laid bare. I have some history I wish could be erased. We all know Paul's claim, 'All have sinned and fall short of the glory of God.' We also know we're saved by grace."

I paused for a quick sip of cooled coffee. For all my rehearsal, I felt like my answer needed work. I set down my cup, hand trembling a little. Just as Mr. Magnusson leaned forward as if to ask a question, I continued.

"My intention is to confess any future transgressions to God and a spiritual mentor, just as I have in the past. As for the Pastoral Covenants of the Lutheran Church—North America, I'm not aware of having violated any since we adopted them two years ago. If I am elected bishop, and if I do violate them, I'll make it known to the Executive Board of the diocese right away."

"So you have some history you're not sharing?" The snake struck. I'd learned from hiking in the Santa Ynez Mountains to stand very still when that happened, and never to run, because the poison would spread faster. I turned to Ellen Olson, hoping she'd apply the tourniquet. She did.

"Thank you, Pastor Larsen. I believe that concludes our questions. As you know, we're interviewing other candidates, and will choose between three and five to recommend to the convention. Our plans are to…" Mr. Magnusson looked irritated, but he didn't press his question, at least then. I suspected I hadn't heard the last of him and wondered if he and Peter Bloch knew one another. "…So we'll conclude with our thanks for your clear and forthright answers. Pastor Larsen, would you dismiss us with the benediction?"

"The Lord bless you and keep you, the Lords' face shine on you…" I drove away feeling elation tinged with guilt. The Lord's face shone on me, but I had hid part of me—again.

# CHAPTER 6

▼

After stopping at the hospital to pray with my treasurer and his wife, I headed home for lunch. Kim hadn't yet returned from the Saturday workday at school, so I slid into the chaise and sipped some iced tea and munched an apple. I felt tense, unable to relax. My cell phone beeped, and I jumped, spilling some tea in the process. I glanced to see whose number showed up—another text message.

DID YOU
TELL THE
WHOLE TRUTH

I'd dismissed the first message as a joke. This one shook me. Surely Peter wouldn't stoop to sending anonymous messages. Still, who else knew I'd interviewed today? I thought about calling to ask him straight out, but my own lack of forthrightness with the committee troubled me more. If only Kim hadn't convinced me to avoid the "whole truth." No, I couldn't blame Kim. I chose to interview. I chose to—lie? Sometime, somehow, I'd become transparent. For now, I'd do my best to let go of my fear and guilt, and concentrate on Sunday's sermon.

I'd preached on the resuscitation of Lazarus enough times that I wanted a new slant. Scripture doesn't tell us what Lazarus did after Jesus gave him a second chance. What do you and I do with the second chances God gives us? My grandmother used to have a saying about that. What was it? I started to make some notes.

＊     ＊     ＊     ＊

The rattle and roar of a motorcycle drowned out my sermonizing. Curiosity got the best of me, so I peeked over the side gate. "Brenda!" She and an old Harley snorted up the street, red helmet strapped to the handlebars, in case the police puller her over, I supposed. Kim's younger sister could have been her twin in appearance, but Brenda didn't take care of herself. Her cheeks showed too much red make up and her eyes showed too much drug use. She braked by slamming into the curb, oil smoke stinging my nose.

"Hey, Righteous Rev'rend, wassup?"

"Hey yourself, Bren. I see you've got new wheels."

"Yup, and needin' a loan." The words slipped off her tongue as smooth as a sales person's patter. She unzipped her leather jacket to reveal a too tight yellow tank top with nothing between it and her body. The seductive move reminded me of other times when she'd tempted me.

"No loans, you know that." The family had agreed after we totaled up how much she owed all of us, and realized we could have bought a motor home and sent her out to the desert. Tempting.

"Shoot man, I've got a job that'll pay enough to get me a place to stay. I'm just a hundred short."

She used some variation on the "just so much short" con most every time. In the past, I'd sometimes ignored the family policy and let sympathy rule. Because Kim demanded tough love, I'd told no one.

"Hey, Good Sam, you ain't gonna pass by on the other side like some priest, are ya?"

"I won't give you money. And why are you talking like that?"

"Because I'm *persona non grata* in this holy family—so I speak the way you see me."

"I see you as someone who keeps asking for money, but never wants to get the help she needs to stay off drugs."

The family seldom talked about Brenda. Her behavior, when she showed up for family gatherings, bordered on the weird. She vomited in the potted plants after Thanksgiving dinner last year. The year before, she'd picked up her birthday cake and had thrown it against the wall because, "I don't want no stupid birthday. I want to die."

We had all cringed, but after she'd stormed out, we'd cleaned up the cake and rationalized, "That's Brenda." Her cries for help, and refusal to accept any, kept us all on edge.

In high school, Brenda had followed Kim and me around wherever we went. Two years behind us, she'd seemed like a good kid who enjoyed basking in the prestige of hanging out with juniors and seniors. I always saw her as a cute, irrepressible pest with an infectious laugh. She wore her blonde hair long and straight, and, yes, I sometimes wondered what she'd look like as Lady Godiva.

After Kim and I left for college, Brenda had seemed to lose her way. The coach caught her in the boy's locker room once, nude, and another time found her parked behind the gym with the quarterback, drinking beer and acting like dogs in heat.

She claimed to be drug free, but when we visited her at UCLA, her room fan argued with the sweet scent of marijuana. The smell won. Kim had told me soon after our wedding about her mother arranging for an abortion during Bren's senior year. Two marriages, a divorce and separation later, she wore out her welcome at home and everywhere else. She survived somehow, hopping from job to job.

Forty-one, going on sixteen, her mental, emotional and social growth seemed to stop after her friends had introduced her to crack in high school. Brenda did what she could to fulfill her death wish, but something kept her alive. Twice, she had slammed her motorcycle into retaining walls. Her broken bones and shattered spirit mingled with our broken hearts and quiet question: "Why?"

She pulled off her jacket, dropped it on the seat, and moved toward me. "I'd make it worth your while, Jon Boy."

"Are you trying to seduce me again?"

"Is it working?"

"We've been down this road before, Bren, and I always say no." I stepped around to the other side of her cycle, fiddling with the chrome handlebars. "So, what kind of job did you get?"

"Gonna sell Harleys. Gave me this used one to demo. Damn thing's got no brakes, though."

"So I noticed."

"Rumor has it you're gonna be bishop, big brother-in-law."

"How'd you find that out?"

"I'm still in the family, you know."

I couldn't imagine who'd told her. I moved toward the house, and she slipped into her jacket.

"If you don't wanna show the love of Christ to a poor prod-i-gal, I ain't gonna hang where I ain't wanted. Just remember…" She paused, tossing her hair and squinting her eyes. "I can always tell the world you paid for my abortion." I stared like a lion protecting his turf against intruders, and looked around. No neighbors visible.

"You're not that kind of person."

"Nobody but you and me know it wasn't your baby. As for paying, well, you have given me money, haven't you, sweetie?" I had, but never more than fifty dollars at a time, and only because it kept her away from Kim. She made sure I noticed her puffed out chest before zipping up the leather. She hopped on the starter and roared down the street, waving as if to say, "I won't forget."

Brenda scared me. I didn't worry about the family, because they knew her well enough to dismiss her accusations as so much manipulation. If the media picked it up, however, they'd be hard pressed to believe a cleric accused of sexual aberrations. The climate was ripe for such things. I thought about calling my congregational president and the chair of the interview committee to tell my side first, but didn't want to dignify Brenda's neurotic threat. I walked back to the garden, determined to talk to Kim about it when she got home.

*          *          *          *

I picked up my hoe and whacked away at the weeds. A half hour and four rows of weeds later, I settled down in my creaky chaise to wait for Kim. She slipped through the gate, face aglow, before I had time to close my eyes.

"So, Mister Future Bishop, did they like you?"

"Not as much as you do."

"What'd they say?"

"They told me you're supposed to love, massage and obey."

She punched my shoulder. "No way. They didn't make you a Viking King." I grabbed her and pulled her down into the chaise with me, crashing both of us through the rotted webbing. We struggled to stand up, but rolled around on the ground tangled in aluminum frame and one another.

"Now can I get a new one?" Her kisses did more than answer. When we settled down on the patio, I told her about Brenda's threat and asked if she'd told anyone about my candidacy.

She scowled. "Just Mom. You didn't give Bren money, did you?"

"Nope."

Kim went for lemonade and brought brownies, too. "Really, did they like you?"

"They said nice things. I tried to wiggle out of it, but..." Part of me always wanted to be liked. Part of me wanted to always do the right thing.

Kim smiled. "You don't need to wiggle. You're a good and kind man, not a worm."

*During the first three weeks, Margrethe rarely looked me in the eye when we were alone, and admitted to holding back about her personal life. I offered to listen. She declined, but her words felt like a caress: "All in due time. You're a kind and good man."*

The memory lingered a little too strong, but I heard Kim ask when we'd find out if I'd been nominated. "In a couple of weeks, when they send out the pre-convention materials."

"So what do we do in the meantime?"

"Wait. And try to figure out who's sending anonymous messages."

"What?" She stopped pulling weeds and did her unique hands-on-the-hips pose. I first noticed it before we got a dishwasher. I'd say something shocking while she had her hands deep in dish water, and she'd pull them out, shake them twice, and strike the pose: feet apart, eyes focused, head bent forward. She kept her hands pointing backward, and put her wrists where the waist touched the upper curve of her hips. "What messages?"

"Anonymous ones on my cell phone. The first one said for me not to even think about it. The second asked if I'd told the whole truth. I figured them for practical jokes so..."

"You think someone's threatening you to say out of the election?"

"I hate to say it, but I'm guessing it's Peter."

"Why would he do something like that? What does he know, anyway? Other than how to insult women and people of color."

"Yeah, he's pretty good at that. And, he's been dropping little hints about my past failures to a couple of the committee members."

Her wrists slipped down her hips and she rubbed the garden's dirt off her hands. She grabbed the hoe like a club. "I can't believe Pete would want to be bishop so bad he'd spread gossip. And make anonymous phone calls."

During the next weeks, both Kim and I immersed ourselves in busyness, partly to avoid dealing with the phone calls and Peter's gossip, and because our careers demanded so much time. The end of a quarter in Kim's school year confronted her with evaluations, book collections and spring picnics. Funerals for the two cancer patients, a minor staff flare-up over office space, and a dozen other matters kept my mind occupied.

$$* \quad * \quad * \quad *$$

Ellen Olson called and asked if I could send her a hundred words about the mission of a bishop. "I guess that means you're nominating me?" I arranged for an afternoon off to meet with Brother David, and headed for the Malibu Center.

Brother David functioned more like a personal coach and confidant than either a psychotherapist or priest. I had lots of friends, but none with whom I could be transparent. David gave me a confidential listening ear and insights to mull over.

He started with the usual question: "Who are you today?" Today's answer, after the "child of God" mantra: "Jonathan Larsen, possible candidate for bishop, looking for a hundred-word mission statement—and to get away from the phones. I hoped you could get me on track."

"Is there any other reason you came?"

"No. Well, I'm still fussing about having accepted the nomination. I didn't tell Kim or the committee about Margrethe." Silence hung over us like morning fog. I shifted in my chair and stared at the floor.

"You believe in forgiveness?" His smile penetrated deeper than his question. "You told me Margrethe said there was nothing to forgive before you left Liberia. I heard your confession and declared God's absolution. What's left?"

I repeated my fears about Peter. "He said he'd keep it confidential, but I don't trust him. I think maybe he's sending me anonymous messages."

"Interesting. What kind of messages?"

"Ambiguous, maybe practical jokes. But they bother me." I told him what they said.

"Not too threatening, really. Could they have come from someone other than Peter?"

"I suppose," I said. "It's not a big deal, I guess. I just wonder what Peter's up to."

We'll get back to this later. There's someone else to consider before we talk about Peter. Can you forgive yourself?"

"Sure—not completely. I sort of forgave myself for falling in love. But I violated my marriage. And the church's trust."

"So, you wonder how you can do justice to your responsibilities as a bishop when you haven't lived up to yours as a pastor and husband?"

"Right."

"Let's think about King David's deception and adultery with Bathsheba. Then consider his long reign, and what he did for the nation. Was his 'good' overruled by his 'bad'?" We talked about other imperfect characters in scripture, and some recent presidents and a Nobel Peace prizewinner. "Most leaders live with flaws," he said. "Even the church is flawed and you love her, right?"

"I fell in love with the church the same way I fell in love with Kim—naturally. Our small town parents brought us to the same Lutheran church where we were baptized on the same Sunday."

I remembered it from all the times Grammom had told me the story. "The pastor said—with his Danish accent—the sacred words. 'Kimberly Yvonne Sondergaard, I baptize you…Jonathan Soren Larsen, I baptize you…' He sprinkled water on us as he pronounced the words, 'Father, Son and Holy Spirit.'"

"Is he still living?"

"No, he died several years ago. He left a powerful legacy, though. Loved babies. He held us both, one in each arm, smiled his heart-melting best, and walked us down the aisle. 'Here they are,' he said, 'the newest members of the church. I predict they'll bring joy and challenge to us all. I can see the mischief in their eyes already.'"

"It must have been quite a sight in black and white."

"Clever. Grammom said we started fussing in unison about the time he made the turn to bring us back to the font. His smile had disappeared and he seemed relieved to deliver us, squirming and squealing, to our parents."

"You've known the church and Kim since you were born—just as God has known you."

"That's true. Kim and I shared a crib in the church nursery. Grammom said our mothers laid our blanket-wrapped bodies crossways on the mattress. While we slept, the attendant played with the older toddlers. When we woke up, she called for help. Kim usually woke me with her staccato squalls, and then I'd join in with mine, more like a siren. Growing up together in the church put us together like Danes adding butter and almond paste to flour and sugar so the pastry always tasted like a bite of heaven."

"Some people would describe you as soul mates."

"I guess we are. Without the lightning strike."

We talked again about Peter and my belief he'd be elected, and agreed the best strategy for dealing with the anonymous messages involved dismissing them. We never got to the mission statement.

Two hours of hiking later, I drove away, still pondering my future. Will Peter and Brenda expose me? Which flaws, and how many, keep one from serving the church? The church has struggled with that question for centuries, and always will. I needed an answer for me, if for no one else. The convention arrived before I reached a conclusion.

# CHAPTER 7

▼

I hesitated in the doorway, looking at five hundred Lutherans crammed into a corner room of the Los Angeles Conference Center. I'd arrived a day earlier, confident Peter would be elected bishop. Beverly Davidson and I had both qualified for the next ballot with Peter still leading. Depending on how the delegates responded to our five-minute speeches coming up, any one of us might win.

When I took my seat at the candidate's table next to the stage, I focused on the hand lettered name cards staring back at me. Mine said, "Bishop Jonathan Larsen." I blinked. Then it said "*Pastor* Jonathan Larsen." The mixed bag of feelings, from dread to desire, gave me the sensation I'd been run over by a horde of Vikings.

A late May heat wave had hit us the day before the convention opened, and the air conditioning system coughed out semi-filtered smog at temperatures just below melt down. A heat source of a different order added to the discomfort. Our church, like many others, faced tensions over sexuality, immigration, church authority and whether or not we should have reorganized, among other things. I wondered how a church with white, northern European roots would feel about electing someone like me.

Fresh roses and carnations on the stage didn't begin to cover the musty smell of sweating concrete or the not so subtle hostile feelings between "inclusive" and "exclusive" groups of delegates. Breathing deep usually relaxed me. Not this time.

"Before the ballot, we'll hear from each of the finalists." I heard the presiding bishop's announcement, but my busy brain begged a question. "How did I end up here?" Because the retiring bishop flattered me? My wife's hugs beguiled me? My father's wish since childhood gnawed at me? Yes. Reluctant, I'd given in to their encouragement, and my own sense of God's call. And, maybe because I didn't want Peter Bloch to win.

Because of his age and experience, no one acted surprised when Peter led every ballot. He'd been on all the right committees and spoke up at pastors' meetings and conventions, always asking us to "do the right thing."

The stage lights made his bald spot glow, and his face looked as if he'd been sculpted from marble. At fifty-six, he could still beat most tennis players in the room. He spoke first, using those sonorous tones associated with cathedrals.

"The church must be a beacon of morality, and a measuring stick of faith. We cannot give in to fluffy theology or dumb down our worship life. We cannot cover up the heinous heresies and unimaginable immoralities of some of our pastoral leaders." After rattling on for most of his allotted five minutes, he concluded his speech with biblical words my father had quoted at me too often. "Let us be a church in which we live up to the call to 'Be perfect, as your Heavenly Father is perfect.'"

Even though most American Lutherans came from Germany and Scandinavia, we'd become a mosaic, like a lot of southern California neighborhoods. We'd changed, but hadn't yet reached our goal of at least ten per cent persons of color or primary language other than English. We still sang Bach melodies, but many others, too, and some folks even felt free to clap during worship services. At conventions, applause after speeches fit the custom, so I wasn't surprised when the delegates clapped for Peter—but they didn't sound enthusiastic.

Few people expected Beverly Davidson to win, yet her wit and wisdom had won enough votes for second place. Somewhere between Peter's five-foot-ten and my six-foot-three, her stature, poise and auburn hair attracted attention. When she spoke, her smoky voice reminded me of Mary in the Peter, Paul and Mary folk singing trio.

She ended her speech in a way I envied. "Jesus told stories about widows and fish, and held squirmy children on his lap. He ate with outcasts and put mercy and justice ahead of rigid rituals. The Word Made Flesh moved among us with grace and love. This diocese needs to follow the earthy Jesus of compassion."

I'd voted for her on every ballot, and knew I'd do the same on this one. The applause sounded louder this time, with a single "Amen, Sister!" from one of the women sitting in front.

From what people had told me, I'd come this far based on two things. First, at forty-three, they saw me as young enough to still have imagination, and mature enough not to chase after fads. Second, as a native Californian with Danish and

Liberian ancestors, I'd worked hard at building bridges among our wide variety of colors, languages, and lifestyles.

I'd become a visual symbol for our diversity, and wanted to say something profound—without sounding phony. No problem. And there'd never be another terrorist attack, either. So, I got up and winged it.

"What kind of bishop does this diocese need? We don't need a bishop who has all the answers—who can do tricks to solve our problems. We need someone to inspire us—to think hard—and work smart—to face tough times with confidence and creativity. We need someone to love us—help us feel like we belong with one another." I used my handkerchief to wipe drops from my forehead. "Lord knows, with all the strong opinions in this church, we need someone who can deal with hot air." A few delegates chuckled, and fanned themselves with their convention programs.

I looked at the clock. Four and a half minutes left. I talked about our complex and expanding immigrant population, the decline of traditional congregations, and quoted Micah about doing justice and loving mercy. I got a little emotional about our call to be peacemakers and healers around the world, using Liberia as an example. I added a few sentences about my family. Still two minutes to go. Five minutes never seemed so long.

"Either Peter Bloch or Beverly Davidson will make a fine bishop for this diocese. They trust God's grace. As for me, I like serving the church as a parish pastor. If you want to vote for me as your bishop, that's your choice. Just remember, I have clutter in my spiritual closet—and my greatest strength is—well, I'm really good at failing." I paused long enough for them to wonder if they should clap, laugh or what.

"Our spiritual ancestor, Martin Luther, told us to 'sin boldly.' He didn't mean arrogantly—or without feeling guilty. We can sin boldly because we trust God's grace. We *fail* boldly because we know we have to keep trying new things—not everything works. Years ago, I learned from my dad to follow God's example as gardeners. If you sow enough seed—water and fertilize it—every now and then, something takes root and bears fruit. A lot dies or gets eaten by birds. I sow a lot of seed—and fail a lot. Oh yeah, I toss fertilizer around now and then, too. Some of you know it by its initials."

Some free spirit in the back shouted, "Amen, brother, spread it around, spread it around." The more traditional Lutherans sat stone still, but laughter rippled around the room anyway.

"We've been asking for ethical transparency from our government and corporations. We need that—and more—from our church. A transparent church doesn't pretend to be what we're not—doesn't exclude or condemn just because someone's not perfect—or is 'different.' A transparent church sees our diversity as a strength, not a threat. It means we don't ignore or cover-up mistakes—we confess them—and let God's light shine through." The parliamentarian raised a "ten seconds" sign.

I took a deep breath. "So here's my statement of mission—personally—and for the diocese. *Be transparent. Fail boldly!*"

Silence. I didn't think to count how long, but it seemed like five, maybe ten seconds at least, as I turned toward my chair. The uprising started when someone yelled, "Yes!" Two loud claps, and the place erupted with applause: the most that stoic and proper Lutherans usually allowed themselves. Foot stomping and table pounding chaos didn't fit the image, but a few dozen enthusiasts cut loose anyway with a rhythmic, "Yes—clap—yes—clap…"

I stood there a few more seconds, stunned. They hadn't responded to either Peter or Beverly that way. I shivered at the thought: what if they elected me?

While the convention heard the announcements about procedure and sang a hymn, I hurried to the rest room. Nausea. It passed as soon as I slapped cold water on my face. With parishioners in the hospital, I never knew when someone would call, so I checked my cell phone. One text message showed up, with no identifying number, as usual.

FAILURE
PULL OUT

I'd decided to treat the other anonymous messages as a joke, but my stomach flipped at this one. I glanced at my reflection in the mirror. From childhood, I'd heard white guys say I couldn't hang out with the blonde girls. I'd heard white pastors say suburban congregations looking for a pastor wouldn't accept me. Yet, there I stood, married to a blonde, serving a church in upscale Anaheim Hills, Orange County, USA, and getting cheered by staid Lutherans, ninety-five percent of them white. I shook my head. I wondered what my Liberian grandmother would think of all this. Most of all, I wondered who'd heard my speech and wanted me to "pull out."

I hurried back into the convention room when I heard the gavel calling us to order for the ballot. Electronic wizardry gave us instant results. Presiding Bishop Bernardo Clemente's deep voice boomed over the public address system, "We have a bishop!" Part of me yearned to hear my own name; part of me hoped to hear Beverly's. No part of me wanted to hear Peter's, but that's what I knew would keep my secret safe. I glanced over at him and noticed his cell phone on the table, but so was Beverly's.

"I hereby declare the election as bishop of the Southern California—Hawaii Diocese of the Lutheran Church—North America..." He stared at the three of us, and then smiled and continued: "...The Reverend Jonathan Larsen. Join me in welcoming him to the..." He didn't get to finish.

The organist broke into "Ode to Joy," and the people jumped up, repeating their earlier rhythmic response: "Yes—clap—yes—clap..."

I felt limp and closed my eyes, not believing what I'd heard. When I opened them, I saw Beverly standing across from me, smiling and clapping, tears trickling down her cheeks. Sad for herself or happy for me? I had no idea. Peter, on the other hand, sat still, his face pasty white. Even though I hoped he wouldn't, I'd always assumed he'd win. "Sorry about that," I said.

Peter hesitated, and then offered his damp hand. "Good luck, Jonathan."

As I moved away through the noise of the ovation, I thought I heard him say to Beverly, "The black-mumble-mumble beat us...he shouldn't have..." but I couldn't stop to ask what I missed.

The joyful noise swept me toward the stage, where I tripped on the first step, almost falling on my face. Flat-on-the-floor prostration would have been a great way to launch my imperfect self into office. I spotted Kim in the visitors' section, waving and jumping up and down. Always the cheerleader, petite and effervescent, she mouthed something. Probably "I love you."

Bishop Clemente spoke to the assembly, but I didn't hear what he said. I stood there, in front of hundreds of people, staring at a huge cross on the wall above the stage. The ancient symbol of sacrifice and new life reminded me I'd hidden something in the darkness of my old life. My bowels moaned, "Unworthy!"

Bishop Clemente sat down, and the delegates followed suit. The few seconds between his announcement and my first words of acceptance seemed like a millennium. For a fleeting instant, I considered turning down the election. Instead, I sunk my soul into the immeasurable power of God's graciousness, or my substantial ego, I wasn't sure which.

"Thank you. I'm flabbergasted. Humbled." I paused and looked around. "Presiding Bishop Clemente, Interim Bishop Madison, delegates and friends. Through you, God is calling me to fail boldly in the name of Christ. If you'll join me in sowing the seeds of love, we'll see God do some marvelous things."

I knew I'd missed something. "Oh—my wife, Kim, her parents, and my two sisters are back in the far corner. I'd like them to stand. Kim, if..." The audience interrupted me with more clapping. Her mother gave a little push, and then Kim floated my way.

"Bishop Clemente, this is where I am supposed to tell you I accept the office . of bishop, and…" They interrupted me again. My upper lip quivered and my fingers ached from gripping the speaker's stand. Their applause drowned out my, "God bless us all" and I turned to meet Kim coming up the stairs.

She hugged me first. Then, she hugged the two bishops, the secretary taking minutes, the parliamentarian, and me again. While everyone laughed and clapped, she gave me a quick kiss and helped me wobble to the side of the stage. She looked at me, both of us with tears in our eyes, and asked, "Are you okay?"

"I probably am, but I won't know for awhile." Her blue eyes sparkled, and she did her little nose-wiggle and shoulder-shrug thing, like when she beat me at tennis. She fit herself under my shoulder, her head against my thumping heart, holding me. "I told you I did the right thing, buying that purple clergy shirt."

"I suppose you packed it?"

"Of course." Kim's confidence in me included providing the best in Lutheran bishop garb. Henry turned to talk to me as the delegates left the convention hall. Kim bounced off the stage. "I'll see you two later. My gosh, this is exciting."

Bishop Clemente wrung my hand, offering warm congratulations and his prayers. Henry gave me a bear hug. "Call me next week, and we'll go over some things. Meanwhile, you need to wind up affairs at your congregation." He handed me a large brown envelope. "Confidential computer disks—a calendar of key events—the discipline process—and one with sexual misconduct charges against some pastors. The password's the Greek word for repentance." Too much for me to absorb. I wanted to shut down and hide. But I listened. Carefully. "You'll need to move on these charges as soon as you're officially installed, Jon. Lives are being ruined."

I swallowed hard. "How soon am I official?"

"Any time between thirty and forty-five days, according to the constitution; whatever works best for your leaving the congregation. I wish you'd start tomorrow."

He grabbed me once more. "Jon, you don't know how happy I am you said yes. I'll tell you more later. There'll be a press conference in about an hour. I'll be there to introduce you." I wondered if Peter would show up.

# CHAPTER 8

▼

When I walked into our hotel room, everyone but Kim's dad, Iver Sondergaard, hugged and kissed me. He grabbed my hand and pulled me toward him in that irksome way he used. "I can't say the church elected the right one here, but they seem to like you. You'd better be good at this bishop thing. And don't leave my sweetie sitting home alone all the time. We'll be watching you." Short and stout, his bluster kept everyone on edge. I learned long ago not to argue with him, so I just smiled, patted his pink neck, and turned to my older sister.

"Call Mom and Dad for me, will you, and see if we can talk for a second?" She pulled out her cell phone and hit the speed dial button for the Lutheran Home in Solvang. "Janelle, the efficient," we called her. She put her natural gifts to good use as a public defender in Los Angeles and as a single mom to a teen-aged daughter.

Kim slipped into my embrace for a longer kiss than we'd allowed ourselves on stage. I hung on and whispered in her ear, "I love you." I glanced around the room to see everyone smiling and holding glasses of wine poured by my younger sister, Michelle. Always the gracious hostess, she honed her skills in the catering industry while she raised two feisty sons with her husband.

"I don't know what to say to all of you, except thanks for being here." I passed on the wine, grabbed a Diet Coke and some peanuts, and sat down at the small desk where I found hotel stationery and a Gideon Bible—just what I needed for writing my opening statement.

Janelle wrapped up her conversation. "No, don't interrupt their dinner. Just tell them their son has some good news and will call back about 6:30. Thanks a lot." I made a mental note to call before the banquet, wishing they could have been with us, but Dad's health wouldn't let them travel. While I flipped pages to the book of Ephesians, the latest anonymous cell phone message crept into my thoughts. I tucked it into a corner of my mind, far from forgotten, while I finished the notes. No pulling out now; just "fail boldly."

Kim kissed me—we'd been doing a lot of that lately—as I went out the door. "Don't forget to breathe." With God as close as the breeze living in us like our breath, we felt we could face anything when we "remembered to breathe." We'd been saying it to one another since our tennis coach drilled it into us in college.

I inhaled, but my ego and worry didn't evaporate. I exhaled, long and slow. Still fretting, but riding the high of election, I strode to the elevator for a ride downward into the unknown realities of public exposure as bishop-elect.

*        *        *        *

The press conference lasted an hour, and felt like two. I opened with a quote from scripture—Ephesians, chapter two, about God's grace, and shared the reality of conflict in the early church. "They argued about circumcision and authority. We argue about sexuality and authority. Scripture doesn't pull punches about human disagreements. I don't either. But I take my cue from the fourteenth verse. 'For Christ is our peace; in his flesh he has made both groups into one and has broken down the dividing wall, that is, the hostility between us.'"

I noticed Peter's absence, but Beverly and the entire Executive Board showed up, along with some curious delegates. The press corps consisted of reporters from two newspapers, a Christian radio station, and one television channel—not quite the White House bunch.

"Our church agrees to disagree, and we aim to do it agreeably. If we keep our focus, we can build bridges instead of walls. That's one of my primary goals."

"What about the clutter in your spiritual closet, Bishop?" The Christian radio reporter picked on the most vulnerable point of my presentation to the convention.

"It's a metaphor. I think it's self-evident. Next question?"

They asked about the usual things: family, vision, staff—and sexual misconduct hearings. I explained our process, handed out our policy, and assured them there would be no cover-ups. "We're interested in justice for everyone, and compassion will be the key."

I wondered what, if anything, they'd print and put on the air, knowing somehow, they'd exploit my color and motto about failing. I hurried back to change for the annual banquet where we feasted on jokes, music, and chicken breast. Pre-

siding Bishop Clemente spoke briefly—a good role model, Kim informed me—
and I introduced my sisters and their families, and Kim's parents to the applauding diners. The silver cloud on which I rode showed only a tinge of foreboding.

*     *     *     *

After lots of handshakes and hugs, Kim and I escaped to our room, and sunk
down on the couch alone. Kim switched on the television. "I want to see if they
gave you five minutes of fame."

"I'm guessing it'll be closer to thirty seconds."

"I hope we didn't miss it. Maybe it'll be after the weather and sports when
they do their tag line thingy."

"Maybe—did you enjoy the banquet?"

"I loved the Hawaiian theme. Everybody looked so cool. And the speaker was
short and to the point—something for you to remember, dear heart."

Kim had worn a multi-colored silky dress, long and tight, with a hibiscus over
her ear. She'd bought me white pants and a reverse print shirt in shades of blue
with small red flowers. "I'm glad your family could be there—except for Brenda,
of course," I said. With Brenda's tendency to mess up family gatherings, we
hadn't invited her. "I loved it when that couple came up and raved about how
you hugged everybody on the stage right after my election."

"I almost laughed out loud when that nice looking old—excuse me—mature
lady said she voted against Peter because he looked like a Bavarian *beermeister*."
Kim sometimes used other words to describe him.

"Which reminds me. Did you see him at the banquet?" The newscast had cut
to commercial.

"No. I saw him leave the convention, though—when you were talking with
Henry. He looked kinda sick. I thought I saw him stop and take a pill."

"A pill? You could see that?"

"No, but I saw a little silver box and his fingers go to it and then to his mouth.
Is that close enough?"

I chuckled. "You'd make a great detective. What do you think the pill was
about?"

She knit her brows and stuck out her chin. "Vell, I tink it vass for hiss bad
hardt."

I laughed. "You sound like your Danish grandfather."

"Does Peter have a heart problem?"

"I don't know." I'd seen his face get red lots of times, and I wondered about high blood pressure, but he'd never confided anything about his heart. The image of Peter suffering a heart attack on account of my election clung to me like a sweaty shirt.

The sports news told about the Dodger and Angel games, and showed clips from the Lakers in the play-offs, but left out the Padres, as usual.

Kim's interest focused on one thing. "Will there be anything tasty from your press conference?"

"I'm not sure what will make it, but the reporter asked a couple of nosey questions."

"Like?" She'd gone to the closet and taken off her dress.

"Yeah, I like."

"No, I meant like what kinds of questions, not—"

"Oh. Well, I do. Like your body. And the questions were something about—lacy bras and—uh—you're taking it all off."

"I always do."

"Not while we're in the middle of a discussion about the press conference."

"You've never done a press conference before." Stark naked. Lovely nude. Sexy woman. Images from aesthetic art to primitive urges waved over me. She slipped a sheer nightgown over her head, and let is slip slowly down over her breasts—and waist—and hips. By that time, I'd moved away from the television to her side.

"I want to…" I drew her close to me for a deep kiss. She pressed closer and kissed me like the temptress she sometimes became. Then she pulled back.

"Wait, the weather's over. They're saying the Lutheran convention is up next."

"Commercial's first. Time for more…" I whirled her around, bending her backward, planting damp kisses from her neck to her ear and eyes and back down again.

I lifted her up, spun us in a waltz step, and pressed her body against mine.

"If this is what getting elected bishop does for you, I'll vote for another election every day." Her eyes twinkled as she rubbed against me.

I kissed her forehead. "I think it's more about your being gorgeous and pregnant."

"The Southern California—Hawaii Diocese of the Lutheran Church—North America met today at the Los Angeles Conference Center…." The announcer cut into our amorous encounter and when Kim grabbed the remote to turn up the volume, she glanced at her watch. They showed the delegates applauding while Kim hugged me on stage, and the voice-over continued.

"…Elected the Reverend Jonathan Larsen the first black Lutheran bishop west of Chicago since 1975. His unusual slogan, 'Fail Boldly,' captured the imagination of the voters. Among his first duties are interviews with dozens of victims of clergy sexual misconduct, hoping, as he said, 'to avoid any hint of cover-up.'"

"No! Not dozens of victims. Dozens of interviews."

"Shh, I want to hear this." Kim kept checking her watch.

"Bishop-elect Larsen admitted to, as he called it, 'clutter in his spiritual closet' but refused to elaborate…"

"Wrong again. I said they'd be bored."

A close-up of the reporter in a hallway showed my secretary, Shirlee, in tears, saying "We hate it that he's leaving," then cut away to the delegates again.

The voice-over continued, "We have been unable to reach other delegates from his congregation for comment. Bishop-elect Larsen will preside at the closing communion service tomorrow morning in the Conference Center. Back to you, Brianna."

"And that's it for news tonight, stay tuned for…"

Kim hit the off button on the remote and studied her watch. "Fifty-five seconds."

"What?"

"You got fifty-five seconds of fame. That's not enough." Kim looked disgusted.

"A bunch of distortions, I'd say." My irritation pushed me to pace.

"What did Shirlee really say?"

"I have no idea, but this—this clip—leaves the impression I'm hard hearted."

"The congregation'll miss you terribly, Jon. But it's not like you wanted to hurt them."

"Of course not. And about the interviews. At the press conference, I told them about Review Panels for accused clergy, and even handed out copies of our policy."

"You didn't think they'd read ten pages on the air, did you?" Sometimes Kim seemed naïve, but rarely got fooled. She'd reminded me lots of times about being too trusting and expecting people to put the best construction on everything.

"No, but the reporter left out important stuff."

"Did I tell you how handsome you look tonight? You're going to be a great TV personality."

She knew how to get me out of my bad mood. I slipped my arm around her waist and led her toward the bed, tugging off the nightgown as we moved.

We'd almost drifted off when she mumbled, "Does getting elected mean you get a raise—so we can get the air conditioner fixed?"

✳    ✳    ✳    ✳

I awakened early, frozen in the fetal position. The nightmare rewound and played again. I stood naked in a town square in front of hundreds of well-dressed white adults shouting obscenities at me. A cackling white face clown with a huge red nose hung a tow chain and crossed tire irons around my neck. A faceless black woman dressed in white appeared, screaming, "No, no! You can't do this." Then I woke up, soaked in sweat.

I lay there, my body paralyzed, almost awake, still asleep. The tingling pin-pricks of my nerves waking up sent a distress signal to my heart, which pumped anxiety through my body. I forced my right arm to pull off the sheet and blanket, gritted my teeth to get one heavy leg across the other limp one, and shoved myself upright with my left arm. I sat on the edge of the bed, head in hands, praying for strength to make it to the shower to wash away the dream.

The cold water jolted me awake, then warmed to the point of pain. I adjusted the faucet to keep the heat bearable, welcoming the steamy water to pound life back into my numbed body. I mumbled a prayer of thanks for the wet reminder of my baptism, and turned the faucet to cold. Shivering to its drumming beat, I turned it off, shook myself, and stepped out into a huge white towel. I dressed in my new purple clergy shirt and best gray suit. I wanted to tell Kim my dream and have her kiss away my guilt, but I ran out of time. I needed to get downstairs to prepare for the worship service.

She opened her eyes enough so I could see the blue, and kissed me good-bye. "I'll be there before they finish the opening hymn," she mumbled.

✳    ✳    ✳    ✳

I'd brought my white alb, cincture and red stole for the clergy procession, but hadn't considered bringing my chasuble for presiding at the sacrament, convinced I wouldn't be elected. Henry lent me his, and helped me prepare to wear the heavy gold, red and white brocade garment. The ceremonial robes, designed centuries ago to hide the celebrant's individual identity, reminded worshippers—and ourselves—we led as servants of Christ, not as ego-driven humans. Presiding

Bishop Clemente, Henry, and I joined the gathering clergy in the back of the hall preparing for the procession.

The congregational singing raised prickles on my spine. Classical hymns done on a pipe organ and sung by hundreds of voices lifted my spirits and gave voice to my sense of wonder. "Lift high the cross, the love of Christ proclaim…" We followed the teen-aged crucifer, holding the processional cross as high as she could reach, and two hundred white robed clergy, singing with gusto, moved up the wide aisle.

The ancient liturgy, based on early Catholic formats, and Henry's sermon led us to the ritual of Holy Communion. Word and sacrament, the essence of Lutheran identity, invited us into mystical community with one another and the gracious God.

I lifted the bread and chalice high, and heard myself, as if watching from a distance, repeat the words of Jesus at the last supper, "…He took bread, gave thanks…he took the cup…given for you…do this in remembrance of me." We remembered and re-experienced and miraculously connected to the people of all times and places who receive the gracious gifts of forgiveness and new life. All the actions, tastes and aromas helped connect me to the awesome mystery of the loving God.

I marveled to myself at the wondrous paradox of the inscrutable and cosmic God as creator and ever present spirit on the one hand, and the earthy reality of Jesus as baby born in a smelly stable and a bleeding man hanging on a sacrificial cross, on the other.

After eating the bread and drinking the wine, distributing it to the assistants who communed hundreds of worshippers, I declared the blessing of God's grace, cleared my throat and delivered the closing benediction while my knees trembled from the experience of God's holy presence. "…The Lord bless and keep you…look upon you with favor, and give you peace. In the name of the Father, Son and Holy Spirit."

Favor? Peace? The words mocked me. God's brilliant light exposed the real me. Nothing but a patient and gracious God could look with favor on my blotchy past. How could I know peace with Kim pregnant and me deceiving her and the church? The glow of worship began to fade into the challenge of going out to "fail boldly."

# CHAPTER 9

▼

A dozen messages waited on the answering machine when we got home from the convention. Ten congratulated me, another told me I'd missed a dental appointment, and the twelfth sounded urgent.

"Congratulations, Jon. It's me, Beverly. Call me right away, okay?"

Her voice trembled, so I looked up her number in the diocesan directory and prepared for the worst. Seven rings, then a weak, "Hello?"

"Bev. It's Jon. Are you okay?"

"Thank God you called. I need to talk. Soon."

"Just say when." Whatever bothered her, I knew she wouldn't ask if she weren't in a lot of pain.

"Did Henry say anything about me?"

"No."

"I need to tell you before he does."

We agreed to meet the next afternoon in Thousand Oaks on my way back from Solvang. It didn't take long to get the feel of the demands on a bishop. I'd been elected for one day and wouldn't be installed for another thirty, yet Beverly called me on official business the minute she got home.

I wondered if Henry's big brown envelope held any hints. I flipped open my laptop and inserted the computer disk labeled "Charges." Before I could open the file, I noticed my e-mail light blinking, so I detoured to check. Five of the six subject lines read, "Congratulations!" The other said, "Election?" I opened it.

DON'T GET TOO
COMFORTABLE

No signature, no explanation, just like the cell phone messages. Kim called out to me from the bedroom wanting to know what time we'd be going to see my parents. They'd pushed my "dutiful son" button the night before when I told them about my election, so I promised to drive up as soon as I finished at the convention. My body said, "Stay home and sleep." My concern for Dad's health said, "Just do it." I answered Kim with a vague, "In about an hour," and turned back to the laptop.

I answered the five messages with, "Thanks. Pray for me. More later." The anonymous message sat in the pit of my stomach like a chili pepper. I tried to forget about it. Kim peeked in the door.

"Everything okay?"

"No. Yeah. Well, most everything, but…" Before I could explain, she walked into the small bedroom we'd converted for a home office. We'd covered the walls with bookshelves, and put a computer table in front of the window facing the back yard. Two rockers and a desk chair for computer work filled the space.

"I thought I heard you mumbling."

"Those special ears of yours pick up everything." I told her about the anonymous e-mail.

"You think it's Peter again?"

"Probably. But maybe it's Brenda."

"Yeah, she'd do something like that. Did a name pop up when you sent a reply?" She walked over and peered at the screen. No name. Anyone who wanted to remain anonymous blocked the mailbox. Changing my e-mail address or phone number didn't seem worth the hassle, since they'd be published in the diocesan newsletter anyway.

I reached to turn off the computer, leaving the bishop's confidential disk for another time, but curiosity got the best of me. I popped it in the computer. The first thing on screen after I typed in the password: "Talk to me about Beverly Davidson's situation as soon as possible."

Ouch. Her call and Henry's request made me uneasy. I'd call him as soon as I'd met with Beverly. First, my parents deserved some time from their newly elected son. The latest anonymous message festered deep inside, keeping me anything but comfortable, but detective work had to wait.

*       *       *       *

Kim drove while I dozed. Driving up Highway 101 to Solvang on a hot Sunday afternoon in May meant fighting through Los Angeles and beach traffic from the Malibu turn-off through Santa Barbara. My mood fit the frustration of stop and go, and the anonymous messages kept me from getting much rest. One scene lifted my spirits: the hazy view of the Channel Islands off the coast at Ventura.

We arrived in time for what they called supper. Mom and Dad lived in a small apartment, but ate their meals in the main dining room. The word had spread about my election, so someone made a computer banner: "Welcome Bishop!" and the kitchen crew baked a cake inscribed, "Bishop Larsen is sweet." Not my adjective of choice, but a nice sentiment.

Solvang's Lutheran Home sat on a hill looking down at the white church styled after *Grundtvig's Kirke* in Copenhagen. A combination of small cottages, assisted living rooms, and a care center provided the residents with everything but an acute care hospital.

The administrator, who ushered us to Mom and Dad's table, assured us that Orpha and Dagmar gladly gave up their places for "royalty," as they put it.

My dad stood up, clinking his glass with a fork to get everyone's attention. "I raised Jonathan to be a good man, and felt mighty glad when he became a pastor. Now, a bishop. Hard to believe, when I think about how…" Mom tugged at his shirt, and he sat down.

Dad once stood a solid six feet tall until gravity and some arthritis shortened him in the last ten years. His blond hair turned gray, the crinkles around his eyes deepened into wrinkles, and his hands, calloused in his beloved garden, turned blotchy and soft. His high expectations of me hadn't diminished much, though.

Mom added a few words about how blessed she felt to have me as her son. "I named him Jonathan. It means "a gift of God,' you know. I always knew he'd make us proud." Then, in honor of her heritage, she said all of Liberia was proud of me, and all of Denmark, and all of California, and that's when Dad tugged at her blouse.

Mom looked radiant. Some people said she looked like an older version of Dianne Carroll. She asked me to stand up for a hug, and planted a huge kiss on my lips. I felt like the child who's too old for his Mom to kiss in public, but smiled and nodded to everyone. I knew they hadn't experienced excitement like this in the Home since last year when one of the residents tried to blow out the ninety-four candles on his birthday cake and set the tablecloth afire.

We walked them to their apartment, visited awhile and said good night by eight-thirty, their bedtime. We drove past the church of our childhood, and cruised the "main drag" the way we did as teenagers. The sidewalks downtown, past the buildings styled in Danish architecture, "rolled up" at sundown, like always. Exhausted from the excitement of pregnancy and election, we collapsed at the motel by nine.

After breakfast and more hugs, we said good-bye to Mom and Dad and a dozen well-wishers who walked us to our car. I always felt reluctant to leave them. Dad's health, at eighty-eight, fluctuated between problematic and "getting along." Ten years younger, Mom seemed to grow stronger each year. I worried about not visiting often enough, knowing each time could be the last with Dad. We kissed them good-bye with promises to spend all day with them one Saturday before I started as bishop. We hadn't told them about Kim's pregnancy, or about the anonymous messages. They had enough to think about for now.

Kim and I chatted about our days as tennis champs while we drove past Santa Ynez Valley High School, and about a couple of class mates who worked at the Chumash Casino nearby. "Remember doing the Danish folk dances in costume every September for Danish Days? I'll bet we could still do 'Little Man in a Fix,'" she smiled.

"I feel like a little man in a fix, Kim. Think we can dance our way through this?"

We talked about our new challenges, the miscarriages and pregnancy, and about Dad and his decline. Most of the time, we gazed off at the Santa Ynez Mountains, still showing some green from spring rains, but turning golden brown the way they'd stay until winter. Like Dad often said, "Nature does the right thing. So should we."

The small town atmosphere in Solvang made it easy, though not impossible, to avoid doing the "wrong thing." The quaint shops, Danish windmills, and a horse drawn trolley all drew people from around the world to visit our town. They'd eat butter-filled pastries, *medisterpollse* (Danish sausage) with red cabbage, and drink coffee so strong the stir-spoon dissolved.

Despite the crowded streets full of tourists, every resident knew what every other resident did, and if they didn't see it first hand, they'd find out soon enough. Every kid in town belonged to the adults, all of whom kept their eyes and ears open so their mouths could pass along the exaggerated details. We found it hard to sneak around and get by with anything in Solvang.

Dad had wanted me to go to a church college. Since Kim had decided on California Lutheran University, I had no problem doing the right thing by choosing it, too. He didn't say to, but I majored in psychology and religion because I knew he'd like the religion part. The atmosphere there helped me discover I enjoyed probing divine mysteries. I had still felt unsure about the bishop idea, though.

I missed Solvang, but not its small town atmosphere. Growing pains rankled people as it changed from a village and farms settled by Danes for Danes, to a cosmopolitan community clinging to the tourist appeal of "Little Denmark in California." The Valley drew celebrities like Michael Jackson and Bo Derek. Wineries and small ranches dotted the landscape. The area changed, but some of the residents resisted anything new.

Driving over San Marcos Pass, past fenced in llamas and Lake Cachuma, instead of the tranquility of the scenery, I felt a growing anxiety about the future. Kim broke the silence on the ride past Santa Barbara, asking if I planned to spend some time in solitude with Brother David at the Center in Malibu. "Yeah, I'd like to spend a couple of days before I take office."

"Good. You're always more in synch when you come back from seeing him." True enough. I needed synchronicity. Balance. A calm center. And, a clear sense of purpose.

∗     ∗     ∗     ∗

Kim volunteered to walk through the mall during my meeting, so she dropped me at Freddy's Coffee Shoppe.

"Thanks for coming, Jon. Bishop Jon. It's going to take me awhile to call you that." Most days, she looked younger than her fifty-four years. Today, she looked ready for retirement.

Overworked, underpaid, and coming off the ego stretch of a bishop's election, she ranked high on the vulnerability scale. I'd admired her quick mind and sharp wit the first time we met at a workshop several years before. Besides learning we had the same personality type, we discovered that those of us most open to the mystery of spirituality are also most open to the mystery of sexuality. That put both of us high on the "seducible and seducing" scales.

I didn't need a workshop to tell me that human and divine passion are inextricably connected, despite what the Victorian Age tried to convince us. My time in Liberia confirmed my vulnerability.

We ordered coffee and their famous cinnamon sticky buns with caramel coating topped with walnuts. Like most Freddy's, the booth showed some wear from the hundreds who had slid across the red vinyl. The waitress wore that "please don't forget to tip me 'cuz I'm not makin' enough to feed my kids" look. The aroma from the kitchen across the room suggested bacon and eggs, but the sticky bun fit my craving for something sweet.

"I told Henry about this, so you'll get his report. I wanted to tell you in person, because..." She looked out the window as if the traffic flowing by on the freeway would give her strength or insight. "Well, I'll just jump in."

Between bites and licking of sticky fingertips, Beverly told me she didn't mention our meeting to her husband, Dean. I'd met him once, and noticed two things: he stood several inches shorter than Beverly, and his large ears literally stuck out.

"Dean likes sex," she whispered, "often and with variety. When the neighbors put in a pool and spa this spring, he started talking about skinny dipping and swapping. I told him if it weren't immoral, I still wouldn't do it because it's such a sexual cliché." She missed her own humor and hurried on.

"Two weeks ago, he went over there without me, came home reeking of wine, and taunted me with what they did. When he threatened to tell the church unless I joined them next time, I told him to quit going over there or leave me."

"You don't mince words."

"Right. He didn't leave, but he didn't stay home, either."

"What do you want to happen?"

"I want him to leave. He's such a pig." She ripped off a piece of the sticky bun and chewed it like beef jerky. "But if he leaves, I probably have to resign because the congregation is so focused on family values, they'd never stand for a divorced pastor, especially a woman." Tears welled up. "And I still love the jerk."

I told her not to worry about resignation yet. "I'm more concerned about you getting the support you need. Do you have a counselor?"

"No. Any recommendations?" I gave her two names. She mentioned having a couple of women clergy she met with once a month, and her sister in Sacramento. "They're my circle of support."

I encouraged her to contact them. "You're a gutsy lady." She smiled for the first time since we arrived.

"Do you have to call a Review Panel?"

"I don't know for sure, but I'll talk to Henry right away. This sounds more like a conflict issue than sexual misconduct on your part. Have you told anyone else?"

"No. Dean and the neighbors know about it, of course, but they don't know what I'm doing about it."

I asked her to think about the plus and minus of making this public, versus waiting awhile to see if their threat to "tell" would pass. We didn't hold hands for prayer, knowing even the slightest indication of affection could be misinterpreted in case someone saw us, and agreed to talk by phone or e-mail in a few days. Before we left, I asked if Peter had said anything to her about my election.

"Nothing I could understand because of the clapping. I think something like, 'Well, he beat us.' He seemed pretty upset."

I let it go at that, wishing for more. I felt like Peter's comment and Beverly's trauma deserved more than I gave it. My plate overflowed. I needed that retreat, and I needed Henry's advice.

When Kim and I got home, I called him. "Beverly filled me in after the election," he said. "I don't see a need to convene a Review Panel. There are no formal charges of sexual misconduct." We talked about the risks of someone else breaking the story, and the possible cleansing and healing if she did go public. "Give her a couple of days to think about it."

A few days later, Beverly e-mailed to thank me. "Dean agreed to go with me to see a counselor. We'll try to work things out. We talked with the neighbors who agreed not to tell anyone, though they couldn't understand why I acted so prudish about a little fooling around among friends. I told them I'd explain some day."

I messaged back that the bishop confirmed we didn't need a Review Panel, and we could talk again after they'd seen the counselor. I felt uneasy, thinking we hadn't heard the last of the neighbors, and probably not Dean, either.

*      *      *      *

Tchaikovsky's *Pathetique* symphony played on the radio in my home office, moving my mood deeper. Sadness oozed into my throat from the lemon-sized lump forming there. Leaving the congregation meant cutting some profound ties. Already, three families asked if I would come back to conduct funerals for their failing relatives. Two others wanted me to baptize their babies expected before Thanksgiving. A couple in college wanted me to do their wedding during their Christmas vacation.

To them in person, and to others I knew might wonder, I explained the reality of my leaving in our parish newsletter. "Once I leave, I can't return for pastoral acts, no matter how much you mean to me. I can't come back for everyone, so returning for anyone would be unfair. Besides, you need to bond with a new pastor."

*"I'd like to show you some of the churches my father and mother helped develop. They've done everything from pounding nails to teaching classes for new pastors. In Liberia, we all do whatever is needed most."*

*"Did your parents ever suggest that you become a pastor?"*

*"Oh no. We've had women missionaries, but never a native Liberian woman pastor."*

*"Some day. You'd make a good pastor, Margrethe."*

*"I want to finish my medical training and become a pediatrician and eventually, a wife and mother."*

The symphony ended, and my eyes began to leak around the edges. I wondered if she'd ever accomplished all she dreamed about. I shook off the thought. Margrethe's dreams belonged to her, and I didn't dare let myself give her energy.

I answered more congratulatory e-mails, cutting corners, as my dad would say, by copying and pasting the same basic message into each one. I added a personal closing, but wondered if people compared messages, and if they did, what they'd think about my short cut. Getting elected and seeing Dad uncovered some old feelings of inadequacy.

I wandered in my garden, wondering what to say in my farewell messages to the congregation, and when I moved toward the Sacred Space and my chaise, I remembered it had collapsed the day of my interview. We hadn't found time to replace it. Or fix the air conditioner. Everything happened so fast. I needed to breathe, but I also needed to wrap up nine years at the congregation, deal with Beverly and my aging parents, go on retreat, and somewhere in there, Kim and I needed to celebrate her pregnancy. Our pregnancy.

# CHAPTER 10

▼

Every time my cell phone beeped, I wondered if I'd get another anonymous message. Beverly's latest call troubled me.

"Dean blew up in our session with the counselor when I told him there'd be no Review Panel." She sighed. "Because I didn't do anything to make me guilty of sexual misconduct." She sighed again, with the kind of catch in her breath we get when we're about to cry. "He called me a selfish bitch for even talking to you and claimed you and I had an affair."

"Whoa! What did the counselor do?"

"Told him to sit down and stop yelling, and then asked why he said that. He sat down and said he knew you and I slept together at that conference last year."

"Where'd he get such an idea?"

"From me, I guess. I came back raving about the conference and how you and I fell in the same personality group, and we'd learned we're vulnerable to sexual involvements with parishioners."

"And he concluded?"

"That you and I slept together."

The thought had crossed my mind. I knew better than to act on it and hadn't even mentioned it to her or to Kim. "Did he say any more?"

"No. He walked out. The counselor suggested I let him go and not feed his paranoia by getting defensive. But I'm worried about what he'll say."

"He could make life miserable for both of us."

"I'm sorry, Jon, I know you don't need this crap."

"Not your fault. Let me ponder it awhile. Meanwhile, don't panic."

I walked in the house wondering if every day as bishop would be like this. I wanted transparency, and instead got exposure—about something untrue.

The kitchen phone jangled and startled me. I hoped for Kim's silky voice asking if we needed milk, but no such mundane luck.

"Jonathan, it's Peter. We need to talk."

I'd called him right after the election, but he'd put me off. Peter acted like his Biblical namesake sometimes—impulsive. I felt like telling him to get over himself.

"Sure. When?" I said the bishop-appropriate words, but my tone had to let him know my irritation. He ignored it.

"I'm in Costa Mesa at my sister's. Wanda's helping her with the new baby. I'll be right over."

\*     \*     \*     \*

I relaxed a little when Peter didn't slam his car door. He turned down iced tea, chose one of our white plastic chairs on the deck, and glowered toward the canyon. I sat down across from him, scraping the chair legs to force some noise into the heavy silence. I noticed a pinkish tinge above his collar.

"Is Kim home?"

"No. She'll be at a workshop for several hours. Why?"

"This is between us." I sipped my tea, while he fidgeted with the cross he always wore around his neck. "You should have pulled your name out before we got to the last ballot."

I touched my fingertips together the way Danny Kaye did in an old movie when he didn't know what to say. On screen, the people thought him wise because he paused before he spoke. I felt awkward. "I figured you'd win."

"You sabotaged me."

"Excuse me?" I leaned forward, forming my fingers into a loose fist and folding my arms across my chest.

The pinkish tinge around his collar moved upward and turned brighter. "You know I'm better than you. You had no business running."

"Whoa there, Pistol Pete. Don't go shootin' off your mouth without thinkin' here."

"Don't give me any of that Santa Ynez cowboy crap. And don't call me Pete. We both know you're not fit to be a bishop."

I winced inside, but wouldn't let him see it. I'd played enough poker with my father-in-law to know how to keep myself looking calm. "Take a couple of deep breaths before you reach melt down, okay buddy?"

He stood up, tipping over his chair, and started pacing. "When we talked at lunch that day, I told you to tell the committee about your secret. I couldn't believe you're so arrogant you let them nominate you."

"Arrogant?"

"Yes. Egotistical. Vain. You're so full of yourself you can't believe anybody else is any good. You ruined my last shot at bishop."

"Ruined?"

"Stop feeding me questions. Damn it, Jon, I wanted that job so bad I almost had a stroke over it." His pacing picked up speed, and turned into figure eights. "Your psychobabble and 'fail boldly' crap pizzazzed 'em. You hoodwinked 'em."

"Hold it, Peter Pop-off. What do you mean, hoodwinked? And nobody says that anymore." I stood up slowly, intending to head for the kitchen to get some more iced tea, hoping he'd take some this time to cool down his head of steam.

"Sit down, dammit, I have more to say."

"Yessir, your eminence."

"Don't smart mouth me, you bastard. Shut up and listen." He leaned over the table separating us, and I sat back down. I knew I could take care of myself if he decided to get physical, but I worried he might have a coronary. He ranted about how he worked harder, lived cleaner, and did all the right things to earn his shot at bishop. "I even married the right woman."

"Are you saying Kim isn't the right kind of woman?" I caught him off guard.

"No. No, Kim is the best part of who you are. No. It's about you." He started to pace again, but slower.

"Peter, I had no idea I'd win."

"But you did. And now I'm sitting on the outside while you get the purple shirt and big cross." He started for the gate, so I followed. "I've said enough"

"You're way too upset to drive. Come on back and have some tea."

"I'm fine. You're not. All I can say is, good luck." He hurried through the gate, pushing it closed with a loud click. In all his bluster, I forgot to ask about his "black something beat us" remark, or if he'd sent the anonymous messages. He drove off without squealing the tires, which relieved my mind about him— not about me, though. I still needed to find a way to say good-bye to a congregation I loved.

The days whirled by, packing books and files, visiting the homebound with communion, completing reports, and more. Kim and I spent our late evenings talking about the baby. Another check up with the doctor gave us some confidence to go along with our apprehension. "New medications and careful exercise will help. I won't kid you. We'll have to watch you carefully."

I knew Kim needed me more than ever. The label, "busy pastor" fit me like a too tight clergy collar. I'd sailed through books and workshops on time management, and could quote Stephen Covey verbatim about the difference between "urgent" and "important." But, something drove me to spend so many hours spreading God's grace around to others, I had precious little left for her. I wondered how we'd handle the pressures of the new job.

Henry called every day to update my calendar for events I needed to attend, and to reassure me I'd do a fine job. I scheduled the forty-eight hour silent retreat at the Malibu Center, and made plans to talk with Brother David some of that time. Before I could escape to the mountains, one major event stood in my way: the farewell roast.

*         *         *         *

I did my best to put on a face as happy as Kim's. She loved to see me squirm. I knew we'd all laugh, at my expense, but I'd been to enough farewell events to know sadness wove its way into good-byes, too. I'd miss the congregation and knew how hard it would be to cut ties with the people I loved.

On the way to the church, I felt a strange sensation near my heart. At first, I worried it might be a reaction to all the stress of the last month. Then, I remembered I'd put the cell phone in my sport coat pocket and had shifted it from bell tone to "vibrate." Another text message.

GOOD LUCK
AT THE ROAST

I showed it to Kim. "Is that a threat? Who's doing this to you, Jon?"

"Somebody who knows my schedule."

"And wants to mess with your head." She grabbed the phone and pushed the "off" button. "No more. We're goin' to parrdee."

I didn't let go as easily. Peter and Brenda, the two prime suspects, might show up just to make my life miserable. Somehow, I needed to find out who continued to bug me.

We walked into the large room we called "Fellowship Hall," filled with familiar faces and gold balloons. Laughter and hugs greeted us, along with the ominous, "You're gonna get yours tonight, Pastor Jon." Kim and I headed to the restrooms to prepare for the long evening of sitting.

Eunice Carlson cornered me as I came out. The oldest member of our congregation tended to gossip at Wednesday morning Bible study, though she called the tidbits, "prayer concerns." In her defense, she also asked the study group to pray for her grandson's battle with drugs, and her daughter's inability to find marital bliss. She didn't hide her family secrets, so I supposed she believed everyone wanted the world to know theirs.

She took my newly washed hand in her withered one, and pulled me toward her tiny bent body. "Pastor Jon, you buried my husband five years ago. You buried my grandson when he overdosed, and you married my daughter to her fourth husband." Her scratchy voice and trembling tears touched me in the deep place where pastors go when they need to keep from sobbing.

"You never judged us. You made me feel secure when you hugged me at my husband's grave. I'll pray for you every day."

I stilled the sob struggling to reach the surface, but silent tears clouded the sight of her beaming, wrinkled face. The sincerity of her words reminded me of the exquisite gift pastors receive from parishioners. They invite us into their deepest vulnerability, confident of our help. Trust got hammered out during hours at bedsides in the hospital, or as we paced the kitchen floor at 3:00 a.m. waiting for a teen-ager long over-due from a date, and whenever we placed a bit of bread in their uplifted hands along with a promise of Christ's presence.

Music moves the soul, and when we all sang John Ylvisaker's gem, "I was there to hear your borning cry," everybody's eyes glistened. The choir led the congregation as we harmonized on the haunting hymn, "There in God's garden stands the tree of wisdom…Its name is Jesus…See how its branches reach to us in welcome…" More tears flowed from some apparently inexhaustible supply deep inside.

Henry Madison and several neighboring pastors talked too long—a professional reality—and they awarded me a silly plaque commemorating the time I baptized a little *boy*, "Emily Kirsten Olson," the squalling baby *girl* I'd already baptized at a service earlier that same day.

My staff sang their own words to the old song, "So long, it's been good to know you" in which they took turns claiming my office furniture, concluding with the plea for plum jobs in my administration. Shirlee, on behalf of the group, presented me with a pair of muddy tennis shoes representing my failed attempts to walk on water, and an elegant padded chaise lounge. "We heard what happened to your old one." Everyone laughed but Shirlee, who shook her head and shed a few tears. Mine joined hers. I'd miss everyone, but Shirlee most of all.

I scanned the room, but saw no sign of either Brenda or Peter. I tried to put the messages out of my mind, when in tromped nine high school youth, smiling like they'd stolen their first kiss. Each one held up a large letter spelling "P-A-S-T-O-R J-O-N." "P is for perfect, which pastor is almost," "A is for awful which he certainly isn't," "S is for silly, which he surely can be," and so on to "N is for nothing, which we'll feel like without him."

No sooner had they finished than three trumpeters blasted the Olympic Overture from on stage. The chaotic procession of children caught me off guard. I held Kim's hand, remembering the struggles she endured convincing the congregation to launch the Tiny Angels of Anaheim Hills Pre-School. Forty of them marched around the room, led by a petite red headed girl dressed in a robe several inches too long, topped with a clerical collar loose around her neck.

They added a twist when they sang, "Jesus loves me," by changing the last line to "and we love Mrs. Kim." The redheaded girl announced in a clear, strong voice, "Now it's time for the sermon." Hands on hips, face solemn as a saint, she took a deep breath and said, "Abba dabba dabba dabba monka sonka wonka. Amen. That's it. I'm outa here."

When we all recovered, the president of the congregation praised Kim for her enthusiastic leadership of the pre-school, and for "keeping Jon sane." She accepted the bouquet of roses with grace, but couldn't speak when she saw the certificate for a five-year subscription to the Los Angeles Symphony.

Last, he asked me to stand alone and invited everyone to take a long look. He spent the next ten minutes telling stories about my ministry among them, and how this "Liberian Danish American pastor invaded the estates and subdivisions of Anaheim Hills with graciousness and compassion. Surrender was inevitable." Turning to me, he said, "You never put politics in the pulpit, and you never let us think simple answers answered complicated social issues. You clothed everything you said and did with compassion."

Eunice caught my eye when she shook her withered fist like a football fan rooting for a touchdown. The president went on, "Things have never been better. It's a great time for you to leave, Jon."

Applause built, but he raised his arms, shouting into the microphone. "Hold on, there's more." He whipped out a thirteen-month calendar. "You've given us more than we had any right to expect. You deserve a reward." He showed the month of June 2003 with three weeks marked with a big red "X." "In order to make sure you take a vacation, we've deposited money in a travel savings account to take you anywhere in the world."

Cheers and whistles joined the shuffling of feet, as everyone stood to honor the love we shared. I felt my knees grow weaker, but gathered myself and gave the president a bear hug.

I paused to let the lump in my throat shrink. "You'll always have a place in our hearts. Your generous spirit and marvelous sense of humor will carry us through whatever lies ahead."

Someone yelled from the back, "How much in the account?"

I hadn't looked. Kim peeked over my shoulder, and we both gasped. The president reached for the microphone and said what we couldn't manage: "The deposit is $4,500.00—five hundred thanks for each year you served us"

Shocked at first, and then honored beyond our expectations, we shouted "God bless you," and stumbled off the stage to shake a mile of outstretched hands.

*        *        *        *

We couldn't wait to get home, sink into the couch, and pop the bottle of sparkling cider the staff gave us. Kim drove, re-living the outrageous skits and moving music. "And what about that trip? Super generous. And the calendar was a great touch."

"How about Hawaii, Kim? Kauai, maybe?"

"Princeville?"

She parked the car in the driveway because I'd filled the garage with boxes from my church office and still hadn't fixed the opener. At least the air conditioner guy had come, and now we had a new chaise. We wrestled with sacks of cards and plaques, and staggered into the house with tangible evidence of the congregation's appreciation. "I don't feel worthy," I said, overflowing with emotional leftovers.

Midway through the second glass of cider, the ringing phone startled us. "Who'd be calling at midnight?" Kim untangled herself from my arms and the couch cushions, and headed for the phone. The Intruder, as I'd come to call the anonymous messenger, had used e-mail and cell phone, not land line. I figured it had to be an emergency.

"It's Mom and Dad. They're in Hawaii—Princeville, can you believe it?" I grabbed the extension in my office, catching Christine in mid-sentence.

"...Couldn't remember how much later it is there. We just finished dinner. Dad tried earlier but said he couldn't get through. Wished we could have been there for the party and wondered how it went." Iver tried to call? That seemed strange. He never called us.

We told about the party, including the travel fund, and our idea of using it to visit Princeville. "As long as you're there, you can make a reservation for next June. Oh, and reserve a crib."

"A crib? Did you hear from the adoption agency?"

"Nope. I'm pregnant."

"I can't believe it. She's pregnant, sweetie. Are you sure? Dad says—well, forget what he said."

We chatted on about babies and parties, their helicopter flight into Waimea Canyon, and how it felt to walk where they'd filmed *South Pacific*.

"Mom, don't tell anyone about the baby, okay? We haven't told anyone else yet."

When we hung up, we dragged our bodies into bed and cuddled together, whispering our love for one another. Kim's deep breathing soon told me she'd fallen asleep, but a clear image flitted through my mind before I dozed off: the two of us with a baby walking on the beaches of Kauai.

Still glowing the next morning, we danced around the kitchen table where the savings account book stood at attention. We conjured up a fantasy about bringing our newborn child to the mystical waters high on the mountain overlooking Waimea Canyon, where we'd create a ritual of belonging and new life in the luxurious landscape.

We imagined out loud we'd write a kind of baptismal ritual to be private for our family of three, and public for all of God's creation, including the birds and flowers, geckos and bugs, sunshine and rocks, all embraced by the fertile and moist Spirit of the Cosmos.

Inside, I suspected she felt the same apprehension I did about the baby.

# CHAPTER 11

▼

Breakfast over, we tucked the dream about Hawaii in our hearts and headed out. Kim drove toward school for another day of teaching. I went up the freeway toward the road winding its way to Malibu Center. I looked forward to re-connecting with the rhythms of the universe in solitude and silence. The friar in charge welcomed me with congratulations on my election, and handed me soap and towels. "You know the way."

The sparsely furnished room included a small kneeling bench for prayer and a simple crucifix on the wall. A single orange flower in a pale blue bud vase brightened the top of the desk. Through my window, I could look out on the desert garden and rugged mountains behind it. Already, my soul began to sing with divine connections.

The setting reminded me of the simple hospitality of Jesus to the *anawim*, the poor and homeless of his day. My weary soul, though far from poverty-stricken, yearned for sustenance, and I knew I could find rest and renewal in this quiet place.

Unpacking became a ritual of letting go. The valley below gradually disappeared with each piece of clothing I took from the sports bag. Besides the basic necessities, I pulled out a pair of sturdy walking shoes, khaki shorts and some tee shirts. I had packed more clean underwear than I'd need, still following the sage advice every mother gives her departing son. A tennis ball nestled in a corner of the bag, left over from another time.

I carried no cell phone, no laptop, just a few pens and notebooks. I changed and headed for the mountain trail, starting an outward trek, taking me inward to the maze of questions festering in my mind.

On the trail, a rabbit stood in my path, wiggling its nose, white tail quiet for the moment. "Good day, Brother Bunny, how goes your hopping this day?"

He hopped once as if to say, "Okay," and stopped.

"You evidently escaped the prowling coyote one more night. I see you've found sustenance for your voracious appetite. Maybe I can fill my insides with insights about what direction I'll be leading the diocese."

The cottontail started down the mountain, then stopped as if to say, "I hear ya', but if you don't mind, I've gotta get goin' down the trail. That dang tortoise is gainin' on me."

"Isn't that the way in life, Brother Bunny? Just when you get into a good conversation and find something tasty to munch, there's a race to be run. Well, you go ahead. I'm going to pause here a couple of days before I get back into the race." The rabbit bounced away, tail dancing in the breeze. I turned up the trail.

I paused now and then to enjoy the expanse of blue water and Channel Islands off to the west and north. The smell of sage and mixture of hot dry mountain air with cool moist breezes from the ocean signaled the variety of insights yet to come.

As my meditation bench, I chose a large rock, worn smooth over many years from hundreds of bottoms shifting on the hard surface. I focused with centering prayer, and the hardness of the rock disappeared, integrated into my confession.

In the silent spaces between my thoughts, I quieted myself to listen, feel, and experience God deep within and far beyond. Like Elijah on the mountain, I listened for the sound of crushed silence, the still, small voice of God. The Spirit's mysterious presence enveloped me, leading me deeper into my darkness.

"I confess my arrogance and selfishness, dear God. I have been unfaithful to my wife, deceived the church, and live in fear instead of trusting your Spirit. Even as I speak these words, I am wondering how to avoid telling the whole truth. I feel crushed by the vise of my dilemmas. Do I keep Margrethe hidden away in my heart the best I can, or do I try to find out if she's safe? Do I deny Kim the sanctity of our covenant of silence, or do I reveal my past so I can live with full integrity? Do I resign before I start, or do I move ahead boldly in Your forgiving love?"

When I stood up an hour later, my body reminded me the rock didn't feel the same as my new padded chaise lounge. Heading down the path, I limped a hundred yards or more before the twinge left my legs. If only I could learn to concentrate on God all the time the way I did while sitting on the rock.

When I'd left that morning, Kim's last words, after "I love you" were, "Don't forget to breathe." As usual. I stopped on my journey for a deep breath of warming mountain air. I yearned for the Spirit to blow its windy truth into my whole being.

I returned in time for noon liturgy and lunch. They served a simple meal in silence, broken briefly by the prayers of thanksgiving and a short reading by one of the friars. Coarse bread, hard salami, torn lettuce, a chunk of sharp cheddar, and rich red wine satisfied my physical hunger. My appetite for spiritual nurture re-awakened when I heard the friar read, "Whoever would be a great leader must first learn to follow."

When I went to my room for *siesta*, I closed my eyes and repeated a simple mantra of relaxation and connection to God. "O God—live in me—I in You." I repeated it slowly, breathing the *ruach*—God's Spirit through the trinity of phrases, inhaling "Oh God—live in me" then exhaling and emptying my concerns into open, loving arms: "I in You" extending the "ou" sound until my lungs deflated.

The mantra drew me out of my ego into the Silent Power where I belonged. Little by little, I left behind the mind chatter, filled with pangs of fear for Margrethe's safety, soaring hopes for Kim's pregnancy, and the drudgery of books and a broken opener waiting in my garage. The mountain air, mantra and wine relaxed me into a deep sleep.

✳    ✳    ✳    ✳

When I woke up, the question rumbling around inside wanted an answer. "Who am I that I should be chosen to lead this challenging diocese, anyway?" Tiny urban churches, shrunken from disuse, abuse and demographic disruption; thriving suburban mega-churches, growing like sunflowers, not beautiful or ugly, but big; in-between churches, alive, but not thriving, all dotting the landscape with bell towers and sign boards surrounded by freeways, mountains, ocean and the Mexican border.

"What do you want me to do God?" I remembered some old messages.

From Jesus: "Be secure in whatever comes. I am with you always. You are precious in my sight."

From Sister Jaqueline, a Catholic nun: "The best we can hope for is to be securely insecure. We have to jump off a cliff every day."

From Soren Kirkegaard, a Danish theologian: "Take the leap of faith."

From N.F.S. Grundtvig: "Our earthly life is a gift of God to be enjoyed."

And from someone, somewhere, who must have said it before I thought of it: "Serenity is a process."

I took out one of my notebooks, jotted down those comments, and began to scribble a poem. What does God want me to do?

> In all things, whatever comes,
> Be content and discontent:
> Content that God is present
> Feeling my feelings, providing confidence;
> Discontent that now is not yet,
> Yearning, risking, changing, growing.
> In all things, whatever comes, I will
> Be content and discontent.

*      *      *      *

I splashed my face with cold water and hurried into the comfortable room Brother David used for consultations. His warm smile and enveloping hug immediately re-connected us. After he congratulated me on my election, I asked him about his trip to Tibet, and we settled into my agenda for the retreat. He started with the usual question. "Who are you today?"

My answer poured out like a fountain, forgetting the poem I'd just written. "I want to define my mission as bishop, and figure out this 'servant-leader' idea. When we last talked, you encouraged me to be open to God's leading, so I accepted the nomination and kinda got swept along on a current like a river heading down the mountain. So, here I am, a new bishop up the river looking for a canoe."

"Slow down, Jon. Before you unpack your head, let's hear from your heart. How is it with you and God?"

"You'll have to ask God."

"This isn't the time to play smart-ass, Jon."

I felt ashamed, like the first time my dad caught me in the bathroom playing with myself the way most boys do around puberty. He'd called me a smart-ass kid, too big to spank, but if he ever caught me again, he'd punch me in a place that would double me over and he didn't mean my solar plexus. Brother David had a kinder way of saying it, but I got the message.

I didn't know how to answer. Did I come here to define my mission, or discover God's mission for me? "Sorry, David. I'm still trying to figure out how things are."

"Tell me your feelings right now."

"Fear. Not dread or panic. Apprehension, maybe? I'm afraid I won't be able to do the bishop's job. I know I'm concerned about Kim having another miscarriage. And I worry about Margrethe with all the fighting in Liberia."

"Are you afraid God's not going to be present for you and those you love?"

"Something like that."

We talked for another half hour about separation anxiety, and the healing power of companionship when facing storms in life. I shared more about my fears of exposure because of the threatening messages, and my argument with Peter. I kept coming back to my deception of Kim and the church.

"Tell me what you think of when you hear the word, 'church'."

"The church is a dragon waiting to devour me. No, sorry, that's a feeling. I think the church is…" I paused, waiting for inspiration. "The church is an organism, living in tension between legalistic nitpicking and cheap grace."

"Uh huh. What else?"

"The church is a human institution and a divine gift of the Spirit."

"Paradox."

"Yeah, the church is a paradox. Same with it's calling: 'Go, make disciples.' We're in danger of aggressive apathy on the one hand and manipulative marketing and patronizing on the other."

"Okay."

"And sometimes the ethical imperatives of advocacy and charity get mixed up in competition with the call to evangelize and teach. Word and sacrament aren't competitors, yet some of us fight over what's pre-eminent."

"You've definitely moved from the emotional to the intellectual."

"Yeah. The academic is easier for me to deal with right now than the visceral."

He ended the session by telling me to leave the intellectual to ripen awhile, and to move back toward my innards. "Write down your emotional concerns. Be specific. Bring the list back for our evening session."

I walked out of his office determined to get right at it. I picked up a diet cola from the machine and headed for my room. The receptionist intercepted me, and handed me a pink message form. Another threatening message? Couldn't be. No one but Kim knew where…I read the words and sucked air.

"Jon—from Kim: Heading for Anaheim Hospital—bleeding."

# CHAPTER 12

▼

The trip down the winding road created more frustration than fear. I swerved around curves, and prayed for an empty path. "Don't let her lose the baby, God, don't let it happen again."

Three freeway interchanges and miles later, I jumped from my double-parked car and ran in the Emergency entrance. The nurse pointed me to a cubicle where I found Kim sobbing. "I lost it, Jon. Dammit, I lost another baby."

"I leaned over the bed, kissed her tears and tried to sound soothing. Inside, I seethed. Just when we felt comfortable to adopt, she got pregnant. Our floating hopes smashed to the ground.

"I can't do this again, Jon, I just can't."

"I know, Kitten. Cry it out."

She moved over and I lay beside her on the narrow bed, holding her shuddering shoulders. Her anger came out in a squeaky voice lubricated by tears. "Damn You, God, Damn You." I hated hearing her say it, and I hated the feeling growing in me to say the same thing.

We lay there, sobbing. I prayed for God to help us feel something good, something solid. "Ask Her why, Jon." I did, knowing, like Job of the Bible, suffering is something we can't understand any more than we can explain why good things happen to bad people.

Gradually, her body relaxed and she whispered, "I'm sorry, Jon. For yelling at God. For losing the baby." I hugged her harder. The doctor came in, so I moved to a chair.

"Your tests are fine. Physically, you're healthy, but I insist you never get pregnant again. We should be thinking hysterectomy for you or vasectomy for your husband." She looked at me. "Your age and medical history make it very unlikely you could ever carry a baby to full term, and your own life could be endangered."

Kim and I looked at one another. We'd talked about a vasectomy last time, but Kim insisted we wait, hoping something would change so we could have our own child. I didn't want her to go through surgery, and I didn't mind the simple procedure on me.

"You're free to go as soon as you feel like walking. Watch for signs of postpartum depression. Even this early in the pregnancy, the body's chemicals behave as if you've delivered a full term baby."

"We know about postpartum depression," I said. "Kim went through it with her miscarriage in San Diego. We're still active in Postpartum Support International's local chapter."

"Good." She fiddled with the chart, handed us a copy of the lab reports, and looked at me. "If you can get away for a couple of days…" She turned to go, and I noticed tears at the edges of her eyes. "God bless. See you later."

"I'm never going to have a child of my own, am I, Jon?"

"Probably not."

"I'm never going to have a child of my own."

The farewell roast had filled us with joy. The brief retreat in Malibu had set me on a positive path. Now this; our dreams for a child of our own gone forever.

We decided to find refuge at our favorite bed and breakfast near San Diego. When I came back from picking up some clothing for our trip, I found her weeping by the window, holding a round paper box. She held it out, tole painted with brilliant blue flowers and shimmering green vines. "It's a memory box. The Spiritual Care Department gives one to every mother who…" She choked on the words.

I took the box and peered inside. It smelled like baby powder. One day before, I had emptied my sports bag, item by item, anticipating a tranquil time for gathering myself together for the future. That day, I emptied a tiny container, tearing me apart as I examined the contents: one tiny white robe, one miniature blanket stamped with foot and hand prints of various sizes, and a small burlap scroll tied with a bright blue ribbon. I untied and read it: "Be at peace; your child is at rest." I replaced the items in the box one by one, joined by my tears.

"Volunteers make these memory boxes so we have something to help fill our empty space."

Despite the sentiment, I felt emptier than when I walked in. When we face the vastness of death, each reminder pushes us deeper into the dark waters of grief, until there's nothing to do but dive deeper, hoping the promise is true: there's an opening at the bottom of the pool. We dove deep, hoping the familiar places in San Diego would show us such an opening.

*     *     *     *

Pelicans, seagulls, and unidentified squawkers floated around us as we wandered along the Del Mar beach. On the way, we passed a cemetery keeping watch over life while holding death in its bosom. Life pressed on, with volleyball players leaping from the sand, spiking the ball into their opponents across the net. We wondered how many people could play at a time, as if talking about the mundane would chase away our profound pain.

At the restaurant, we ordered lobster bisque and a Caesar salad and listened to diners talk about losing at the racetrack next door, and alternating time between their house in Rancho Santa Fe and "the condo" on the golf course in Carmel. A wee one sat in his high chair near-by, smushing his crackers into bits, and sprinkling them in the glass of water.

We drove into the city before rush hour, and wandered through the shops at Horton Plaza, munching on a piece of pizza and a churro. The symphony poster said, "Brahms Tonight in the Park." We caught the summer preview concert, aware that everything would remind us of our loss.

One or the other of us spent much of the night standing in silence at the window gazing at the moon dancing on the tumbling waves, alone in our thoughts, then holding one another again, on the bed in darkness.

"We need to call your parents." Waking up to sunshine by the beach gave me some energy despite the restless night.

"Okay, but let's go to the Wild Animal Park today, and call tonight." Kim enjoyed the regular San Diego Zoo, but loved even more going to Escondido where the animals had acres to roam. "We can have lunch out there, and then go to our favorite Chinese place on the way home." Familiar anchors in the storm.

We called Kim's parents to break the sad news, and to make sure they hadn't told anyone else. We slept better that night, and headed for home after a breakfast of muffins and cocoa on the beach.

"I need to pick up my gear at the Malibu Center. You want to ride along?"

"Sure. Could we do a little service in the chapel? Like we did for the others— for Hannah and Ruth?" Both were tiny fetuses, without clear identity. We chose the names because they signified love and service. We didn't ask if their sex could be identified. Somehow, it didn't matter.

"Good idea. Have you thought about a name for…?"

"I wondered about Stephen."

"I like it. Soft to say, but strong underneath." The New Testament Stephen served the widows and died from stones thrown by jealous zealots. He knew strength lay in compassion. "Yes, I like the name."

\*　　\*　　\*　　\*

Brother David met us as we drove into the parking lot. I'd called to explain, and he anticipated our needs. His long arms encircled Kim with warmth and strength. "Use the chapel as long as you like. I'll light some candles, and leave you to your solitude. I'm in my office if you want anything."

Kim walked to the altar and lifted the memory box above her head. She gently set it on the altar, and stepped back to stand beside me, hands holding my arm, body leaning against my side.

"Nothing can separate us from the love of God in Christ Jesus." I wanted to believe the quotation, and did at some deep level, covered over with layers of anger and disappointment. We knelt on the cold stone steps, praying by breathing, afraid to put our grief into words. "We commend Stephen to your care, dear Lord. He reminds us that the smallest of creatures is precious in your sight. Rest eternal grant him, O Lord, and let light perpetual shine on him. Amen."

"Amen." Kim breathed deep, almost fell forward, then caught herself and stood with me holding her close. We moved to go, carrying the memory box along with our grief, and said good-bye to Brother David. He handed me my re-filled sports bag with a strong embrace. Three days of torment. The Easter light would shine again, but fog hung heavy over the hills.

\*　　\*　　\*　　\*

Grieving our loss brought up memories of the past. In the fall of 1988, Kim and I had made a huge mistake. When she miscarried for the second time, we'd decided to tough it out and get right back to work, both of us. No therapy. No time away for grief work. After all, we'd been through it before. Then, she began to feel listless and sad, and had trouble getting up in the morning because she hadn't slept well during the night. She'd stopped eating and started crying in the middle of a sentence.

When we called the doctor, she explained postpartum distress and depression, which led us to therapy and support groups, sandwiched between our jobs and volunteer commitments. Despite all our efforts back then, neither of us had found the peace we'd known before the miscarriage.

No longer depressed, she'd seemed angry and distant, and I found more and more reasons to stay at the office. We'd tried to re-connect, but our sex life suffered. Over what I hoped would be a romantic New Year's Day dinner at the Coronado Fish House, I'd blurted, "I'm going to ask for three months off from work." She'd looked up, eyes wide.

"You'd do that for us?"

"We need it. The therapy and prayer have helped us, but we need some time free to re-build our marriage. We've—I've—kinda felt like sister and brother through all this. I need us to be lovers again."

"I haven't felt much like making love, and you always seem so tired at night."

"You're right. Yesterday, I read this article about clergy burnout. I've got some of the symptoms—headaches, fatigue, and resentment when people ask me to do things I used to enjoy. They recommend a sabbatical every five years."

"Would the church give you the time?"

"It's in my contract."

She'd shifted in the chair like the idea didn't fit. "What would you do?"

"Maybe spend a month at the seminary in the Bay Area. A month writing. And, I got this in the mail today." I'd handed her an envelope from Ben and Edie Christiansen inviting us to spend time with them in Liberia. We hadn't seen them since college days and had lost track of them until the invitation arrived.

"I don't get a sabbatical." Kim sounded worried.

"But you get the summer off. We could make it like a honeymoon."

We'd discovered the church board had already made some plans. The president sat down in the overstuffed chair in my cluttered office and sighed like he didn't want to say what he came for.

"You're worn out, Pastor. You go to the hospital four days a week, you teach two classes, visit all the newcomers, and keep this church running like IBM. You and Kim have been through hell. Everybody loves you, and we worry about you." I rubbed my jaw and twisted in my leather chair. "You've got bags under your eyes. Your usually great sermons wander. And you bit the secretary's head off over a mistake in the newsletter. It's time for your sabbatical." He'd spit it out like he couldn't wait to be finished.

I felt like dancing, until he told me they'd found an interim pastor to cover April through June. "I hoped to take it in the summer when Kim wasn't teaching."

"Interim pastors are hard to find. He's available those three months, but that's it. Can you adjust?"

Kim had cried when I told her. "I can't leave then, Jon. Even if I could get a sub, I wouldn't want to be away from my kids at the end of the school year. Besides, Liberia's so far away."

"Yeah, but think of what we can learn."

"I wouldn't be comfortable there."

"How come?"

"It's, well, so hot and sticky, and I won't know anybody. I'd miss my kids. Besides, it's your sabbatical and your country."

"I'll do something else. We'll go another time."

"No. No, you go."

We'd worked out a compromise. The first two April weekends, I'd flown home from the seminary in Berkeley, and Kim came to be with me in San Francisco the other two. She loved tromping around Ghirardelli Square and Pier 39 with all the shops and restaurants on the bay. Street musicians and mimes worked the crowd, sea gulls stole fish and chips off the tables, and hawkers tried to sell us tee shirts every half block. We feasted on seafood, walked in the windy salt air, and kept an uneasy silence about Liberia. San Francisco held a mystical charm for us in the past, but the weekends suffered from tension over my approaching trip. Seeing young mothers with their babies in strollers didn't help any.

I'd made my plane reservations, feeling lousy about Kim's reactions to Liberia. I could still hear her dad during one of our arguments. "Africa for Africans, America for Americans." I couldn't believe Kim felt that way, but her resistance surprised me.

In my study time, I'd reviewed Martin Luther's struggle to gain God's favor. As a sixteenth century German monk, he fasted, beat himself, and slept on the stone floor of the monastery. He felt unworthy. I, on the other hand, had been eating too many doughnuts, skipping my tennis matches, and falling asleep in the big chair by the television every night. Burnout symptoms nibbled at me into the last week of April.

Like Luther, I could out-guilt anybody, and I couldn't quite grasp the gracious brass ring. I preached grace, taught it, and applied it—to everyone but myself. Luther studied scripture and came to a new understanding about God's graciousness. He gave up trying to win God's favor. I relearned how to do that, or so I hoped.

Getting away from Kim didn't seem right, but I'd found it hard not to look forward to time alone. I'd wondered what I'd see when face to face with myself without her around.

I'd brought Kim a May basket full of bright spring flowers. Saying good-bye didn't come easy. She'd stiffened her body, smiled like she didn't want her picture taken, and brushed her lips on mine. When I had asked what I could bring her from Liberia, she stared at me for a long, uncomfortable minute, holding a deep breath. Before she exhaled her whisper, I knew what she'd say: "Bring me a baby."

I didn't bring Kim a baby from Liberia. Instead, I brought a lachrymatory and a half-truth. When I gave her the tiny antique vial and told her, "It's a gift of love for tears from our shared grief," she shuddered and tiny rivers ran down her cheeks.

In all the years since, I'd started to tell her the whole truth a dozen times. I didn't know how much longer I'd be able to keep my secret from her, but telling her on the way home from Malibu didn't fit. Too much grief.

*     *     *     *

When we walked in the door from Malibu, the answering machine blinked its demanding welcome, so Kim jotted down numbers while I unpacked the car. "All the other messages can wait, but Peter called three times. He sounded strange on the machine."

"I need to be with you."

"I'm okay. I'm going to lie down awhile."

I punched in his number, more out of a weird sense of duty than anything.

"Guess you've been away." He did sound strange.

"Yeah."

"I want to get together."

"Now's not good. Kim and I have plans tonight, and I'm moving books to the office in the morning. How about middle of next week?

"This can't wait. I need to apologize for my temper. In person. I'll come by mid-morning. Might even help throw some boxes in your trunk."

He hung up before I could protest. I'd never heard Peter apologize for anything.

Kim and I wanted to be strong for others, and we had work to do. Grieving for ourselves came in a distant third. We spent the rest of the day calling family and close friends to tell them our news, and timed our call to Solvang when we knew Mom and Dad would be alert.

"Kim and I have some sad news."

"Oh dear, are you alright?"

"Sort of. Kim had a miscarriage."

"Oh no! Oh my goodness. Dad, Kim had a miscarriage."

I heard her repeating everything to my father, about naming him Stephen, praying in the chapel, and the memory box. Dad cried a lot since his stroke, and the sound of his sobbing in the background made conversation harder.

"We're holding up okay, Mom. Don't worry about us." I wanted to reassure them.

"We love you son. Let me talk to Kim a second." Mom had come to stay with us after the first miscarriage, because Kim's parents were traveling, and she offered to come this time, too.

"Thanks, but we're okay. You stay and take care of Evald."

"Yes, he needs me, too."

"Bye, Mom. Love to Dad." It's what we always said when we called. The sameness of the ritual seemed trite sometimes, but not to say it would have left an empty space. We wiped tears from one another's eyes, and walked toward the back yard to watch the sun go down. Daily letting go would help our grieving in the months to come.

I slept in fits, sad at our loss and angry with myself for letting Peter ignore my boundaries. Underneath it all, nothing bothered me as much as my own inadequacies.

# CHAPTER 13

▼

In contrast to the beach birds we'd enjoyed at Del Mar, crows and blue jays greeted us at home the next morning, darting from tree branch to fence, cawing and cackling in their irritating way. Back to reality.

Kim looked at me with moist eyes. "I'd like us to see a counselor together."

My own grief and concerns about my workload needed attention, too. I hoped counseling would help me find the courage to tell her about Margrethe. "Me too. Let's call and I'll get it in my date book before the office fills it up."

Peter arrived at ten sharp, dressed in jeans and an old shirt. Kim waved from the kitchen window, but didn't come out. I stopped loading book boxes long enough for him to shake my hand, but he didn't bother.

"I meant what I said on the phone about feeling bad I got so upset last time. But there were some things that needed to be said. That still need to be said."

I heaved a box into the Volvo's trunk and took a deep breath to be ready for verbal judo. I'd already spent ten minutes in the shower searching for my calm center.

"I still don't know why you weren't honest with the nominating committee. With your charm, they probably would have nominated you anyway."

"Thanks." So much for his apology. I picked up another box.

"I'd make a better bishop."

"Humpf." My grunt, along with the sound of a heavy box hitting the trunk floor seemed like the appropriate response. "Did you want to help me here?"

"Sure. What with?"

"You could fix the garage door opener if you're not going to touch the boxes."

"Oh. No, I don't know anything about electronics." He picked up a box, grunted, and dropped it in the trunk. "You're probably a better parish pastor, but…"

He'd never paid me such a high compliment. Damning with faint praise still damned. "Uhnh." One more box elevated into my arms while he stood by, watching and talking.

"You're a good guy, Jonathan, but you've got to have tough skin when you're a bishop."

I held the heavy box against my chest, tempted to toss it his way, just to see what he'd do, but I knew. "What do you really want to say, Pete?"

"Peter." He said it under his breath, but what came next carried the full weight of his passion. "You won't get away with it, Jon—a—than." He emphasized each syllable of my name and sounded like a jealous ten-year-old.

I set the box down by the car and glared. "Peter, our whole relationship has been about competition. You usually won on the tennis court, I've won the election. You came into my home a month ago and yelled so loud the neighbors called. Today, you've lifted one box to my six and told me nothing I don't know already. I get the message."

"You don't need to get huffy." He kicked at a couple of boxes, and walked away like they were too heavy for him. "I just wanted to clear the air."

"The air is clear as it can be. Thanks for all the help." He either missed the sarcasm or thought lifting one box qualified as help.

"No problem. Well, I need to get going."

Peter Bloch handed me a pick and shovel that sunny Saturday morning, either to dig my own grave or a deep trench for a concrete foundation. I chose the latter, and had no doubt he'd huff and puff every time we met, not to mention what he'd do behind my back. Once again, I let him get away before confronting him about the "black vote" and cell phone messages.

\*     \*     \*     \*

Kim went with me to deliver the first load of books. The bronze nameplate on my office door looked more permanent than I expected: Bishop Jonathan Larsen. The scent of new carpeting hit me with the same intensity as my apprehension about serving as bishop: a nice surprise, but tinged with unpleasantness. I slid a box of books onto the wide oak desk, and tested the huge burgundy swivel chair. For the next six years, if I lasted that long, I'd make my imprint on the seat, and stack the papers high and deep on the desk's surface.

"You look good sitting there."

"Come sit on my lap."

"Should I?"

"Who's bishop around these parts?"

She slid into my lap, circling my neck with her loving arms, and I felt more complete than I had since we got married. My lover and best friend kissed me and we bonded spirit to spirit. The feeling made my deception all the more painful. I shifted in the chair.

"Okay, big guy, I'm getting up now, but every time you sit in this chair, I want you to feel my imprint."

"I'll always remember today."

"And don't forget to breathe." She unlocked herself from me, and walked over to the bookcases. "Your dad would love to see you sitting here."

I wanted him to be pleased. But I knew, despite my election, he wondered if I always did the right thing. I didn't mind it so much when he said, "Here he comes—the bishop—and he wears no clothes." He kidded me on our last visit about my wearing a sport shirt and shorts instead of the vestments of the pastoral office. But, like the child about the emperor, he also meant, "I can see right through you. You're a fake."

Are all emperors—or their tailors—and bishops fake, as we strut around in our soiled underwear? I'd wanted to be transparent all my life, partly driven by Dad's demands. I got up from the chair and walked around the desk to leave, knowing I hadn't yet achieved all he expected—all I expected of myself.

On the far wall, I noticed large block letters on diocesan stationery. "The church ain't perfect, but she's what you've got to work with." Henry's scrawled signature across the bottom identified the giver of the parting gift. Next to the message, a cubist print of a green, orange and teal church hung in a chipped ornate gold frame. Picasso deserved better, and so did the church. So much for Henry's sense of humor. I got his message, though. We went home for another load of books, reminded that no human institution—no human being—is perfect. Transparency? Not quite yet.

*       *       *       *

I walked into my office on Monday morning, and studied Henry's farewell gift again. The diocese elected me to preside over an imperfect institution full of imperfect people—a good fit for an imperfect bishop. I didn't have time to ponder details of my fitness or lack of it, because Teresa buzzed me into the staff meeting.

They gathered around the same table where I'd been interviewed, with the same art on the wall. Their t-shirts caught me off guard. Every member of my staff stood up and gave me a sloppy salute with one hand and pointed to their chests with the other. The white shirts blazed with red lettering: FAIL BOLDLY!

"We all voted for you and we're really glad you're not Peter Bloch." Teresa's infectious laughter got us off to a great start. Long black hair, probing brown eyes and dark complexion revealed Teresa Gomez's Central American origins. After losing her husband to a violent death in Guatemala, she emigrated and worked as a waitress, maid, secretary, and recently, as Henry Madison's Administrative Assistant. A devout Roman Catholic when she arrived, Lutheranism rubbed off on her enough to make her think about pursuing ordination.

"Bishop Madison told me you can do anything," I said to Teresa.

"I hope he's right. He told me the same thing about you." We'd have plenty of opportunity to find out.

I knew the six field staff members, but didn't know their deepest hurts and hopes, or the priorities in the territories they served. I asked them for stories about both, and watched the puzzle begin to emerge from scattered pieces into a coherent picture. All of them served the diocese part time, so I heard something about their other jobs, families, and frustrations about the high cost of housing.

The priorities ran the gamut from two congregations needing pastors, to plans for congregations in the desert, blooming with new houses. A conflicted congregation called for a Reconciliation Team, but a Prevention Team earlier might have kept the pastor in place. Campus ministries, social services, and advocacy in our two state capitols all clamored for attention. The days and nights on my calendar filled quickly, leaving precious little time for Kim and me to grieve. When our staff member specializing in personnel issues, Loren Westland, reported, I felt anxiety build.

"As you know from Bishop Madison, we have two pastors in the diocese charged with sexual misconduct. You need to interview about a dozen people before the Review Panels are convened." He hunched over as he talked, and the lines on his face gave away his pain. "I know the church has the responsibility to hold its clergy accountable, and people need to be able to trust that a congregation is a safe haven. But I hate seeing pastors get chewed up."

Sexual misconduct dogged my journey into the new office. Interviews, assessment documents, and confrontations poked their heads above the surface, but more lay hidden away in the unknown darkness of denial and secrecy. My job: expose, cauterize and heal the wounds.

"Excuse me, Bishop, but Pastor Poulson is here insisting on seeing you. I told him you were in a staff meeting." The receptionist looked irritated.

"Thanks. We're about to take a break. Ask him to wait in my office."

"Hi Jon Boy, howya doin'?" Larry Poulson burst into the room, slurring words and breathing noxious fumes from some near-by tavern. We'd been friends since seminary, but hadn't socialized for several years.

"Let's go to my office, Larry."

"The hellya say. I'm not good enough to grace this holy gathering?" I walked toward him while the staff watched to see how this new bishop would handle an obnoxious intruder. I shook his hand and drew him toward the door, but he pulled away. "I jus' want you all to know how much I 'preciate you guys callin' me in front of a firing squad."

I tightened my grip on his arm. "Larry, we're going to my office."

"Okay, okay, no need to get pushy." I hooked my arm through his and this time, he didn't resist. "I'm comin', Jon, you ol' coot, you. Made bishop jis' in time for my trial. Way ta go."

"Have a chair, Larry, and tell me how you're doing."

"Messed up, Jon. Been doin' a lil' drinkin' since ol' Henry and Loren put the screws to me. Not feelin' real chipper. Prob'ly flu or somethin'."

"I planned to visit you in later in the week. I want to go over your version of what happened with the two women in your congregation."

"I screwed 'em, Jon, or so they say. Hell, man, they wanted it worse than I did."

"We'll talk about it when I come down. How'd you get here?"

"Hitched a ride with a drinkin' buddy. He's waitin' outside."

I walked Larry to the car and told them to get coffee before driving to San Diego.

"You're mighty uppity, Jon, bein' bishop and all."

"Good friends don't cross boundaries on good friends. You crossed one today, Larry. Go home and get sober."

No sooner had I returned to the office than the receptionist buzzed me. "Sorry to interrupt again. You have a call on line one, Bishop."

Edward Fount, the other pastor facing a Review Panel, sounded as respectful as Larry had been the opposite. "Bishop Larsen, Bishop Madison no doubt informed you I have been accused of having an affair. I would like to relate my story in person." His Yale training and New England breeding expressed itself in his voice and choice of words.

We arranged to meet on Friday morning for breakfast. Edward had worked hard to gain acceptance as a gay pastor, and earned respect for his ministry far beyond City of Angels Lutheran Church. His partner's accusation of adultery tarnished his reputation, and opened him to criticism from everyone who questioned ordaining gay pastors. After I hung up, I pushed away from the broad, solid desk. I needed shoulders like my desk, and arms that could stretch around the wide spectrum of this diverse diocese.

I walked back into the staff meeting, wondering how I'd ever get a handle on this job. "Tell me, Teresa, how much time did Henry spend on conflict compared to all the other things a bishop does?"

"It varied. Some weeks, it seemed like that's all he did. But over a year? Maybe a month."

"How much of that month dealt with sexual misconduct conflicts?"

"This year, most of it. We had two cases last fall, and now the two you know about. The other conflict took him about five minutes to settle."

"That's my kind of conflict. What happened?"

"The pastor cancelled Christmas Day services when only one of the twelve council members said she'd be there. It really upset some of the older members. We got half a dozen calls here, and the pastor got even more. Some of the calls came from people who hadn't been at a Christmas Day service for years, but they still got upset he cancelled it."

"So what did Henry do?"

"He met with the pastor and council to work it out, but they'd already decided when he got there. They spent the whole hour talking about ways to avoid conflict in the future."

"Well, what had they decided?"

"To ask a retired pastor to conduct Christmas Day services and get a substitute organist. If attendance fell below ten, they'd announce right away there'd be no more until twenty signed up a month in advance."

"Sounds like a plan."

The rest of the staff meeting purred along without incident, ending in time for me to check my e-mail before heading home for a late dinner. Two dozen congratulatory messages popped onto the screen, but no anonymous ones this time. Thank goodness. My suspicions of Peter and Brenda had grown to the point of scribbling down ways to find out which of them deserved confrontation. Tomorrow. Today's troubles were enough for the day, as scripture says, so I packed up my laptop and slung it over my shoulder, glad to leave my first Monday behind.

# CHAPTER 14

▼

I pulled into the parking lot of St. Michael's Lutheran Church in San Diego, plugged into the electricity and attached a water hose. The motor home, as Henry had promised, made life on the road easier. The donor's will had said, "Let the bishop sleep in style." Henry left me a map and instructions for parking in every segment of the diocese. Someone dubbed it, "Galloping Ghost," an oblique reference to the circuit-riding preachers of pioneer days.

One of my sad duties as bishop, I'd learned, involved presiding over a ritual for Closure of a Congregation. They'd held no Sunday worship for months, and Henry had helped them complete the documents to disband the congregation. When the seven remaining members met that night, we signed the papers, prayed the prayers, and celebrated the decades of ministry to Scandinavians. They had never found a way to reach out first to the African American population, and now a mosaic of Hispanic, Korean, and Hmong.

Closing some congregations and planting others demonstrated how the rhythm of life in the church reflects life in general: birth, growth, decline, and death. Some lived a few years, others made it past a hundred. Healthy congregations found a way to keep growing despite changes in their communities.

When the last members—Petersen, Carlson, Johnson—had walked sadly away, I climbed into the Galloping Ghost and flipped on the television. No cable, so I had to adjust the roof antennae before I got anything but snow. The one clear channel delivered the end of a not-too-old movie, "The Mirror Has Two Faces." Jeff Bridges and Barbara Streisand stood in the street where he admitted he found her sexy and said, "I love you. I want to be married to you," and Barbara reminded him they were already married. The orchestra and chorus faded in with Puccini's haunting aria, *Nessun Dorma* (no sleeping.)

The volume built as Pavarotti's glorious tenor soared into the deserted early morning street. Looking down from his apartment window, a balding man in underwear and bathrobe lip-synched while the orchestra's strings vibrated with passion. Barbara and Jeff melted into one another's arms, as the closing line built to a climax: *Vincero Vincero, Vincero.*

*Vincero.* I will conquer. I will win. When I thought about my election, some said I had conquered. I had a long way to go before I felt like a winner, especially at integrity. That moment, I felt overwhelmed by the memory of sitting with Margrethe in Monrovia, hearing the climax of the opera, and moving to the epitome of our relationship.

I dug into the storage pocket of my brief case, and pulled out a computer disk marked "Sabbatical." I'd never shared it with anyone, and hadn't looked at it for many years. During the month in Liberia, I had kept notes, written observations, and, just before leaving, crafted a farewell note to Margrethe. When I bought my first personal computer, I had transferred it all to disc, and burned the paper evidence in the fireplace.

I typed in the password, "occasionforsin," and watched the words fill the screen. I skipped the notes and observations, and stopped at the farewell.

May 30, 1989

Dear Margrethe,

I wanted to leave some small part of me behind, so wrote this while you went to work this morning. Last night brought me more joy than I could ever imagine. Today brings an equal amount of sadness because I must leave for home. I know we'll say all the right things about moving on and letting go, but I don't know how I can ever forget the love I have for you.

The first day we met, I felt the electricity, but didn't know if it came from you or visiting the land of my grandmother's birth. As the weeks went by, my feelings for you and the country wove together in a tapestry of intense hues and strong strands. When you showed me the cemetery where you said you'd be buried, I felt as if I were dying. I knew by leaving, I'd lose you and the sacred land of my ancestors.

I love you and this place in a way I can't comprehend. Our lovemaking last night seemed as natural as harvesting fruit from the tree in your courtyard. Now, I must go, but I will never forget you, my soul mate.

Tears clouded my eyes so I had to stop reading. For all I knew, Margrethe had already died. Maybe she'd been tortured and killed. Or, maybe she escaped to London to be with her brother and family. The kind of love we'd shared defied limits of values and determination to hide it away in some dark corner of my being. I never should have looked at the disk. It tormented me with regrets, so I went to bed and tried to sleep.

I woke up feeling cramped and stiff. The digital red clock on the television flashed 12:45 a.m. Nobody had blackmailed me to run for bishop. Nobody threatened to reveal my affair, unless I counted the anonymous messages as threats. Something deep inside struggled to answer the riddle of integrity. "What is right when both paths lead to pain?"

My thoughts turned to the pastors we'd call before the Review Panel to determine if they were innocent or guilty, and what kind of justice fit their situation. My fate and theirs intertwined. I tried again to relax and sleep.

Still no sleeping at 1:30 a.m. How could I uphold the discipline of the church when dings and cracks zigzagged my own clay pot? I must have slept for a while, because the clock clicked to 6:00 a.m. the next time I checked.

I showered, ate, and worked on my sermon for Sunday, and then re-read more of Larry's file. At noon, I maneuvered the motor home across the city to their condominium.

\*       \*       \*       \*

Larry and Ginger greeted me at the door with sad faces and warm hugs. Ginger excused herself to finish preparing lunch, and Larry suggested he and I go for a walk in the park across the street.

"Sorry I didn't make your installation, Jon. I figured I'd embarrass you."

"I understand. You missed some great music. An Episcopal choir came from the San Diego cathedral with the bishop. That and the mass choir from the Orange County Lutheran churches made it sound like the Mormon Tabernacle Choir."

"Lots of pomp and circumstance?"

"No more than when you were installed here as pastor. Just a few more bishops, is all."

"Good food?"

"My sister Michelle catered it. What can I say? Nobody went away disappointed."

Larry stopped at the entrance to the park. "Are you disappointed in me, Jon?"

"I want to hear your story, Larry." He looked thin and pale.

He lingered a few silent seconds, then poured out more than I wanted to hear. "It started eight years ago when Ginger got shingles. She couldn't stand it when I touched her. No sex. No cuddling. Nothing more than a little kiss now and then. I respected that, but I went crazy inside. I need a lot of touching. I'm a sensual-tactile guy."

We turned into a park and circled the playground and gazebo. He led us on an asphalt path around a small lake, talking non-stop. "I need sex too, but the holding and caressing—I missed that a lot. We talked about how it didn't matter if we had sex. We had so much more going for us. We laugh together and never say a harsh word. We're a darned good brother-sister couple."

"That's what showed in public, Larry. But you had something else going."

His words tumbled over one another. "I went to a massage parlor a couple of times, but felt so guilty, I didn't go back for a long time. Then, about five years ago, I started playing around on the Internet and found some 'personals' sites. I clicked on and registered, just as a lark, wrote an ad and waited, but nothing happened for two weeks. So, I checked out the ads women had written, and e-mailed six of them. I heard back from all of them because I didn't mention being married."

"When did you start meeting with them?"

"Almost right away. One of the women I contacted was godawful eager. We met for lunch and she right away told me she liked the way I looked."

He paused at a bench, so we sat down. San Diego afternoons in June could be cool and foggy, or hot like today, when the wind blew off the desert.

"She wasn't ugly, but must have weighed under a hundred pounds. So I lied and said I liked the way she looked, too. She invited me to see her condo. When she finished the five-minute tour, well, we ended up in her bedroom."

"Really?" I'd led a sheltered life.

"Well, hell, by that time I felt so horny I couldn't turn her down. We got naked and jumped in bed. I thought that if it's that easy, I'm going to like this Internet dating thing. She invited me to come back any time for a 'day time delight', and I thought maybe I'd found a way to meet my needs. I had second thoughts while I drove home, and decided I couldn't do that. God, Jon, she was so skinny. So I e-mailed her, and told her my values wouldn't let me do this. She said she understood."

"She probably knew which value she violated."

"Yeah, my 'no bony broads' rule. So, I messaged a dozen others, shared a few lunches, but no one else offered sex. My insides felt like a cement mixer. As long as I kept looking, I kept flexible. If I stopped looking, I hardened and got grumpy."

"Can you take a breath, Larry? You tend to talk in paragraphs. Long ones."

"Yeah, I know I do. There's just so much to say. I started reading Updike the other day, his old *Rabbit At Rest* book. He says it takes a lot of strength to have an affair—to put up with its danger, its performances on demand. You get preoccupied with it and with the constant threat of its being discovered and ended."

"Updike writes about a lot more than sex. Have you read all his books?" I needed a little break in his sex report.

"No, just the one. Anyway, I think sex is about ecstasy, but it doesn't have to be about commitment. Sex can be just as meaningful if two people want to share it as part of their friendship, but not as the defining essence."

"Defining essence? Sounds pretty theological, Larry."

"Yeah, well, you catch my drift. Anyway, after a couple of years even marriage doesn't have sex as its defining essence any more. Are you with me so far?"

"Not really, but you have a lot to unpack. You haven't mentioned your visit to my office."

"What visit?"

"You don't remember?"

"Like I said, what visit?" I wondered if he'd blacked out or didn't want to discuss it. He hurried on. "I don't think what I've been doing is so bad, but the church won't buy that. Hell, my wife won't buy that. Mostly, I didn't want to hurt her, so I never told her."

I'd used the same rationalization for not telling Kim. It sounded so clear when Larry said it, and so shallow. "Maybe that's your answer about being bad or not."

"You mean 'cuz I could hurt my wife? Or because the church has rules against it?"

"Both, Larry. You made a promise to your wife and to the church. In the promises, you said you'd be faithful. It's not just because the church has rules that it's bad to have affairs. It's because you've broken your promises. The church can't trust what you say." I felt like I was talking to myself as much as to Larry.

"Bull! The church can trust what I say. It just doesn't like what I do in secret."

"It's not secret any more, Larry. Two women have reported that you had sexual intercourse with them. It's on the record. You've broken trust with the church and with your wife. Do you expect us to ignore those things?" My voice cracked and my eyes glistened.

Larry's face turned red. He talked through clenched teeth. "Damn it, Jon, you and I both know there are plenty of pastors out there having affairs."

"There aren't very many. But does even one excuse yours?" I tried to keep calm.

"And they're gambling, drinking, swearing and all the other sinful things we're not supposed to do. And, no, their affairs don't excuse mine. It's just that…" Larry's words trailed off as two tears slid down his cheek, hinting at the flood to come.

I grabbed Larry's shoulders and embraced him. His penitential tears soaked my shirt, and his shudders moved me to hug him harder. I wondered if anyone would hug me when I confessed.

✳   ✳   ✳   ✳

"How'd your visit with Larry and Ginger go?" Kim knew I couldn't tell her the details, but they'd been friends of ours, and she could see I didn't feel happy when I got home.

"Okay. We had a tense lunch. Ginger's looking old and Larry's drinking too much. He looks like something's eating away from inside—not just stress. He said he'd go see a doctor—hadn't been to one for years. He was long-winded, as usual." My tone of voice suggested Kim not pursue it.

"Brent and Andrea invited us over for dessert and baseball. Feel up to it?"

Anything to get my mind off sexual misconduct. "Sure. Who're the Angels playing?"

"Oakland, I think. Maybe Seattle. It's a west coast away game, I know."

"Important series. Our division. Gotta say they've got a long way to go to make the World Series. They could use a couple of superstars."

Andrea had whipped up a chocolate mousse to die for. A dollop of real whipped cream on top made me forget about Larry or closing churches or anything else. Brent set up some TV trays, and shooed the kids off to the kitchen to do dinner dishes.

"So, Jon, did you hire Shirlee to work at your new office?"

I'd been surprised Henry's secretary resigned, but she said retirement looked appealing, and besides, I should have a choice about who kept me in line. I'd called Shirlee and after she quit blubbering, she said she'd be honored. "Yes, she starts in two weeks. I'm stoked."

Kim and Andrea gave up on the game when the Angels fell behind in the fifth inning, but Brent and I kept hoping. During a commercial, I asked Brent if he remembered the anonymous messages I'd been getting.

"Yeah, you ever find out who the practical joker is?"

"I'm not sure it's a joke. The last one said, "You deserve to suffer.""

"Whoa! You think somebody's out to get you?" Brent leaned forward in his chair and hit the mute button on the remote.

"I've never heard of a Lutheran bishop getting a death threat," I said.

"I thought I read about a pastor getting shot not long ago?"

"Yeah. Kim reminded me of that one. Back in February. He'd counseled a woman to go to a shelter and file charges against her husband, because he was beating her."

Brent stood up. "And the husband came after the pastor?"

"At the church one night, without warning" I said. "Wounded him. The police caught the guy an hour later."

Brent glanced in the living room where our wives were busy talking. "Is Kim worried someone wants to shoot you?"

"Well, a little. But why would they?"

"Maybe because you're black?"

"I'd hate to think there's anybody that full of hate."

"Even Lutherans go crazy, Jon."

"I faxed the messages to a detective I know from the Anaheim police department. He was an usher at the church. I'll see what he has to say."

"Good idea." Brent held up the remote. I shook my head affirmatively. He cut the volume back in just as another Angel hit a home run with two on to tie the game.

"Good timing!" We both whooped, bringing Kim and Andrea from the living room and the kids from the kitchen. We watched the Angels pull out a win, and all did a little monkey dance.

# CHAPTER 15

▼

I made my way through the early morning Los Angeles traffic to meet Edward Fount. I recognized him from his picture when he walked into the hotel coffee shop. Handsome face and black wavy hair, he looked like Pierce Brosnan. His smooth gait revealed the years of basketball stardom for the Yale Bulldogs. He wore a tan suit with black clergy shirt, along with a pained expression.

I'd read his file and Henry's summary: "Pastor Edward Fount's partner, Gary Temple, demanded Edward resign as pastor because of adultery, and declared he'd have nothing further to do with Edward. Fearing Gary would leak the story, Edward sent a letter to me and to the congregation revealing the incident."

Edward preferred not to order breakfast, so I suggested we go outside with our coffee to the deserted deck overlooking a golf course. The white plastic chairs felt uncomfortable, and so did I, as Edward unpacked his story.

"I invited a gay friend of mine from college days—Don—to stay with us for a week while he attended a conference here in the city. We'd never been lovers, but there had been some magic between us back then. When he came to stay, some of the magic re-appeared." A foursome whooped over a long putt that dropped, but Edward ignored them.

"I felt attracted to his humor, and he to mine. We laughed and enjoyed reminiscing and thought my partner, Gary, enjoyed it, too. You know Gary's my partner, don't you?" I nodded. "Gary told me later that night he resented Don."

He paused to sip his coffee, staring out over the manicured green of the fairways below. I imagined what he must have felt about confessing to a bishop, and what I would feel were I to confess to Bishop Clemente.

"The night before my old friend left for home, we went out to enjoy a cappuccino and cinnamon roll, much the way we had during our college days. He touched my hand during the conversation and asked, 'Is it well with you my friend?' I began to weep right there in the restaurant."

Tears pushed their way to the edges of his eyes and he stopped talking. I gave him some time while he wiped away the dampness with his handkerchief. "What kind of things were you going through before your friend came to visit?"

"Crappy things. Pardon me, Bishop, but, not everyone in my congregation is comfortable with my being gay much less living with Gary in a covenant of fidelity. I don't blame them. They've heard from the church all their lives that homosexuality is a sin." He started to pace. "Much as it hurts, I know how hard it is for them to get over their fear or whatever it is they feel. My Lord, I'm just now getting accustomed to the freedom of being public about it myself."

I nodded. When the church reorganized, one of the "agree to disagree" issues focused on allowing congregations to call pastors living in a covenant relationship. Until two years ago, our church body said we didn't ordain or allow pastors who were homosexual to live together in love. Either they stayed celibate, lied, or were removed from the roster.

"Our church may have officially said it's a private matter, but some people can't stop themselves from poking their heads into the bedroom. A few of my members still look at me as if I'm contaminated." He slunk down in the chair, looking defeated.

He went on. "Fear of sexuality comes in a wide variety of packages. Some of the most devoted and prominent church members wear masks of acceptance, but harbor deep and distorted fears about what happens in private. Some worry they'll be propositioned. Some don't want their children exposed to the sexuality spectrum. Some just need somebody to judge."

Edward coughed, sipped his coffee again, and then spoke more to the trees on the golf course than to me. "Long hours at the church aren't rewarded with visible signs of success. I often came home late and found Gary asleep. He's not exactly enthused about my ministry, to be honest, and we've had words about it. Our sex life had deteriorated to a little smooch before going off to sleep, and then only if he hadn't dozed off."

I shifted in my chair, not sure I wanted to know the details that seemed to be coming.

"So when my friend touched my hand that night, the dam broke. I needed that touch. I needed someone to care for me. We left the restaurant hand in hand, went home to the guest room and made love. Gary wasn't supposed to get home from his seminar in San Francisco until the next day, but he finished early. He walked in on us, and here we are."

Edward's grief overflowed and my chest tightened over my inability to console him. He sat down and I explained the procedures for the Review Panel and confirmed the date two weeks from Saturday. We left the hotel, both looking like defeated warriors. He'd already lost his lover and respect from some members. Next, he'd probably lose his position. Me too?

*      *      *      *

Henry Jordan loved the Angels even more that Brent did. He and his wife bought a used motor home and followed the team to away games, and hosted tailgate parties at Edison Field. One Sunday afternoon, he woke me from my post-preaching nap and asked if I wanted to go to a Sunday night game, because Priscilla was baby-sitting grandchildren.

Kim said, "Go, go, you baseball nut. I'm into Jan Karon's latest book anyway."

Sometime along the middle of the fourth inning with the score tied at three, I'd finished my second hot dog and diet drink, which freed my hands to talk. I talked okay without them, but not as well. "Henry, tell me, now that I've been on the job awhile, why did you say at the convention you were especially glad I'd chosen to run? Did you know about Beverly's problems?"

"No—well—I knew right before the speeches. She came to me in tears during the break. She didn't expect to get to the final three. I sympathized with her, because it didn't sound like she'd done anything wrong except marry an insecure man. But when she asked if I thought she'd get elected—she was surprised to get as many votes as she did—I told her I honestly didn't think she would. No, the real reason was what I heard in the pre-convention caucuses, especially the Asian and Latino pastors."

"Really." I knew the African-American caucus hadn't met since January. I'd been attending since my internship.

"Yes. It's tough to be so few in a white dominated church. They asked to meet with me in confidence—wanted find out what they could do to keep Pete from being elected."

"They figured he'd patronize them?"

"Yes, and cut out the special funding efforts and change the way we make sure they're represented on the boards and committees."

"What do you think would have happened if Pete—Peter—had won?"

"I don't know, but it would probably have caused a big split in the diocese—between those who think we ought invest our mission dollars in growing suburbs and those who think the inner city needs more." Henry had worked hard to keep the funding balanced.

"I've heard Peter wants to get the Mission Committee to reallocate ninety percent to suburbs and new communities," I said.

"The next meeting is set for August—be ready." An Angel home run broke the game open. "Man, these guys are good. They could win it all this year."

"Relax, Jon, it's never happened, and it never will. It's more likely the Ducks will get into the hockey finals. Which reminds me. Where did you come up with that 'fail boldly' motto in your speech at the convention?"

I laughed. "No idea. I had big time notes about facing up to being consumer Christians instead of servant leaders, and how we needed to sow seeds of grace all kinds of ways, even if they didn't grow, when it dawned on me."

"The motto?"

"No. That I'd guarantee failure in my election if I used too much jargon."

Henry laughed. "So you tossed your notes and spoke from the gut?"

"Yup. When I heard Pete talk about being perfectly heavenly and Bev say we needed to be earthy like Jesus, I figured somebody needed to get a plug in for experimenting. And look at those Angels—failing boldly—another error, another run."

"And the transparency thing?"

"I'd been reading about all the corporate fraud and everybody wrote letters to the editor demanding transparency from business—then our president started blowing smoke about finding bin Laden and justifying all kinds of missile pointing, and the editorials started in about political transparency, so, it just kinda came out."

"It's not an easy word for lots of us, Jon. It means so many things. You'll have to work at helping people see through, if you'll pardon the pun, what it means for the diocese."

"You're right. Kim and I did the whole dictionary discussion one night when I first brought it up. I don't remember all of them, but one was about letting light shine through without distortion—I liked that because of the 'Christ as the Light of the world' idea."

"And I suppose there was one about being clear enough to see through—like so people understand where you're coming from."

"Yeah, but the one Kim liked best was 'diaphanous' or 'sheer' because she said I always got turned on whenever she wore her transparent nightgown."

"Oh, man, another error. How many's that? Three in two innings? They're lucky they've still got the lead."

"Transparently."

"That's a stretch."

"No, that's not until the seventh inning."

"Jon, I think you've gone over the edge. Let's drop it, okay? The Angels need our concentration."

\*        \*        \*        \*

Teresa stood in the doorway of my office, eyes like slits and lips tight together. "You look like someone ticked you off," I said.

"It's that Pastor Vanhorst again. This time he wants us to censure some pastor out his way for blessing a lesbian couple."

"He doesn't believe in blessing same sex covenants." I'd stated the obvious.

"And he thinks anybody who does it should be tossed out of the diocese."

"Any pastor has a right to bring a complaint against another, but he won't get anywhere on this one. Congregations and their pastors can decide for themselves, just like the age of first communion and a lot of other issues."

"He's mad about you ordaining Vivian, too."

"He can get mad about whatever he wants. Someday, he'll figure out what it means when our church decided to 'agree to disagree agreeably' on issues like that. I ordained Vivian because she's qualified to be a pastor. She and Nadine have a covenant of life-long fidelity. I've explained that to him. Vanhorst likes to rile people up."

"I'm not riled. I'm just tired of him calling with nothing but complaints." She sputtered out of my office.

"Hey! It's okay to be riled. He gets to me, too. Let's take a coffee and cookie break."

"*Bueno*, Bishop. I like your style. Shirleeeeee! C and C time."

Shirlee baked cookies at least once a week and brought some to share at the office. Her husband ate too many otherwise, she said, and besides, she liked getting crumbs in the computer keyboard. The "coffee room" consisted of a counter, cupboards, mini-refrigerator, a round table and four mismatched chairs, gifts of a semi-thoughtful pastor who'd bought a new kitchen set.

She also made the coffee every morning, not because anyone said it was her job, but because she thought hers tasted better than anyone else's. She was right. Besides, she got to use "fair traded" coffee from Guatemala, courtesy of Teresa's first hand experience with abused pickers back home. "Anything we can do to help the workers," Shirlee said whenever anyone asked why we used the more expensive beans.

"Who else's in the office today?" I hadn't peeked out from behind my desk for a couple of hours, and the staff tended not to interrupt.

"Loren came and went. Copied some forms to take to a congregation tonight so they can interview a new pastor like Jesus—without long hair. Sandra is due in later with financial reports. Nobody else." Shirlee kept track of comings and goings like an air traffic controller. "Oh, and while you and Teresa were plotting how to tolerate the Reverend Mr. Vanhorst's intolerance, you got a call from Edward Fount's parents."

"Are they in California?" I asked.

"All the way from Hartford. They're in LA and want to see you as soon as possible."

"Okay, fit them in my schedule somewhere."

"I will as soon as we get these envelopes stuffed." Shirlee sipped coffee, munched a chocolate chip cookie, and stacked envelopes into three piles—all at the same time, it seemed. "You and Teresa are cordially invited to join the contest—first one through with their stack gets another cookie."

"Did Henry stuff envelopes, Teresa?" I'd helped Shirlee back at Anaheim Hills a few times, partly to help out, but mostly because I enjoyed seeing something get finished.

"He did, but usually came in second to me when we raced. He claimed no other bishop stuffed envelopes, at least that's what they said at the big meeting they all go to." Teresa winked at Shirlee like I didn't see.

"Okay, you're on. Just so you know, I lettered in envelope stuffing in high school."

Shirlee snorted. "That's ancient history. Ready, set, stuff."

I lost, but ate another cookie anyway.

# CHAPTER 16

▼

Nathan and Samantha Fount stood in the doorway of my office, looking as if I had the power to sentence their son to death. Tall with white hair, they carried themselves like I'd expect of wealthy aristocrats from Connecticut. "We've come to plead our son's case," he said.

I welcomed them, pointing to the couch.

"Please," she said, "we'll stand. We won't take much of your time."

"Your son is a good pastor," I said.

"And a good son. He never gave us a minute's trouble." She looked at her husband who nodded. "We know he's made a mistake, but..." They looked to one another in the silence.

I felt a spasm in my heart when I thought about my own mistakes. "You've been through a lot." I indicated the couch again. This time, they sat—on the edge of the cushions.

"We can't believe you'd put our son on trial for..." Mr. Fount didn't seem to find the word he wanted.

"Your son will meet with a Review Panel to help decide what's best for him and the congregation. It's not a trial—more like a family conference when someone has broken a house rule." I noticed they glanced at one another, as if remembering some sessions like that over the years.

"But Edward said he could be removed from his congregation. He's already lost his partner." Mrs. Fount blinked away some tears.

I felt the lump forming in my own throat. "Nothing has been decided about the future. Edward is on temporary leave. I've suggested a reconciliation retreat for him and Gary"

"I'm not sure that's a good idea. Gary coming back, I mean." Mr. Fount twisted a button on his blazer. "They aren't good for one another."

"My husband doesn't mean because Gary's a man." She touched her husband's arm as if to calm him. "We've accepted Edward as gay. We know he'll have a man as his..." This time, Mrs. Fount searched for the right word.

"They've had their troubles," I said. "All couples do." I wanted to move the conversation away from the pain of unfaithfulness—for myself as much as for them. "Did Shirlee offer you some coffee?"

"Oh yes, thanks, but we know you're in a hurry." Mrs. Fount shifted, ready to stand.

"Please, don't worry about the time. Tell me what you'd like me to know about Edward." I slid back into my chair, hoping they'd follow suit.

Mrs. Fount sat back, but Mr. Fount stayed on the edge, back straight, feet flat on the floor. She patted his back and said, "Our son never gave us any trouble. He and Nathan played basketball in the driveway from the time he was little. They built a soapbox car out of packing boxes and we all climbed mountains together in Vermont. He never gave us any reason to believe he was—gay."

"You weren't expecting it."

Mr. Fount shook his head back and forth, lips tightened, eyes staring a hole in the carpet. "I always thought gay people were effeminate. Hated sports. Hell, he starred in basketball and track in high school." He blushed. "I'm sorry, Bishop, my language..."

I waved away his concern.

Mrs. Fount looked embarrassed. "He came to me first, not sure what his father would say. I cried. Not so much for my sake, but for his. I know how most people, even church people, think of homosexuals."

"I didn't believe it when Samantha told me," Mr. Fount said. "So I went to him, asked him how he knew. He asked me how I knew I loved Mom. I told him I just did. He said he'd always known, too. He just didn't understand until he was in college."

Mrs. Fount shifted her gaze to me. "A professor—what do they call it—came out. The students all loved him. The administration fired him. Not because he'd done anything. Just because he told the truth about who he is." She paused. "Is it wrong to tell the truth?"

I shuddered inside. "The truth is meant to set us free. Sometimes, the truth hurts, doesn't it?"

"We told him we loved him and suggested counseling. He said no at first. We told him we wanted to go together so we could figure out how to live in a world that hates queers." Mr. Fount's ears reddened. "I guess that's not a good word, either."

"I've learned that 'queer' is a badge some wear with pride." I also knew some hated the label, especially when they were slapped in the face with it. "And you're right. Society has many—the church has many—people who fear and hate and denounce anyone who is different somehow. But there are more of others like you than you might suspect."

"I'd like to believe that, Bishop," Mr. Fount said.

Society and faith communities have struggled with differences forever. Who's in and who's out? Purity laws among the Hebrew people separated out those who ate the wrong foods or suffered from certain diseases. Early converts from Judaism disagreed with Gentiles about the importance of circumcision. Ranchers fought with herders in the early west. Beliefs about racial superiority, among other things, spawned a world war. The most controversial issue facing courts and congregations in recent history is how to understand sexuality.

"Did you find a good counselor?" I asked.

"Yes, and she helped me understand it wasn't our fault," Mrs. Fount said. "It's not anybody's fault. Eddie certainly didn't choose to be that way. Nobody would be so ignorant as to make that kind of decision when…" She began to shed more tears.

Mr. Fount put one hand over his wife's knee. "I've read all the stuff on both sides. I know what the Bible says about perversions. I know some scientists say there's good evidence it's not learned, and it's not a moral choice. That doesn't make it any easier."

"Some theologians agree with those scientists, and modern scholarship has called traditional scriptural interpretations into question," I said.

"We went to a support group for parents at a church in Hartford. They had some brochures about all that." Mrs. Fount dabbed at her eyes with a lace handkerchief.

"A parents and friends group?" I asked.

"I think so," she said. "It's part of that national group that helps gay people."

"They've had several names over the years. They include parents, family and friends of persons who are lesbian, gay, bi-sexual and transgendered. Their web site calls them PFLAG for short." I'd read their literature and met with some representatives about their mission.

"Yes, that's it. We learned about the Metropolitan Community Churches there. They do good work with people like Eddie. But we like our Lutheran Church better, if only…" Mrs. Fount shook her head.

"The Lutheran Church—North America welcomes your son." As soon as I said it, I knew they could challenge me. "Officially, at least."

"Not if he makes a mistake." Mr. Fount stood up. I looked up at his stern face. "If he weren't gay, you wouldn't have bothered about a little one night stand."

"All pastors—gay and straight—agree to certain covenants. Faithfulness is one." I kept my guilt under control by thinking about their feelings, not my own.

"Why can't you just forgive him? He confessed." Mr. Fount sat down again, shoulders slumped, looking defeated.

"I've already reminded him of God's forgiveness. I don't have the power to keep him from the Review Panel, though."

"Then for God's sake let him stay as pastor. They love him there." Mrs. Fount's tears began to flow again.

"I'll do what I can. Edward is fortunate to have parents like you." We prayed for God's guidance and strength to face the future, and they seemed more at peace. I couldn't do what they asked, but they left knowing God loved them—and Edward.

I knew God loved me, too, but my time with a Review Panel loomed in the future, just as soon as I found the courage to confess.

*    *    *    *

Dean Davidson called again to berate me for not doing anything about calling Beverly to face a Review Panel. We went through the same question and answer game as before. Once more, I asked for evidence, and again, he said he'd get it. "The neighbors took pictures."

I knew he lied. Beverly would have noticed a camera, had she been there. I believed her when she said she didn't join them, and told Dean that.

"The bitch is lyin', Mister, and you're gonna get your ass dragged into court."

"Have your attorney call our diocesan attorney."

"I don't have an attorney. I just want you to know you can't get away with it."

The conversation went nowhere, so I told him to deliver the pictures to my office on Thursday by 10:00 a.m. and I'd deal with it from there. I called Beverly and told her about the threats, and agreed he was bluffing—probably.

I also called my sister-lawyer. "Janelle, do I need a personal lawyer besides the diocesan attorney?"

"You might. Let's see how it rides out. If you need one, I can find you a good one. It just can't be me. I'm a little biased."

*      *      *      *

On my way to interview the two San Diego victims of Larry Poulson's sexual misconduct, I noticed the El Cajon Boulevard exit as I drove down Interstate 805. The memory of another time, a dozen years before, flashed through my mind. I'd seen a therapist after I got back from Liberia, and had taken that exit to get to her office, and noticed a lot of streetwalkers, even in the middle of the day.

I decided to detour on the Boulevard to see if things had changed. They hadn't. Somewhere around 35$^{th}$ Street, a young white woman leaned against the street sign pole in the "uniform" of her clan: boots with high heels, bare legs leading upward into short shorts, and a tank top.

I had no business being there, but something had drawn me. Curiosity? Probably. In seminary, I'd debated legalizing prostitution in ethics class. I took the position in favor, affirming hookers as society's helpers, much like pastors. Sensitive listeners. Providers of consolation. Once I hit the streets of Los Angeles on internship, the naïve notions of a seminary debate faded into the harsh reality of disease, drugs and violence. I kept driving.

The meetings with Larry's accusers revealed stories worse than the file had summarized. He'd conned each one into believing he loved her, alternating between the two about once a week. Their embarrassment almost exceeded their hurt and anger. I worried about their recovery from the betrayal, and felt better when each said she'd begun therapy. They declined my offer of financial support from the diocese.

*      *      *      *

That night, I stopped to chat with my neighbor out front mowing his lawn. "How's it going?" he asked.

"Tough day—interviewed some people about a sexual misconduct hearing coming up."

"Someone cheating on his wife?"

"Can't talk about the details. Confidential," I said, and turned off the car's engine.

"Can you tell me anything? Like how many there are?"

"I can't tell you unless they become public. I can tell you the statistics for sexual misconduct Review Panels in the two years since reorganization are a lot less than most people think. Most pastors live moral lives. Some get tempted and fail to live up to their values. Some get falsely accused."

"How's the church handling the gay issue?"

"Better than some thought. There still are a lot of people scared that we'll be taken over by the promiscuous and abusive ones. But those folks aren't in our churches."

"Wouldn't it be nice," he said, "if we no longer had to worry about revealing our sexual orientation any more than our preference in cars or baseball teams? Wouldn't it be nice if we could be black or brown or any color skin and people would see us as beautiful pieces of a mosaic instead of someone to discriminate against or label or make jokes about? Wouldn't it be nice if we could all just get along? Or is that simplistic?"

"Wow! I pushed your button."

"Sorry. I guess my persecution syndrome kicked in."

"You're right about it's not being simple, certainly. However, if each of us took one small step in owning our racism or sexism or ageism or any of the other isms with which we're infected by our culture—if we could listen more than speaking, study more than labeling, then maybe, just maybe, we could move the twenty-first century culture into a paradigm shift." He'd pushed my button, too. We agreed, it would be nice. Not likely, but worth trying.

"Are there other things pastors get in trouble for besides sex?"

I laughed. "Sure. Things like excessive gambling, alcohol abuse, spousal abuse, child endangerment…"

"Frequent?"

"No. Much less than the general population. Fewer suicides. Fewer arrests. Fewer civil suits. The one thing we found disturbingly high in our survey was how many speeding tickets clergy get."

"And that includes you, right?" He laughed.

"Guilty." Not just of speeding, but Brent didn't know that.

✳     ✳     ✳     ✳

As I expected, Dean Davidson didn't show up on Thursday. Maybe he'd come to his senses, but I wouldn't bet on it.

# CHAPTER 17

▼

Two phone calls urged me to "get to Hawaii as soon as possible." One came from a committee interviewing candidates for their pastor, and the other from the pastor where they'd defaulted on their huge mortgage. I adjusted my appointments to allow for five days away from the office, and took some good-natured ribbing from Teresa.

"Tough job, you've got—flying off to paradise."

"Yeah, but Henry warned me I might not see much of it. He said every time he went, all he did was look at faces and walls in meeting rooms. He never did get to lie on the beach." He'd encouraged me to add an extra day whenever I went, and to take Kim.

"True," Teresa said, "Hawaii looks like all scenery and scents, but underneath it all, they live with tough stuff."

"Like what?"

"I only know what Dr. Geoff said at staff meetings." Glenda Geoff worked ten hours a month for the diocese and the rest of the time offered psychotherapy and marriage education classes on the islands. "She said too many suffer from limited wages and high cost of housing for service workers. There's a lot of culture conflict between the *haoli* and local kids in the public schools, and too much domestic abuse."

"Henry told me the churches barely get some leaders trained when they move on, or those who stay get burned out. The military people transfer a lot, and mainlanders come looking for jobs in paradise and discover they can't afford to enjoy it, much less survive."

"Dr. Geoff says she loves it there, though, except for the humidity, bugs and tourist traffic."

When I called Kim, she said she didn't know if she could go along, but made it clear she had already tired of my travel schedule. "School doesn't start for two weeks, and my room's not ready."

Our discussion later that night didn't go well. Kim stood in the bedroom, hands on hips, not glaring, but almost. "You can't just drop things on me like this and expect me to jump at the chance to take off for five days."

"I'm sorry, but it came at me, pardon the pun, out of the blue. I know it's fast, but I'd really like you to go with me."

"What will I do while you trot off to your meetings?"

"We'll have a car, there are lots of interesting things to see in Waikiki. You love history, and there are some great museums. Remember your parents had a good time in Honolulu and on Kauai."

"Can we go to Kauai?"

"I've scheduled an extra day so we can spend it wherever you want."

The discussion warmed up from there, and we started talking about going to Waimea Canyon like we'd dreamed about for Stephen's baptism. I promised I'd keep an afternoon free on Oahu, too, so we could see some places together.

The five-hour flight from Los Angeles to Honolulu used the best part of day one, but it gave me a chance to read files and nap while Kim finished another Jan Karon novel and read about all the sites to visit. The pastor serving in Pearl Harbor met us with the traditional lei greeting, and helped us find our rental car.

Kim caught a tour of Queen Emma's Summer Palace and the Bishop Museum, wandered in the Foster Botanical Garden, and spent a lot of time at Iolani Palace. She even managed to pick up a few credit card slips for goodies at the International Market Place. "The contrasts here are amazing—so much beauty and native history competing with commercialism—all in such small space." She didn't like sitting in the hotel alone after dinner while I went to more meetings, though.

On my free afternoon, we visited the "Punchbowl," formally known as the National Memorial Cemetery of the Pacific in the hills above Honolulu. When I read the history of World War II battles painted on the walls, and looked out over hundreds of military graves, I felt humbled by the sacrifices. We wound down to the harbor and thought about the attack on December 7, 1941. I choked back tears as I read the long list of names at the Pearl Harbor Monument and stared silently at the dark hull of the USS Arizona beneath the water. War is hell, and the island of Oahu holds many reminders of its huge cost in human suffering.

When I finished the meetings, we flew to Kauai for a quick evening visit with the pastor of the oldest church in the diocese. Founded by German sugar cane processors, the church building, gleaming white inside and out, reminded me of pictures I'd seen of village churches in Germany. The pastor arranged for us to spend the night in Lihue at a bed and breakfast inn overlooking Nawiliwili Bay where cruise ships come and go.

The next morning, after a walk by the bay to see one of the ships at anchor, we headed our rental car toward Waimea Canyon. We put the north shore's Princeville and Hanalei on our "next time" list. All the way up the winding mountain road, we talked about Stephen and our shattered dream for a child of our own. Adoption didn't feel satisfying, and the process seemed to take forever. Still, we couldn't see any other option.

The view back toward the valley below stayed clear, and we marveled at the pineapple plantations and experimental farms dotting the landscape. The coastline, with its turquoise and dark blue waters, made its way from south to west, and we imagined seeing Captain Cook's ship landing where it did in 1778 near Lauaokala Point.

We kept hoping the sun would break through the clouds and fog, but the higher we drove, the more it rained. "The angels must be shedding their tears with ours for Stephen," Kim said.

When we pulled off at the lookout above the Grand Canyon of Hawaii, umbrellas kept our heads dry, but our eyes wept in remembrance of losses: Stephen, Hannah, Ruth, Grammom and Grandpappa, Kim's grandparents, the casualties of war, and so many others. We couldn't see the green and lush mountainsides or the sheer cliffs and waterfalls Iver and Christine had raved about. "Another time," I said, and we stopped at the museum to buy post cards. "At least they get sunshine once in awhile to take these pictures," Kim grunted. She wept most of the way down. "I wanted to see the canyon. I wanted to have my own baby with us. Life sucks sometimes."

We'd forgotten about lunch, so by the time we arrived down the mountain, we searched for a place to eat and stumbled on the Camphouse Grill in Kalaheo. A rustic looking place, we learned it had withstood Hurricane Iniki in 1992, despite severe damage to homes and businesses and loss of electrical power all around. In fact, the waitress said with pride, "As soon as it stopped blowing, we started the generator running, and kept the beer flowing and the burgers frying." We could have split one, but I managed to polish off a huge burger overflowing with mushrooms, cheddar cheese, and fresh pineapple slice, and Kim devoured hers covered with Swiss cheese and a maxi-slice of Maui onion—she promised not to breathe on me—plus a huge stack of fries. Before we left, I checked my cell phone. I wished I hadn't.

YOU ARE THE
WRONG COLOR
FOR HAWAII

We'd wanted to "get away" to renew, and for a few hours, at least, we had, even though we'd missed seeing the canyon. The message, like the others, could be understood as a joke or a taunt. We needed to find out which—and who.

"I'm getting sick of this, Jon. I'm sick of threats, I'm sick of your traveling, I'm sick of eating dinner alone…" The flight home felt like a trip to the dentist for a root canal. I couldn't sleep, we didn't talk, and the movie stunk. Kim was right. Life did suck, sometimes.

\*          \*          \*          \*

Kim and I worked on having more time together, and that meant postponing some meetings and telling people I'd be sending a staff member instead of coming myself sometimes. I felt frustrated at not having enough time for everything, and confused about how to make it better. I loved Kim, and I loved my job. Now and then, I'd experience those memory flashes of Margrethe and my feelings became even more confused about how to deal with them.

*"I love walking along the harbor with you." We inhaled the aroma of African Jasmine, and listened to the soft slap of some boat's wake on the dock's posts as we strolled.*

We'd stood close enough to feel mysterious vibrations from one another. Still, she always seemed emotionally distant, avoiding any conversation about her personal life, talking instead about the children she tended at the hospital, her dreams of becoming a pediatrician, and asking me questions about what I'd seen and learned.

Finally one night, she'd started to pace. "I can see in your eyes that you care for me, and I care for you. I've kept you at a distance because I have a secret I've been afraid to tell anyone."

I'd stood still, watching her graceful body move as she stood first on one foot, then the other. "I was afraid you didn't like me intruding into your life."

"Oh, no, I've enjoyed every second with you, except…"

"You have this secret," I'd said. "Secrets have a way of poisoning the keeper."

"I know. I need to tell you." She'd hesitated, paced a little, and then poured out her story. "Rape is common in this country because of the testosterone-driven soldiers. The doctors at the hospital have the same drive, they simply don't admit it." She'd tilted her head, and taken a breath so deep she could have sung a full aria. The expelling breath told the shocking story. "A doctor kept asking me out, but I turned him down because he's married."

"But he didn't back off?"

"No. One night in the parking lot, he stopped me at my car and grabbed my arm. He said, 'If you don't go to bed with me, I'll tell the administrator you stole drugs from the laboratory.'"

"Oh God, he didn't."

"With his influence, he could get me fired. I'd never get into medical school. I let him come home with me, but I told him never again. He rejected my plea. At least once a week for three months…" She'd stepped closer to me, her eyes like slits and her chin like the prow of a boat. "He won't leave me alone."

I'd moved closer, wanting to envelop her in my arms. I didn't know what to say. She'd pounded my chest with clenched fists. I'd touched my hands to her shoulders, and she'd stopped hitting me and slid her body close to mine. "Oh dear Jonathan, how I wish you could take away my shame, my hatred for that man. You are so kind and good."

We'd embraced for as long as it took for her sobs to subside. I'd held her as if she were one of the dying children at the hospital. When she'd raised her face to mine, our lips inches apart, I resisted my deepest impulse to kiss away her tears. Instead, I'd pulled her head to my shoulder and stroked her back. "You're so precious to me, Margrethe."

She'd pressed even closer. Her whisper touched my heart. "Thank you, Jonathan. Thank you for caring and thank you for not taking advantage of me. I want you, but I know it's wrong, and you must know, too."

"Yes. It's what the Catholics call 'an occasion of sin.'"

We'd drunk coffee and talked late into the night, alternating between how she might trap "the evil Dr. Shebenay," and how difficult we'd find it to give up our mysterious connection.

Then, I flew home, and other feelings confused me. The anonymous messages kept me on edge.

＊      ＊      ＊      ＊

Detective Earl Adrian, member at Lutheran Church of Anaheim Hills, answered my earlier fax with one of his own. "Our expert on terrorism and threats thinks your messages are not dangerous. However, I'd be glad to swing by your house and check your security system."

Our security system? Some of the window locks didn't work, and I could open the back door with a table knife. Kim talked about alarms once, but neither of us got excited about it going off when we'd forget the code or something.

I called and asked him to come by some time and give us some ideas, but we'd never gotten any hints of violence—just ambiguous messages. When he saw our locks, he laughed. "No alarm company in the world will hook you up until you get some dead bolts and better window locks. Why not get those fixed and wait on arming a system?"

Kim felt better after talking to the officer, and we stuck some dowels in the windows and added dead bolts to the front and back doors. He'd also suggested always locking our car windows and doors when we drove, and keeping the cell phone ready to call 911. "Even when you're out on the patio, it's not a bad idea to keep your cell handy."

"Maybe we should move back to Solvang. Life seemed simpler there," I said.

"Maybe life isn't so simple there anymore, either," Kim said. "Mom said Dad installed alarms on both cars and the house."

"Speaking of your Dad—do you think he could be the message sender? That one about being the wrong color for Hawaii sounded like him."

"I can't believe Dad would do that. I mean, he's racist, we know that. But he tells us that stuff to our face. Why would he send anonymous messages?"

'You're right. It doesn't make sense."

I couldn't rule out Peter as the sender. Brenda? She probably didn't have the technology. I decided to call Iver and meet him for lunch. Before I did, my life turned upside down.

# CHAPTER 18

▼

Peter called a Mission Strategy Task Force for the second Monday in August. As chair of the group, he had every right to set the date, but I'd vowed to take Mondays off, and he knew it, irritating me one more time.

For some reason, I'd forgotten to turn off my cell phone, and "Ode to Joy" interrupted Peter's exasperating speech about starting new congregations in places where we'd get fast pay-off. I glanced to see the number on the little screen: Solvang Lutheran Home. I left the room to answer.

"It's your dad. He's had another stroke."

"How bad is it?"

"The doctor thinks he could die anytime."

"Where is he?"

"At the hospital here in Solvang."

"Tell my mother I'll be there by noon. And tell Dad not to die."

I re-entered the meeting in time to hear Peter say, "I know Jon doesn't agree with me, but we can't afford any more new mission churches in Spanish speaking communities."

"You're right, I don't agree, Peter, but I can't stay to debate the merits." I turned toward the other committee members. "My father is near death in Solvang. I'm going right up. Could we take a minute to pray for him?" Peter looked surprised, but bowed his head while we prayed for Dad's comfort and peace. Murmurs of comfort and hugs sent me on my way.

As I drove, I called Kim at home. Always the practical one, she said, "You go straight up there. I'll pack some clothes and tell Andrea we'll be gone. I'll drive up as soon as I get things together. Tell your dad I love him. And hug your mom."

"Thanks, Kim. I guess we'll have to postpone the adoption review tomorrow."

"Oh. They called this morning after you left. They're so far behind with requests, they wondered if we could wait until fall. What could I say?"

I concentrated on driving as fast as I dared, and what I would say to Dad. "I forgive you, Dad." I did, but a son didn't say those as his last words to his dying father. Maybe instead, I'd say, "Forgive me, Dad. I did my best, but I can't be perfect."

Somewhere around Calabassas, I remembered my grandmother's funeral, and how everyone gathered around our family to show their support. She'd died a few months short of her eightieth birthday. I'd been in college, and when they called, I hurried to Solvang. Mom and Dad had met me at the front door.

"Your grandmother doesn't have long to live. The cancer…" My mother had started crying and my dad wrapped his arms around her. Grammom's breast cancer had spread though her whole body. She lived on pain pills and milkshakes.

"Go to her son. She's waiting for you." When I went to her room, Grammom moved toward the door to greet me. She shuffled along, using a walker, wearing her tattered chenniel robe from Christmas ten years ago, even though we'd given her two new ones. "It's comfy," she'd say. She told me to sit in her comfortable chair crammed with pillows. "I want to stand as long as I can, and talk to you. I have things to say, and my walker is my pulpit to lean on."

I sunk down in the big chair by the window overlooking Dad's well-tended garden. Before she got cancer, Gram did her part, too. She'd come to live with us when Grandpappa died soon after I turned five. As long as she could bend, she'd pulled weeds and clipped off dead flowers. As long as she could walk, she'd inhaled the aroma of the roses and fresh black dirt, even when the fertilizer smell drove the rest of us away. As long as she could see, she'd sit in her big chair by the window and look out, marveling at God's gift of fecundity. "Look out there, Jon, and see what can happen from a few seeds. Plant and water, and God takes care of the rest. Overflowing abundance."

"It's amazing, isn't it? Are you sure you don't want to sit down?" I couldn't bear the thought of not hearing her voice. Grandmothers should live forever. Grandfathers, too, but I hadn't connected with him like I did with Grammom. She'd treated me like I could do no wrong.

"Hush, my boy. God's going to welcome me when it's time and not a minute after. I don't know when it will be, but I want to be ready." She'd rolled her aluminum frame closer and leaned over like an evangelist about to rouse a congregation from sleep. "I have stories to tell and…" She made that little "sucking air" noise when pain stabs the body, and winced. "And your job is to listen and pass them on when I'm gone. Except for the secret."

"Take your time, Gram." I'd heard all the stories a dozen times, but I'd listen to whatever she wanted to tell me. What secret?

"My people lived in tribes, and we had our customs and ways that ran deep. When the people came from America in the 1840's—many of them free black folks from the north going back to Africa—our people didn't like it. Tribal chiefs made deals, and carved out boundaries for a new nation without caring what happened to the souls who lived there. The black folks from America decided to call the place 'Liberia,' and named the capitol city for President Monroe." She shifted her weight and took a deep breath.

"Please, Gram, won't you sit down?"

"Hush. I'm just getting started. It was 1847 when they formed Liberia's government on the model of the United States, and 1860 when the first Lutheran mission started up. Reverend Officer from Pennsylvania arrived and got some local men to help him clear a space on a hill above the St. Paul River." I thought she'd tip over, so I started to get out of the chair.

"No, sit still. Just give me a few seconds" Her weak voice trailed off, then her eyes brightened and off she went again. "The missionaries planted all kinds of trees in the clearing: banana and pawpaw, guava and orange, coffee and palm— and lots of sweet potatoes." I hadn't heard that part before, and it registered why she always asked for her milkshakes to be made with a guava.

"By fall, they had land and buildings, but no children for the school. About that time, some United States cruisers took over a slave ship—1500 souls from Congo on board. Reverend Officer rescued twenty boys and twenty girls, took them to the school and found out nobody spoke their language. What to do? Well, the missionary decided he'd best figure out what to call them, so he wrote names of American church leaders on cards and hung them around their necks with pieces of string. That's why the first Congolese children to attend a Liberian Lutheran school had names like William Passavant, John Heck, Samuel Schmucker, Alexander Imhoff and so forth."

I'd chuckled. I'd heard those names the week before in an American Lutheran Church history class. "What did he call the girls?"

"I don't know, but I do know his timing was awful if he wanted any help from the United States. That terrible War Between the States broke out about that time. When he died, the mission struggled until a young couple named Day arrived." Interesting name for a new beginning. "They added more buildings, planted more crops, and built a little steamboat to run rice and coffee the twenty-five miles to Monrovia. Some folks didn't want to listen to his Bible stories, so he decided to do a miracle."

"What kind of miracle?" I asked. She smiled like a poker player with a bad hand, and she hadn't yet given even a tiny hint about the secret.

"Well, he told them that in America water got so hard you could walk on it. They laughed and laughed—called him crazy. So, he imported an ice machine—cost him a hundred dollars—a fortune in those days. When it came, he made a block of ice, chipped some off and gave it to one of the big laughers. The ice burned his mouth and he screamed and ran off and hid for days. It wasn't long until the tribal chiefs asked Mr. Day to start schools a hundred miles around."

"Great story, Gram." Her breathing seemed shallower and she closed her eyes, as if lost in thought. I started to get up again.

"Don't you move, I want to tell you something important." The walker creaked as she shifted her weight. "The missionaries had three big things they wanted to do: teach the Bible, teach the language, and heal the sickness. My tribe, the Kpelle, was big and stretched many miles up and down the St. Paul River. In 1915, when I was…"

Her eyes glazed over as if she were seeing the past flow by. I interrupted. "Five? After you were rescued from your village and raised by the missionaries?"

"You sure do remember my stories, don't you, son?" The crinkles around her eyes slid down to meet the corners of her huge smile. "Where was I? Oh yes, in 1915 they started building Phebe Hospital. Took them six years. Trained women to be nurses and men to be medical helpers. It was wonderful what they did with so little."

She started to waver. "Gram, you've got to sit down."

"No, dear, I'd better lie down." I squirmed out of the deep pile of pillows in the chair and helped her to the bed. She sat on the edge for a minute, and then settled down on her side. I pulled up a bright colored afghan and covered her to the waist. She squinted and shuddered, no doubt from pain.

"Water, Gram?"

"No, let me finish my story. The best part's coming. I've never told anybody."

"Maybe you should rest awhile first."

She gave me the disgusted look she used when Mom and Dad argued about some silly thing. "Hush. I've got to tell you about your Grandpappa Soren. He'd learned some English in Denmark but had trouble speaking and writing it when he to came to Liberia with the Scandinavian Missionary Society. I'd learned English well from the missionaries who taught us orphans—so we'd know our country's official language." She coughed and held her side, but I knew I'd never stop her story telling.

"I taught him English, he taught me Bible. We fell in love the minute he arrived, but we never spoke of it for six months. Then one night after the group Bible study, he walked with me toward my dormitory." A few tears trickled down her cheek, so I reached out to stroke her shoulder.

"There we were, alone in the moonlight, and he whispered, 'I love you Lydia.' I melted. We kissed and kissed and stumbled into the jungle to a knoll above the river. I'd gone there many times by myself and dreamed of making love to him."

"Are you sure you want me to hear this?" I knew about love making, but I'd never entertained the idea of my grandmother lying naked in the grass with her Bible teacher.

"Hold my hand and listen. I conceived your mother that night. And nobody living but you and I know." My free hand went to my ear. Illegitimate? My mother? I didn't want to keep that kind of secret. "When your mother and father are dead and gone, you can tell your wife and family if you have one, but not until, promise?"

"I promise." I hoped I could keep it, and wished I didn't have to. I wanted to get off the delicate subject. "But why did you leave Liberia when you loved it so much?"

"We didn't want to embarrass the mission with a baby born to a thirty-four year old Danish missionary and an eighteen year old Liberian orphan girl, and even if we got married, people could count."

"So you came to America?"

"Yes. Your grandpappa knew some people in Solvang, and they needed an assistant administrator at the Home. We got married in Monrovia before I started showing, and set sail for a new start. People need second chances, Jonathan. Don't ever forget it. People need second chances."

Her breathing slowed and her eyes fluttered. "I'll always remember, Gram. Now get some rest."

Lydia Rasmussen had died in her sleep three months later. We buried her in the Solvang Cemetery after a service full of great singing, celebrating her life, and the pastor talking about her honesty and inner beauty.

Even my transparent Grammom hid a secret in her heart. I wasn't the only pastor who'd fallen in love with a beautiful Liberian woman. I'd never told anyone my grandmother's secret. My mother deserved to know, just as the church deserved to know about my deception. But I'd been sworn to secrecy. Maybe my transparency would have to include secrets.

*"I loved you the minute I saw you, Margrethe."*

*"I could see it in your eyes. They glazed over when I welcomed you."*

*"Didn't you feel anything?"*

*"Of course. Who wouldn't? A handsome man from America with eyes as blue as the ocean—yes, I felt something strong, too. I didn't dare think it could be love."*

*"I could lay here with you the rest of my life."*

*"Oh, Jon, I don't want tonight ever to end either, but tomorrow you…"*

*"Shh. Don't say anything more."*

I'd driven an hour remembering Grammom without noticing the traffic or brilliant blue Pacific. When I got to Santa Barbara, I turned off the 101 to take San Marcos Pass and cut off time. I marveled once more at the rugged peaks of the backcountry beyond Dad's beloved Santa Ynez Valley where his gardens had flourished. "Keep breathing, Dad, I'm coming."

✳    ✳    ✳    ✳

Mom met me with a long hug. Hospital smells, mixed with dim light, made me want to be anywhere else. "Janelle and Michelle are on the way. He's still with us, but not for long. I told him to wait for you."

I touched his hand, intravenous needle in his arm, chest moving with each shallow breath, eyes and cheeks sunken. No evidence of his familiar pinkish tinged cheeks. No wry smile curling his lips. No voice to greet me with his attempts at teasing about my position as bishop the way he had on the phone last week: "How's it goin', Your Eminence?"

I crawled up on the bed beside him, scrunching my warm body next to his cool one, and touched his cheek with the back of my hand. "I'm here, Dad. I love you." If he felt my presence, he didn't show it. I took his limp white hand in my dark one and squeezed. "You're in good hands, Dad. God and you have been friends forever. You've got a place waiting for you."

The nurse brushed by Mom, and looked at me as if I'd stolen her last thermometer. "Bishop Larsen, what are you doing?" I suppose the sight must have seemed a tad strange, given my formal gray suit, purple clergy shirt and gold cross dangling from a chain touching Dad's chest. I hadn't taken time to change.

"I'm telling him his son loves him and that's it's okay to leave us if he wants to."

"Oh, of course, I just meant…"

"I'm on the bed because when I was a pre-schooler, I'd crawl up on his side of the bed at night if I had a bad dream. He always said, 'You're in God's good hands.'"

Most of my bad dreams had come after Dad scolded me for some silly thing. I wished I had a dollar for every time he quoted Jesus at me: "Be perfect, therefore, as your heavenly Father is perfect." I'd have enough dollars to start several Spanish-speaking missions. But when I crawled up beside him in bed back then, he'd always hugged me.

I slid off into the chair beside the bed, and hung my suit coat and cross on the back. My eyes focused on his face while I prayed. No eyelid flickering, no lip movement, even with the Lord's Prayer, no sign of life except the shallow breathing. He and Mom had signed papers requesting no heroic measures, no ventilators, nothing but pain medication. His withered hand lay in mine like a cornhusk. The nurse, relieved to see me in a more appropriate position, took the vital signs, checked the intravenous drip, and left us alone.

Mom sat in the other chair and began to hum. She hummed me to sleep many times in childhood, and now offered Dad the same comfort. I recognized the melody from "Go, my children, with my blessing," and hummed along. Dad's chest rose and fell, slower and slower. Several times, I felt sure he died, but the chest rose once more, like a small, late wave coming into shore. After what must have been an hour, the chest stopped rising.

"Good-bye, Dad." I hadn't noticed my sisters slip in. They stood across the bed, watching his now quieted chest. I raised my bowed head and lifted my hand from his diaphragm, where I last felt connected to the life force, now extinguished.

Mom leaned over to kiss his forehead, as each of us did in turn. The quiet ritual of leave taking, repeated in countless hospital rooms, took on our unique family touch as we recited together the blessing we used at the close of all family gatherings. A few words dropped out when they caught in one throat or another, but somehow, we managed to say, "May God who goes before you show you the way; may God who walks behind you give you courage; may God who lifts you from beneath give you strength; may God who sees you from above give you peace; and may you know the indescribable joy of God's gracious love, until we meet again."

The nurse looked on as our moist embraces told the story: Evald Henry Larsen, crusty, kindhearted husband and father, breathed no more. She glanced at her watch to note the time of death, moved to disconnect the monitor, and told us to take our time saying our good-byes. The trauma of death invited the comfort of ritual and routine, tears and termination duties.

# CHAPTER 19

▼

Walking into Solvang's Lutheran Church felt like coming home. For my first eighteen years and many visits back home, I had occupied space in the third pew from the front on the left side, because that's where my parents and grandparents always sat. Baptized at the font, confirmed and married at its altar, this sacred space blessed me in a familiar way.

As always when we entered the church, our eyes lifted to the small sailing vessel, a Viking ship, hanging above the aisle. It symbolized the journey of faith, the launching into dark waters, confident of reaching our destination, trusting the movement of wind on sails, the breath of God on hearts, the forceful currents sweeping us into safe harbor.

On this funeral day, they ushered our family into the front pew on the right, because that's where families of the deceased always sat, despite having to crane our necks almost straight upward to see the pastor in the high pulpit. Some traditions are meant to be broken. I suggested we move to our normal place. Mom agreed. Janelle resisted. "Someone's already sitting there, and…" Michelle nodded with vigor. Kim pushed me on my way.

I moved to the old family pew and asked if they minded exchanging places. "This place is where Dad would sit if he were here." They graciously moved, and we settled in to hear the prayers and scripture, sang the great hymns of faith, and listened to the pastor proclaim good news.

Kim touched my hand, and gave me a look as warm and loving as any I could remember. For all we'd faced with my long hours and travel, her miscarriages and troublesome younger sister, and those infernal anonymous messages, she never wavered in one thing: she comforted me when I needed it most.

The pastor's voice gently intruded. "We speak the language of faith, which always must be more poetry and art than science and mathematics, more musical and mystical than definitive and physical, and we hear words from Jesus giving us comfort and hope. 'Let not your hearts be troubled; believe in God, believe also in me. In my Father's house are many rooms; if it were not so, would I have told you that I go to prepare a place for you?' All of us want to know we have a place."

I thought about my place in this congregation, and my role as the grieving son. The office of bishop meant nothing in this moment. My dad had died. Like everyone else, I grieved my loss.

The end of the service and our procession to the cemetery happened without my awareness. My thoughts wandered from one set of grandparents to another. As a child, I had often visited their graves in Solvang Cemetery, tracing their names with my small fingers on the gray granite headstones.

The pastor gathered us around the Larsen family plot. "We come to this quiet place of rest, and will return here in the months and years to come, as a place to mark our memories. We ask God to bless us in our remembering and in our living onward. 'If we live, we live to the Lord, and if we die, we die to the Lord; so then, whether we live or whether we die, we are the Lord's.'"

I looked around at the rich green of trees and grass, and the black of earth. I felt the Spirit's presence, supporting my weakened knees. I inhaled the flower-scented air, and felt the Spirit's refreshment. The pastor closed the service. "In the sure and certain hope of the resurrection to eternal life through our Lord Jesus Christ, we commend to Almighty God our brother in Christ, Evald Henry Larsen, and we commit his body to the ground. Earth to earth, ashes to ashes, dust to dust. Amen."

My dad had worked at Solvang Lutheran Home as the caretaker of buildings and grounds for more years than I could remember. He called himself, "The Gardener." They offered him a better title, but he said, "'Gardener' was good enough for Adam, so it's good enough for me." His biblical scholarship tended toward the literal and mystical, but his commitment to responsible care of the earth was rooted in pragmatism. Now, not a half mile from those precious gardens, his physical body became one with the earth.

When the others moved toward the road, leaving me alone, I picked up some of the rich black dirt and sprinkled it on the simple pine casket he'd picked out several years before. "Good-bye, Dad. I'm not perfect. You weren't either. You did your best. That's what I'm doing, too. I promise I'll confess my secret. I've put it off long enough."

*     *     *     *

A week later, I cruised north on Highway 101 over the hills past Calabassas and Camarillo, along the coast through Ventura and Carpinteria toward Santa Barbara, drinking in the fresh ocean air and aroma of eucalyptus. The view of the Channel Islands always inspired me. As I passed through Montecito, I wanted to skip the meetings and instead go directly to Solvang to see Mom. Dad's death left her needing my love more than ever.

The first meeting at St. Ann's promised to be full of tension. The pre-school director and pastor were talking past one another, blaming the other for the break down in communication.

The second involved Our Saviour's Church where the pastor had retired. Adjusting to a new pastor presented a significant challenge to the congregation, because they'd known his leadership for twenty-three years.

I dressed in my usual garb for official functions. Somehow, church members seemed to respect the office of bishop most when the external attire didn't call attention to fashion, but role. I knew my real authority rested in whatever gifts God gave me and in the competence with which I used them.

The St. Ann's meeting completed, I walked away wondering if I did more than calm the storm temporarily. "Time for a coffee and cookie break," I thought, and headed down State Street in my aging Volvo. Some scary noises suggested I make a note to check on a new one next week. And the garage door opener. Tension began building in my neck. The cell phone chirped. "Yes."

"Bishop, it's Teresa."

"I know you're Teresa, what is it?" My curtness surprised me. Teresa and I had already developed a wonderful working relationship. At my first meeting as bishop, I asked the Executive Board to revise her job description and title to reflect the heavy responsibilities she carried beyond word processing and filing. Her new nameplate read, "Bishop's Associate Teresa Gomez."

"You need a C and C break, Señor Reverend Bishop, Sir. But before you do, I need your permission to tell Pastor Vanhorst to go jump off the Pomona over-pass. He's bugging me again about an appointment to tell you you're a heretic."

"Permission granted. But just in case you chicken out, put him down for two weeks from Thursday for lunch. I'll be out his way for a meeting and could swing by to pick him up at noon. And what's with the title?"

"It's what I'll call you when you sound like you've forgotten your humanity. Don't forget to stop for C and C. One cookie."

"I'm headed for *Paseo Nuevo* right now."

"Ooooo, *bueno*. What's there?"

"It's an open-air-square surrounded by shops and restaurants just off State in downtown Santa Barbara. Good for people watching. And there's a great cookie and coffee place."

"Enjoy! *Adios*."

"Bye, Teresa. And thanks for keeping me sane."

"No problem. When I get ordained, I'll probably drive you crazy."

"Fair enough. Meanwhile, you're a great associate!"

I finished my meetings right after lunch and headed for Solvang. The executive committee of the congregation had agreed to a yearlong interim to "adjust," and the retiring pastor indicated he'd be moving back to Minnesota. "It makes it easier for the new pastor," he said. A wise man.

Besides Mom, a nagging issue needed my energy. The threatening messages hung around the edges of my mind, yapping like hungry puppies. After thinking more about Peter, I'd pretty much dismissed him as the culprit. Brenda rated low. I'd wondered more about Kim's father. Iver disliked me as a teenager, especially when I'd called him a bigot one day when he rattled on about lazy Latinos. He objected to our dating, and almost ruined the wedding with his crude toast. "Here's to the happy couple. May they try a thousand different ways to make me a grandpa." He seldom talked to me. When he did, he often included an insult. I'd talk to Kim about him as soon as we could carve out some time together.

\*        \*        \*        \*

Mom and I signed some papers, packed a couple of boxes for the Thrift Shoppe, and reminisced about Dad's quirks. "The gardens here never looked quite as nice after he retired." I agreed. The hours passed while we looked at pictures, and painted our own with remembrances. We cried and laughed until we had nothing left but silence and our breathing.

Before I left the next morning, she grasped my arm. "I have a secret to tell you before you go." I didn't want to get involved with any more secrets, but she looked too serious to turn her down.

We sat in her room, rearranged to suit her now that Dad's things were gone. After a deep sigh, she began. "When your grandmother was dying, and you came to visit her, she told you a secret."

"I thought you had a secret you wanted to tell *me*." I didn't want Mom to ask me what Gram told me.

"That's the secret. The day before she passed, she told me she'd asked you never to tell anyone until after your father and I had died." I fidgeted, but her eyes held me like a vise. "She died before she could release you from that secret, but she told me you could tell me when Dad died, not before. That's my secret. Now, what's your Grammom's?"

"I'm not sure now is a good time."

"I know. No time is a good time to find out you're illegitimate."

"What do you mean?"

"I was born eight months after they got married. And no one ever said anything about being premature." She kept talking before I could get a word in. "Grammom seemed to love her land so much. Poppa never said much one way or the other. I guess it wouldn't have been easy for them to be a mixed family there, either. They had tough time here, sometimes."

I didn't want to get sidetracked, but I'd wondered. "Were people mean to you?"

"Not most people. But some, even in the church, acted like we weren't quite good enough for them. Momma was a proud woman and she gave me that same pride. I got in fight at school one day because of it."

"You, Mom? I can't believe you'd get in a fight."

She sighed at the memory. "I was sixteen and a boy asked me to the prom. One of the Danish girls liked him and wanted him to ask her. When she found out he'd asked me, she cornered me in the hall and told me what a—let's see, what did she call me—a 'brazen hussy.'"

I snorted. "Wow, my Mom's a brazen hussy?"

She shook from laughing. "Can you imagine? Well, I had no idea what 'brazen hussy' meant, but I knew I didn't like the way she talked to me, so I up and slapped her across the face."

"Mom!"

"She was so surprised she just ran off. She never bothered me again."

"You are something else."

"That's another one of my secrets. I never told anybody, not even your dad. But it made me curious about why your grammom and grampoppa came here instead of staying in Liberia, and that's when I started my detective work."

"What'd you do?"

"I started asking her questions about why they left Liberia, and when she and Poppa got married. She always put me off with another story about the 'lush jungle,' and the wonderful opportunities in America."

"So what made you think you might be premature?"

"I ran across her wedding record from Monrovia when I went through her trunk. I'd gotten a copy of my birth certificate when I married your father, and compared it to the license. I counted. I'd wondered if I were illegitimate."

"That's not the right word. No child should be called illegitimate. We're all children of God. It's a beautiful love story, Mom, and if you're up to it, I'll tell you."

She winced when I told her how reluctant I'd felt about learning my grandmother had been naked in the grass with her Bible teacher. She smiled at the part about not wanting to upset the people in Liberia. "That's the way Momma and Poppa were: always concerned for everyone else before themselves."

"We seem to like protecting one another. But I'm glad you know, Mom. I hated keeping that secret from you."

"Secrets are part of life, son. Some are best kept forever. Some are best never hidden in the first place. The trick is to know which is which."

*    *    *    *

Brother David welcomed me with his usual warm embrace, inviting me to be comfortable in his small study overlooking the ocean. I'd met with him after my father's funeral, and he'd urged me to think about the "confession" to Kim and the church for a few days. I came back, thinking I was ready.

"Who are you today, and are you prepared to make your confession?"

"I confess I am a sinner of God's redeeming, but one who has not made amends with everyone for my transgression. I continue to deceive Kim and the church by withholding my encounter with someone not my wife. I've written my letter of confession, but…

"No 'but' yet. Go with 'and.'"

"And, I don't want to give up being bishop."

"Suppose you start by telling me why you think you fell in love with Margrethe?"

"I didn't think about it all. It just happened."

"You arrived there still feeling burned out, is that right?"

"Burned out? If spiritual fatigue—physical, emotional, mental, and social—means I felt burned out, yes. The first month off kept me running to classes, flying home or having Kim in Berkeley. And the way we parted, well…"

"So when you landed in that place you'd yearned to see…"

The images as we circled to land lifted me beyond time and space. "I saw holy ground. I felt a primal connection. I fell in love with the land before I ever saw Margrethe. And when I did…"

"Lightning struck?"

"So vibrant. So beautiful and black. She personified Liberia and all it meant."

"Quite different from Kim."

When I fell in love the first time, it felt as natural as a potted camellia growing into a blooming bush in the garden. The second time felt like spontaneous combustion. "Yes, quite different. Still, I knew Kim was my soul mate when I first heard the term in college. She was the key that fit my lock, and when she told me she felt the same way about me, we 'clicked.' It was like some soul mates talk about when they first meet—like they'd always known one another—we had. We'd been friends from the crib onward. We liked being together. We knew a lot about what the other was thinking and feeling."

"There's more than one kind of soul mate."

"There must be. My love for Margrethe was born instantly. It blossomed into a mystical flower that demanded we draw in its scent and savor its aroma."

"Why did you decide to sleep together?"

"Decide? There was no decision. We went to the opera with a month of unexpressed feelings. The passion of the music tore us open. Nothing could have kept us apart."

"And now you feel guilty." Brother David knew how to bring me back to earth.

"Consumed."

"You made a moral choice when you left. You've never connected again?"

"Never. Well, not true. Not by human means. But there are times when I experience her, hear her, feel her touch. It's eerie."

"But Kim is real, and you want to be honest with her." I got up and paced. The surfers bobbed on the distant waves, and the sun glanced off the water making the image almost as mystical as my encounters with Margrethe.

"It's hard work, confessing. It's even harder to rebuild trust," he said.

"I know."

"It's even harder if you make it public by confessing to the church authorities."

"The books I've read tell me I'll have to do a lot of talking. Answer all Kim's questions. And let her decide when I tell anybody else. I wish I'd known some things before we got married."

"Like what?"

"Like skills. I took drivers training to drive a car. I took tennis lessons and typing lessons. After four years of college, I went to seminary three years and interned a year to get ordained. But I never took one class to learn about the five love languages or how to do a family budget or how to make conflict into a positive at home. I never thought about using all the leadership courses in my marriage."

"Men, especially bright and congenial men, don't think about skill training for getting along with others. But for marriage, you're right, you need all the education you can get—before and during."

"I guess I thought I learned everything I needed to know by watching my parents and Kim's parents. That, and what someone said about not letting the sun go down on your anger."

"Life isn't lived just with simple formulas, no matter how helpful they are." Brother David came to stand beside me, looking out over the gardens to the ocean beyond. "Healing won't come quickly. There will be times of regression. Like those surfers out there. They just get up on the wave when they crash and have to paddle out again. Not easy. But possible, Jon."

"Yes, possible. But so hard."

He gave me some affirmations to repeat and I left with a feeling I could do it. Maybe.

# CHAPTER 20

▼

The garage door opener repairman handed me the remote controls. "These should last a few years. Call me if anything goes wrong."

I wish he could fix the past so I didn't need to resurrect it. The Sacred Space had welcomed me early that Monday morning—my day off. Since my mind wouldn't quiet down, I'd opened the book lying beside the chaise. Anthony de Mello. I'd read the story about two monks coming to a wide river. A beautiful maiden stood wondering how to cross. The first monk picked her up and carried her across, and then set her down and went on their separate ways. After several hours of silent glances, the second monk lashed out, "How could you do that? We are not allowed to touch women."

The first said, "I put her down hours ago. It is you who is still carrying her." Guilty. Margrethe continued to nestle in a niche in my heart. I couldn't put her down.

I didn't want more memories. I couldn't meditate. The phone rang, giving me an excuse to roll out of my chaise, and move toward the house, still unclear how and when to tell Kim and the church.

"I need to see you right away. I'll be there in five minutes." Before I had time to tell Brenda not to come, she hung up.

Kim had left earlier to do some shopping. I'd planned to work in the garden awhile before the sun burned through the gray gunk the weather report called "low clouds leading to hazy sunshine." A dark cloud moved my way, riding a Harley. Every time Bren called or showed up, she asked for money, and once, tried to seduce me.

A few months after we'd moved to Anaheim Hills, Brenda had invited us to her apartment for dinner. She worked for a caterer at the time, and part of her pay included left over food. Kim had left for a quick parent-teacher conference as soon as she finished eating, and said she'd be back soon.

I had sat in the one piece of decent furniture Brenda owned: an upholstered love seat covered with red, white and blue hand knit afghans, courtesy of patriotic Grammmom Larsen. Bren brought another glass of champagne for me, plopped down with her own, snuggled up close and way too personal, and asked me what I'd like while we waited for Kim to come back. "Coffee and an after dinner mint." She brought the mint, unwrapped, and popped it into my mouth as she slipped onto my lap.

I'd tried to get up but she put her arms around my neck. I pushed her away, but she hung on even tighter. She said something about living in the moment.

Kim knew her sister too well to trust, so we'd agreed she'd come back in five minutes. When Bren started unbuttoning her blouse and I squirmed out from under her, Kim had banged on the door. I don't remember everything Kim said to Bren, that night, but we didn't hear from her for months. I'd last seen her the day of my interview.

I decided to meet her out in front, and not let her inside. Her Harley popped its way up the street, just like last time, sputtering to a stop when she cut the engine.

"I have some bad news."

"For you or me?"

"Both. I'm pregnant, and I'm blaming you to the press."

I stared at her with the hardest look I could muster, trying to imitate Kim. Brenda knew where to apply pressure. Even the slightest hint about a bishop who cheated on his wife would spread distrust like summer pollen on the wind. The media needed something new, since people were getting tired of Catholic bashing.

"You must want money bad this time."

"Ten thousand."

"I'll give you a hundred thousand."

"Don't mess with me, Jon, I really need the money."

"I'll give you a million."

"Dammit, Jon, if I don't come up with it, I go to jail. Or my boss will drag my rear to the Long Beach Bridge and drop me over."

"You stole from your boss?

"Borrowed. He owes me. He's the one who got me pregnant." She started to cry. I knew the ploy.

"I recommend going to a treatment center, Bren."

"Damn you! You'll get yours, smart ass." She rode off with a roar.

*       *       *       *

I shuffled into the house, hoping I'd called her bluff. I looked for a snack, poured another cup of coffee and settled in front of the computer. A message from Bishop Clemente startled me. "The situation of the Lutheran Church in Liberia is critical. Countless members are dying from violence and disease, many more are homeless or fleeing the country. Church buildings and medical centers have been vandalized or burned. We need someone to bring them a word of hope from us, and return with first hand information for a special funding effort. Because of your heritage and experience while in Liberia for a sabbatical, you are the logical choice. It's dangerous, but urgent. Talk to me when you come for the Bishops' Meeting."

My first reaction carried me heavenward. To represent the church and visit the churches in Liberia meant a fulfillment of a dream. My second reaction scared me as much as the first filled me with elation. Margrethe. I sat still, imagining what it would be like to see her—hold her. No!

I heard Kim come in and met her on the patio. "We've got to talk. I can't do this any longer"

"Do what?" Concern washed across her face.

A couple of mocking birds chattered in the eucalyptus, and the aroma of sage brushed our senses, but nothing inspired me to speak. I didn't want Kim to feel the pain of my confession, but I couldn't turn back again. "There's something Peter knows that you don't."

"Yeah, right. He knows more than you, too. Is he sending the messages?"

"No. I mean, I don't think so, but that's not what—I mean he knows something about my past."

"Oh God, Jon, not that again."

"At first, I didn't tell you because—well—I was scared. I thought I could keep the secret safe. But now Peter wants—"

"What secret, for God's sake? Now you're scaring me."

"Well—"

"And stop saying 'well'."

"I slept with a woman in Liberia."

The color drained from her tanned face, her eyes narrowed, and her chin quivered. She stood up, knocking the chair over. "You crap head!"

"I'm sorry."

"You sonovabitch!"

"I never meant for it to happen."

She spit at me. She'd never done anything like that. Ever. Then she spit again. "You make me sick."

"I knew you'd be hurt. That's why I didn't say anything."

"Hurt? Hurt, hell! I'm pissed!" She spit at me again.

I backed away. I'd never seen her so out of control. I tried to wipe the saliva off my forehead while I kept one eye on her. My insides felt like they were in a blender set on "liquefy."

She kept moving toward me, and I kept backing up. "You had an affair a few months after my miscarriage? After all that counseling?"

"I did a terrible thing."

She caught up with me and dug her nails into my shoulders. "You bastard! How could you do that to us?" I had to catch myself when she shoved me out of the way and slammed her way into the house.

I waited a few minutes, and followed her. I found her standing at the mantle in the living room holding the lachrymatory I'd brought her from Liberia, crying.

"I didn't know she'd be there," I said. "Then her parents had to leave for London, and..."

"Who? Who's 'she'?"

"Ben and Edie's daughter, Margrethe. She's a nurse."

"Your cousin?"

"Not really. Ben and Grammom weren't related by blood, just..."

"Cut the crap, Jon. I don't care about her ancestors or her job, I wanna know how in hell you could stand there at the airport and give me this beautiful vial and say how much you missed me, and now you tell me you—"

"I'm sorry, Kitten."

"Don't call me that, you bastard."

"It just happened. The night before I left, we went to the opera and I took her home, and then..."

Kim slammed her hand across my face, and stormed toward our bedroom. "You sonovabitch!"

My face stung like I'd been hit full on with an oversize ping-pong paddle. While I stumbled after her, I gingerly checked for blood. The greatest pain settled somewhere between my broken heart and my groin, which I knew could be the next point of attack.

When I came to the bedroom, she bounced a bottle off the door, sending the sweet smell of cologne into a losing battle over the stench of betrayal. The shattered glass and mutilated trust mixed to make a dreadful mess. I peeked into the room, and she sailed her shoe past my face. "Get the hell out of my room, you pig." The other shoe skidded across the floor as I backed away.

"I know you can't forgive me right now, but…"

"Now? Try forever!" She swore again and slammed the door, rattling the family pictures lining the walls. I retreated down the hall to the den and slumped into the couch.

An hour later, she walked out of the bedroom wearing a mask of reddened and swollen eyes and determined chin. "I knew about her all along."

"You what?"

"I knew you did something in Liberia you couldn't tell me."

"How?"

"I can always tell when you're keeping something from me. I hated your passion for Liberia. That's why I didn't go with you."

"But…"

"And you've always had a mistress. The church takes you away from me all the time."

"But…"

"So when you came back and showered me with attention, I knew you'd done something more than fallen in love with your homeland."

"I did fall in love with it. Margrethe kind of came with it."

"I'm sure. Nice try." She kept moving toward me, one small step at a time. I didn't dare move.

"I've never done anything like that, and…"

"And you'll never do it again. And you'll never lie to me again. And we'll keep going to counseling as long as I say so." She didn't give me a chance to do more than nod my head.

✻    ✻    ✻    ✻

The counselor's office looked like a living room in a well appointed home. Pastel colors and soft fabrics lent a mood of calm. I didn't feel calm. Tall, middle-aged, and looking stern, the counselor told us we could expect at least six months of sessions. "Jonathan, you need to apologize over and over, and give Kim reassurance it won't happen again. She'll let you know when she's heard it enough." She gave us a sheet of things we could do together to nurture our marriage, besides what she'd suggested to help us through our grief over Stephen: taking walks, eating out, and going to movies. "Don't talk about the affair all the time. Set aside specific times for talk, and for doing things you both enjoy."

We met twice a week over the next month, and each session began with reassuring Kim, and me apologizing, which is the way we started and ended every day. We saw more Angel games and movies than ever before in our married lives.

When Kim said okay, the counselor brought up forgiveness. "Kim, when you can forgive him, you can begin to heal. Jon, when she forgives you and you can forgive yourself, you can begin to heal. Without forgiveness, neither of you can heal." She explained that forgiveness is a choice, just as my unfaithfulness had been a choice.

Some weeks were worse than others, when Kim's voice had an icy edge and her stiff body refused to return my tentative hugs. Two weeks passed before she'd do more than buss my lips before we turned over to go to sleep. After the fifth session, she kissed almost the way we had before my confession. "Now you can tell the presiding bishop whatever you need to."

✳     ✳     ✳     ✳

While the counseling sessions for Kim and me helped us become more and more transparent to one another, I continued my meetings with Brother David, too. Each one felt like undergoing an MRI of the soul. The comfortable leather chair would morph into a conveyor belt, transporting me into a dim coffin-like tube of semi-consciousness, while his deep-set dark eyes probed somewhere beneath my level of awareness where my most vulnerable feelings hid.

"I want you to write a poem about forgiveness, Jon."

"I'm not ready to forgive myself."

"All the more reason to write the poem. It's important before you confess to the bishop." He stood up, tossed me a yellow lined pad and pencil, and turned on a Mozart piano concerto. "You've got thirty minutes."

Three deep breaths settled me to the task. I moved to the table from my comfortable chair, and began to scribble out some feelings.

"Tears tumble down my cheek." I scratched it out. "Teary eyed, I sit wearied by the wearing war within." Still not right. "Safely sitting beside the stately oak…" Nope. I crossed it out. "Serenity seeks safety in the gift of forgiveness." Hmmm, maybe something usable there.

I scratched and wrote, tore off pages, crumbled and tossed them toward the wastebasket. More missed than made it, sort of like my attempts to write poetry, or maybe like my sorry attempts at living transparently. Fail boldly! The words emerged:

> trembling tears like willows weeping
> signal dreams of safety, serenity
> beyond our reach except for a
> minuscule glimpse of forgiveness

A psalm came to mind, but I couldn't remember the exact words. Something about "Thou hast searched me and known me since I was knit together in my mother's womb."

I began to tremble, tears forming from deep inside. My eyes clouded over, but I kept pushing the pen to give vent to my intensity. If I could just see the Forgiving One who has known me from before my birth—see the sad eyes of the One who gave his life on the cross—see the nail pocked hand extended to lift me up. If only. I thought about the color of his hair and eyes, the pain of nails driven into his hands and feet, the message to the penitent thief hanging beside him, "Today, your sins are forgiven."

I began to write again. Colors, bright and dark, flashed in my imagination—blue, crimson, green—ten minutes to go. I wrote:

> Forgiveness is woven from
> the threads of broken promises
> hateful words despicable behavior
> colored with crimson stains of back stabbing
> yellow edged cowardice
> dark blue hues of depressing denials
> brilliant green of cemetery grasses
> lined on line with stark white crosses
>
> The fabric of forgiveness is woven
> from the spun glass of intense pain
> and silky smoothness of dark deceptions
> bringing unspeakable peace when received

When I stopped, I read between the tearstains, and discovered I'd been able to put into words some of my deepest feelings. I picked up the page and went to find Brother David, and handed in my "soul work." He began to read aloud, but his eyes brimmed with tears when he came to, "spun glass of intense pain." He finished and handed back my poetry. "You're catching on, Jon. Keep at it."

# CHAPTER 21

▼

Before I had a chance to open the meeting, Pastor Fount moved his half-closed eyes around the room. "This is humiliating! Imagine being called before a body of your peers to talk about adultery. Your own adultery! It's shameful. At least, I feel shame being heaped on my head."

"Excuse me, Pastor Fount," I interrupted. "We're not here to inflict shame, but before we begin to talk about why we are here, I want to set out some ground rules. And before that, I'd like to invite us to pray." Pastor Fount stiffened, started to speak, then his bowed head joined the others as I prayed.

I looked around at the seven-member panel, seated in comfortable chairs in the carpeted and spacious lounge of St. Barnabas Episcopal Church. We'd borrowed it both for the sake of privacy and for its ambience. "Pastor Fount, you have been accused by your partner of being unfaithful to him. Our purpose today is to discover the facts and together work out a way to move ahead with integrity." I took a deep breath.

"Your partner, Gary Temple, has publicly charged you with unfaithfulness and unworthiness to be a pastor. The written summary is in our notebooks. We know this is painful and we'll take the time necessary to deal with both feelings and facts."

I looked around the room, noticing the intensity of everyone's attention. I felt tentative about conducting a Review Panel, but so far, things had gone according to plan. Pastor Fount outlined what he had told me when we met. When he finished, he let out a huge sigh, along with tears streaming down both cheeks. A foot tapped, someone scratched an ear, a tissue wiped away a tear, and Peter picked at a hangnail. Each nervous gesture gave both physical evidence of the tension in the room, and the uncertainty of what good could come of our deliberations. After discussion and more prayer, we made our decision.

Because the congregation already knew about his situation, the Review Panel recommended he receive a public censure, and suggested the Executive Board appoint a delegation to meet with the congregation to interpret the action with hopes they might retain him. I agreed with the decision, and walked to the car with Edward.

"Have you heard from Gary?"

"Yes. He called and apologized for dragging me through this mess. We even talked about getting together."

"There are some excellent programs for couples who want to reconcile," I said.

"They want married folks, and we don't qualify. No one will take on a gay couple."

"I know someone who will."

"Yeah, and he's gay, too, or a lesbian, right?"

"No, but he's helped a lot of couples, gay and straight, lesbian and bi-sexual."

"Really?" Edward looked at me out of corner of his eye. "Every workshop or seminar leader I've contacted talked about the one man one woman marriage institution—not us."

"Try this one." Edward hesitated, and then took the card I handed him.

✳     ✳     ✳     ✳

I hadn't anticipated vengeance from Peter. True he lost the election for bishop, and his rants at meetings about funding and cost effectiveness didn't get him anything but embarrassment. But, a professional leader in the church ought to know better than to spread damaging gossip. His reaction after the convention seemed like the way any wounded man would behave, and I assumed he'd heal over time. However, Beverly Davidson's phone call made me wary.

"Why is Pete out to hurt you, Bishop?"

"What do you mean?"

"He called and told me you didn't deserve to be bishop. Something about holding out on the diocese. What's up with that?"

"I'm not sure. Did you suggest he call me directly?"

"No. I forgot. Guess I should have remembered what we learned about triangulation. But only an idiot would figure I wouldn't tell you."

"Peter's no idiot, but he must be angry." I'd heard from two other pastors in San Diego about Peter saying much the same thing to them. I punched in Peter's office phone number.

"Oh hello, Bishop. How nice to hear your voice. I'll find Pastor Bloch. He's been out prowling around the playground, making sure the toddlers stay inside the fence." Just like a perfectionist. Or did I need to give him some slack? He'd always seemed to like little kids. Protectionist, maybe?

"Yes, Jonathan. What's on your mind?"

"Our friends are talking about us, Peter. It's time you and I sat down and talked about the strain between us."

"What strain?"

"You know what strain. How about tomorrow for lunch at the Pastrami Palace in Pacific Beach?"

"Not sure I can make it."

"I'll be there at noon. We can get take out and talk in the park while we eat."

"I'll think about it."

\*        \*        \*        \*

Peter showed up on time, as always. He maybe didn't want to be there, but punctuality permeated his personality. He ordered sliced turkey breast on whole wheat, non-fat mayo and no tomato.

"I'll have your special," I said. The Pastrami Palace served the most succulent, calorie laden pastrami in San Diego: fresh baked rye bread, Russian dressing, Swiss cheese, a lettuce leaf, and piles of hot, juicy pastrami. They always topped off the order with a kosher dill pickle. It smelled as good as it tasted.

He chose a drink free of sugar and caffeine, while I ordered an O'Doul's to go. The clerk smiled as she rang up the check, "You two don't look like you should eat together."

We ignored the comment, and walked across the street to a pocket park, empty except for two moms and their babies in strollers walking through. "Peter, I've decided to tell the Executive Board about my affair in Liberia." He spilled his drink.

"Why?"

"Because it's the right thing to do."

"Yes, but you should have told the nominating committee in the first place."

"I should have done a lot of things, but I can't live with this secret any longer."

"We'll no doubt ask for your resignation."

"I'll accept whatever the Board decides."

"Yes, but you'd give up the office of bishop just because someone might find out about your old affair?"

"No, I'd give it up because I respect the church too much to deceive it any longer."

"You're nuts."

"And you're delighted."

He stared at me and took a giant bite from his sandwich. Chewing like a paper shredder, and too polite to talk with his mouth full, he shook his head, "No."

"I know you've been trying to pressure me through our friends."

He swallowed hard. "You don't know what you're talking about."

"You've talked to Beverly Davidson and Ron Miller, and at least one other. You told them I have secrets. No one else knew."

"So, Detective Larsen, what other speculation do you want to exercise?"

"I want to know what you said to Beverly the day of my election. It sounded like 'The black something or another beat us.' I know you were hurting, Peter, but are you that paranoid about the African-American caucus that you blamed them for your defeat?"

"I don't know what you're talking about. I don't remember saying anything. My God, man, I'd just lost the election. It felt like a heart attack."

"I'm not going to press that issue. I saw how white you turned. And I know you wanted me not to interview, and once I'd gotten votes, you as much as told me to withdraw. In fact, I suspect you're the one who's been sending me anonymous messages."

"Anonymous messages? What're you talking about?"

"The first one came right after I'd been asked to interview. 'Don't even think about it.' Then after my interview, 'Did you tell the whole truth?' And right after our speeches. 'Failure Pull out.' Another said I deserved to suffer, and while we were in Hawaii, I got one that said I was the wrong color. Those anonymous messages."

His face turned pink. "Is this part of your transparency crap, Jon? Do you think I'd hide behind anonymity?" He looked more angry than guilty.

"I think you're hurting so bad you can't help yourself. I think your pain at losing has made you so mad you'll do things you're ashamed of. I think you need therapy."

"Good God, you sound like a bishop."

"I am your bishop, Peter, and maybe it's about time you honored that."

He picked up the rest of his sandwich and drink, dumped them in the trash, and stomped toward his car. He threw his barb over a disappearing shoulder. "Just because you're a liar and a fraud doesn't mean I am. You'll be hearing from me—Bishop." He pushed the last word through a sneer.

I shouted above the traffic noise. "Remember, Peter, you've taken a vow of confidentiality. If you break the news before I do, you're as bad as I am."

"Yes, but…" He slammed the door before I could hear him finish. I watched him go, wondering if he'd said, "Yes, but I don't care, and I'm telling."

I called Janelle again. "Can I get a restraining order against someone who's threatening to violate the rule of confidentiality?"

"What?" She sounded like I'd lost it.

"I've got a pastor in the diocese who's threatening someone to reveal a confidence. It's not a crime or anything, it's about something personal."

"And it could mess up, like maybe a marriage or something?"

"Something like that." I didn't want to get specific.

"I doubt a judge would issue a restraining order, but you might get a good lawyer to write a tough letter."

"Okay, just wanted to know. I'll be in touch if I need you."

"Jon?" She sounded like she wanted to know more.

"Yes?"

"You're not in trouble are you?"

"Why would you ask?"

"Because usually when we ask about something for a friend, it's really about us."

"You've been watching too much television. Relax. I just needed an excuse to talk to my big sister." Even if her answer hadn't satisfied me, hearing her voice calmed me down.

*    *    *    *

Kim sounded tense. "Brenda called from the Betty Ford Center. Her boss pulled some strings and got her in. She wants to make amends. It's the ninth of the twelve steps." Kim's voice sounded calm, but she left no doubt we needed to listen to Brenda.

"Does it have to be in person?"

"Yes. Step Eight stays to make a list of people you've wronged, and determine to make amends. Step Nine says to make direct amends whenever possible except when to do so would injure them or others."

"So when would this happen?"

"She gets one Saturday morning a month for visitors. Her next one is this week-end."

"Then we'll go." I checked my calendar, already showing three appointments, but I'd postpone them. Part of my therapy included practicing forgiveness.

High winds and late September heat faced us on the drive to Palm Springs. I hoped Brenda wouldn't try to blow us away or melt us down.

She told us more than we wanted to hear, but her honesty gave us hope. She'd told her boss about taking the money. He'd agreed to support her and the baby, once she'd proved paternity.

Outward sincerity doesn't guarantee inner authenticity, but her tears and apology touched us. Transparency? At least for now. Telling us about all the stunts she'd pulled didn't shock us as much as what she told us about Iver.

"Dad's sending you anonymous messages."

"Dad?" Kim's eyes became slits, her brow gathered into tight lines, and her tiny ears turned deep pink.

"Says he likes to needle you."

"How did he always know where we were?"

"Because you always told Mom, Kim, and Mom told Dad. He also knew I'd tried to seduce you, Jon, and so he blew that up into a 'secret' to warn you about. He laughed when he told me about finding software to keep both his cell phone and computer messages anonymous. Seemed pretty proud of himself, except it irritated him you never mentioned the messages."

Kim swore she'd slap him silly. I felt like joining her. We decided to postpone confronting him until I got back from the bishops' meeting.

\*        \*        \*        \*

I welcomed Larry Poulson into the Hearing Room, and prayed for God's loving care for all of us. The same Review Panel, the same cold fireplace, and the same stifling tension made me as uncomfortable as when we met with Pastor Fount.

I turned to Larry, who sat to my left, with the Review Panel circled around the room ending at my right. Accusing an old and dear friend with his transgression felt like self-exposure.

I turned to address the Review Panel, opening the black notebook filled with damning information. "Researchers have taught us what looks like consent to the pastor, and may even sound like consent by the member, is, in fact, coercion by the pastor. The role of pastor is a powerful one that invites trust, caring, and even obedience. The two women awakened to his abusive nature when he threatened each one with spiritual damnation if they ever revealed anything about their sexual involvement." Larry shifted as if he wanted to say something. I held up my hand, and he waited until I finished.

"He denied threatening them with damnation. Our decision relates to the fact of sexual behavior between pastor and parishioner. Deciding about consent belongs in civil court, if anyone decides to sue. The women have chosen not to pursue the issue of psychological abuse relative to threats of damnation. Our decision relates to the fact that Pastor Poulson committed adultery with at least two women. I say, 'at least,' because I received communications from others who will come forward if needed."

There were no questions. When I asked Larry for his statement, he stood up and said, "You've got my letter. This is all bullshit anyway." He looked weak, his cheeks hollow, and his complexion blotchy. I wondered if he'd ever seen the doctor like he'd promised me. We excused him so we could make our decision.

I noticed Peter had been sitting erect with a stern face throughout my comments. He spoke in deep and measured tones. "Bishop, I have a question. In scripture, Jesus asks whoever is without sin to cast the first stone. How is it that we as a church have made a rule to cast all our stones at the transgressing pastor? Are we letting these seductive women off without so much as a censure?"

Before I could answer, one of the female pastors snapped her head around to stare at him. "Are you saying the victims are guilty of something?"

"Not necessarily. It's just that…"

"How dare you even suggest they seduced him?" The discussion gathered momentum, but unlike the Edward Fount situation, the inevitable conclusion merely waited to be said out loud. We invited him back to read our conclusion: "We find you guilty and will recommend to the Executive Board that you be asked to resign from the roster of ordained ministers.

"Don't bother. I've already written my resignation. And I've called my lawyer. There may be some legal action coming your way, Bishop."

# CHAPTER 22

▼

I didn't look forward to going. When Kim kissed me good-bye at the airport, she said, "Tell Bishop Clemente they'd be crazy to remove you from office." I'd answered his e-mail to let him know I'd be glad to discuss the Liberia mission, and asked for time to share a matter of "significant concern." I'd also called the Executive Board president and set an appointment for two days after I returned. The road to revealing my deception led through those two stops, but I didn't know where it would take me next.

On the flight, I rehearsed what I'd say about Margrethe. The thought of maybe seeing her again almost made me forget everything I'd learned in counseling.

*"When I cup your breast in my hand, my entire body resonates with a thousand cellos throbbing their melody." She pressed closer, brushing my forehead with the back of her hand, moving slowly to run her fingers through my hair. Wrapped only in our ecstasy, her body melted into mine.*

*"I feel the synchronization of our souls, Jonathan. No one but God could grant us such wonder, such pleasure."*

I knew then, more than ever, I couldn't go to Liberia. Once I confessed, the bishop wouldn't send me. How could he?

\*         \*         \*         \*

The quarterly meeting of bishops of the Lutheran Church—North America vibrated with one major concern: sexual transgressions. We sat in a large conference room at a hotel near the airport in Kansas City. Thirty-five of us fiddled with coffee cups and our notebooks full of information. Bishop Clemente opened the meeting with prayer and scripture, and then launched into his "state of the church" address.

"The Cardinals returned from Rome, the American Catholic bishops voted on how to deal with sexual abusers, the pope has spoken, and the media has quieted down. The pain of the victims lives on. Lawsuits continue. The shame of the family and friends and parishioners of abusers lives on. And, the abusers live with consequences of violating a sacred trust."

His voice sounded calm, but we couldn't ignore his intensity. He stood straight and stared at each of us for several seconds before moving on to the next bishop in the circle.

"I have no qualms about discussing sexual issues with you. We are living in a time when much of the world would have us reduce our standard of morality for them, and raise it for everyone else. You all know what it is to live in tension between two goods, two evils. We can't ignore the crisis in the Roman Catholic Church. Sexual abuse issues sap the energy from every church body, including ours. When boundaries of sacred trust are crossed, the church must speak."

The presiding bishop spoke with the accent of a man born in El Salvador and educated at Luther Seminary in St. Paul, Minnesota. His pronunciation carried the heritage of Central America, and his phrasing and deep voice reminded me of Garrison Keillor.

"It doesn't much matter if we have fewer reports of molestations than promiscuity. One is too many. Receiving three reports of pederasty in the past two years breaks my heart. Two single and five married pastors are under review for sexual misconduct. Reports come in about once a month regarding pastors downloading pornography from the Internet. Can we rejoice that a very small percentage of our colleagues commit sexual transgressions?"

The bishop from Philadelphia sitting across from me raised his head at the question. I wondered if he had the same reaction as I. It sounded like the presiding bishop wanted to cover the pain with percentages, but he didn't stop there. "And I'd like you, as bishops, to know how important victims—or even apparently willing participants—are to me, and, I hope, to you. No one should suffer the consequences of a violation of trust by clergy, either in crossing the sexual boundaries, or because bishops covered up the transgressions."

I glanced around the room at my colleagues. One indiscretion deserved our dismay as much as fifty. With plenty of responsibility to go around, blaming victims didn't fit anywhere in the equation.

He concluded, "We dare not abuse the trust people place in us. We have more than a legal responsibility to report sexual abuses of any kind. The church should be a role model for morality, an example to the world. If our people can't trust us, whom can they trust?"

Compassion for victim and abuser didn't mean backing away from consequences. For the victim, a lifetime of pain couldn't be overcome by our sincere apologies and financial support for therapy, important as they were. For the abuser, a terrible mistake required consequences.

The bishop from Boston stood to his full six feet six inches and spoke with a voice like James Earl Jones. "Compassion for victims must come first. And for the congregations defiled and disrupted for years to come. And for family members of the pastor."

"Agreed," said a piercing tenor voice, coming from a stout bishop at the far side of the room. "But what about compassion for the broken, repentant pastor? Can we forgive the pastor even as we carry out discipline?"

The discussion revolved around the tension between law and gospel, regulations and graciousness, boundaries and forgiveness. A middle-aged female bishop stood up and began to speak with intensity. "Forgiving the sinner but not the sin just doesn't work for me about sexual abuse. A human being is a whole being. We condemn the whole person for immoral actions. We discipline the whole person. And, we show compassion to the whole person."

"When is a transgression serious enough for public exposure?" The other female bishop rose from the circle and paced as she spoke. "Is every sexual indiscretion worthy of ruining a family's life, whether victim or pastor, by exposing it to the media?"

No one answered. I wondered about my own, and about Edward Fount's back in Los Angeles. Edward's situation became public because his partner decided to make it known. Mine could stay secret, except for one thing. I couldn't live with deceiving the church any longer.

After the break, our colleague from Pennsylvania brought a resolution from the Liberian Lutheran bishop urging the United States government to bring the warring parties to the negotiating table. Leaders in Sierra Leone and Guinea agreed to aid displaced persons, repatriate refugees, enhance border security and promote economic development, but Liberian president Taylor had stalled negotiations. We also called attention to allegations by humanitarian workers about sexual exploitation of refugee children in the three countries.

We recognized another tragedy: the AIDS crisis. Just as the Gulf War diverted America's attention away from Liberian civil strife in 1990, the terrorist attack on 9/11/01 and the invasion of Afghanistan had diverted our attention from AIDS, human rights violations, continued fighting, and economic disaster in many parts of Africa, including Liberia.

Lutherans, Episcopalians, Catholics and many others from around the world contributed to feeding programs, but high unemployment meant more needed help than there were resources. The situation in some outlying areas of Liberia resonated with the sounds of war.

The United Nations refused to lift sanctions, which helped or harmed, depending on one's point of view. It helped by sending a message that the world would not tolerate selling diamonds "dipped in blood," so called when profits from their sale bought weapons used to incite revolution in neighboring countries. Harm resulted because the common people clamored for food, clean water, medical supplies, jobs, education, and a return to stability in their country. Most of Monrovia lived in darkness, without electricity, telephones, trash pick up or functioning sewer systems. No one questioned the need to assist the Liberian people. The discussion broke up for dinner, and Bishop Clemente invited me to his office.

*         *         *         *

Red carpeting and wine-colored draperies brought a cardinal's garb to mind, but Lutherans don't have cardinals. The room confirmed our presiding bishop's reputation for art and aesthetic comforts. Two elegant but comfortable looking chairs faced one another with a coffee table between. His modest maple desk and leather chair sat under a large picture of a white church with green steeple, surrounded by rubber trees.

*I walked into Margrethe's apartment, where her living room wall held a picture of the church she loved—small, white, with a green steeple topped with a cross. I stood speechless when she showed me another picture in her bedroom: an exquisite nude portrait done when she attended college in London. The potent sensuality of her female form superimposed itself over the presiding bishop's painting.*

"I'm glad we can talk about your going to Liberia. But your request to talk with me about a matter of significant concern is troubling."

"I am troubled, Bishop."

"I'm surprised. Your board president sent me glowing reports about your first months in office. Peter Bloch's complained a little, but I don't pay much attention to old Pete. He was in my seminary class, brilliant and persuasive, but he always had more complaints than compliments. Is this about Pete?"

"No, though he and I have our moments—including his insistence on being called Peter rather than Pete by his friends. This is something a lot bigger than Peter's carping. I don't think you'll want to send me to Liberia after you read what I've written." I handed him the note and watched him unfold the single sheet revealing my deception of the nominating committee. His brow furrowed . with concern.

"You lied?"

"Yes. I failed to explicitly describe a transgression from thirteen years ago. I told them I had confessed past sins to my spiritual mentor, and I wasn't in violation of any pastoral covenants of the Lutheran Church—North America."

"But there's more?"

"Yes. The transgression—I had an affair during my sabbatical in Liberia in 1989."

"I see." He shifted in the chair opposite me, and then put his feet up on the coffee table, carefully placing his heels on a magazine. A metaphor hung around the edges of my mind, but I couldn't quite get it. Something about not scratching the polished surface of the church while he stretched to find a wise response.

"Bishop, I'm prepared to be disciplined. I've drafted a letter to you and the Executive Board." I handed him a copy. "I trust the church to do what's right."

"I need to think about it before I respond, Jonathan. I'll read the letter tonight. I must confess my deep dismay."

"I understand, and can't begin to tell you how much I regret…" My words drifted off into the air of foreboding in the room.

"We can get together after breakfast tomorrow." His feet dropped onto the soft carpet, and he stood to shake hands. "God's wisdom is never easy for any of us to discern. Pray tonight, Jonathan, and I'll do the same."

The next morning, he agreed with me that I needed to tell the Executive Board. "There is part of me that thinks more harm will come from telling than not telling about an indiscretion from so long ago—one you confessed to your wife and God. We need you to reach out to the Liberian Lutheran Church. But not to reveal it smacks of cover-up, and we've seen that abyss all too clearly in our sister church. I must distinguish between God's forgiveness, which is freely given in Christ, and the duties of the ordained. I can offer forgiveness in the name of Christ. I can't ignore a violation by someone entrusted with responsibilities as pastor or bishop. I will abide by whatever your Executive Board decides. They have responsibility in this matter. And, I will keep praying for you, Jonathan."

# CHAPTER 23

▼

On the drive home from the airport, I filled Kim in on the meeting. "He gave me the round trip ticket to Monrovia he'd already authorized. Said I could turn it back to him if I don't go."

"Sounds like he doesn't quite know what to do with you."

"True. But it's up the Executive Board anyway, so that's the next step."

When we walked into the house, I wondered how we'd be able to make the payments if I had to resign. If we were forced to sell, we'd owe Kim's parents half the equity because Iver had insisted on "helping" by giving us half the down payment. Our plans to buy him out landed in the "never got around to it" category.

"Go out and fire up the barbeque for hamburgers. I'll get stuff ready in the kitchen and we can talk about it while we watch the sun set and listen to the play-offs." Kim's connections fascinated me. "If the miracle Angels can get into the World Series, I know you'll have a miracle at the Executive Board meeting, too."

The smell of smoke from the barbeque aroused childhood memories of small piles of leaves burning in our Solvang garden. I'd helped my father rake some to burn after we stuffed as many as we could into our composting bin. We didn't always welcome the aroma of smoke, of course. It aroused fear in anyone living on a canyon in Southern California, especially on a hot and hazy October afternoon with santana winds.

I alternated dozing and meditating in my new chaise lounge under the Monterrey pine. Now and then, I glanced at the canyon's dry grass and bushes beyond the block wall. Across the canyon, I concentrated on a community of oak and eucalyptus trees, hosting complaining crows and who knows how many invisible critters. I sat there hoping for some profound insight—an igniting spark—a fresh breeze—to set me on the path toward living with my resignation and starting a new life far from California.

The choir of eucalyptus across the way, stripped of bark by years of weathering, seemed to be sending messages. "Even when one is tall and strong looking, a brisk wind can snap huge branches as if they were thin sticks." I owned a tall and strong body, but my reputation? On the thin stick side. "The Spirit blows where it will. Tongues of flame, like rain, settle on the just and unjust." The reality burned a hole in my soul, luring me into fantasies bordering on the megalomaniac on the one hand, and the self-destructive, on the other.

My shadow side had threatened to take over my better judgment. I'd clung to my titles: bishop, pastor of pastors and overseer of congregations. Spiritual leader. Model of the godly life. But, "flawed vessel of awe" and "clogged conduit of grace" described me better.

The aroma of smoke mixed with the incense of my meditation. In the hazy edges of my mind, I saw smoke and flames rising from a patch of brush in the canyon. I flew into the house to call 911, but learned the whole neighborhood had beaten me to it. I gathered up our picture albums and the packet of important papers we kept in the refrigerator, threw some clothes in a suitcase, and yelled for Kim. She didn't answer. I loaded the car and turned it toward the street, ready to leave in a hurry. I shouted at the neighbors across the way; they shouted back. Fear rolled over the canyon neighbors like the smoke swirling ahead of the wind gusts.

The eucalyptus grove across the canyon looked and sounded like a Fourth of July fireworks show. As the sparks from the brush ignited the dry leaves, branches and trunks turned into torches; they popped and banged as pockets of sap detonated. Fireballs flew from tree to brush, igniting new flames, whipped by the santana winds.

I noticed the fire moving away from my house. "Thank God." But what about all the homes in the path of the firestorm? And the humans and pets and wild animals—how would they escape?

Sirens wailed from all directions. The crisis exploded across the canyon, climbing mountains, roaring it's way forward. The fire, except for smoke, disappeared over the hills, out of sight. Hundreds of visible acres sat blackened, with patches of dull green sage and juniper here and there somehow surviving the onslaught.

Kim jiggled the chaise. "Wake up, dreamer. The coals are ready for you to barbeque the burgers." I jumped up and stared at the quiet canyon, still golden brown. The oaks and eucalyptus waved at me as if to say, "Do we have your attention?"

Transparency meant allowing someone to hold my feet to the fire. The special Executive Board meeting loomed like a giant canyon fire. But first, Kim and I had a distasteful job to do.

*    *    *    *

Kim jumped out of the car the second it stopped rolling. Me, too. Confronting Iver about the anonymous messages didn't rate up there with watching the canyon burn, but it ran a close second.

Kim started. "Father dearest, you always told me I could have anything I wanted. You've given me a wonderful education and generous gifts. When you helped us buy our house, I wasn't surprised. You've always been more than available to give us advice about how to live our lives." Her sarcasm grew with what appeared to be the mercury in a thermometer as the red moved from the base of her neck upward. Her small ears must have reached a thousand degrees centigrade about the time she got to her next sentence.

"So what I'd like to know is what in God's name were you thinking when you sent Jon those stupid messages?"

Christina stepped between Kim and Iver, as if she wanted to protect him from a full frontal assault. My grim face can't have given her much reassurance. "Whatever do you mean talking to your father like that? What messages?"

"I've gotten a half dozen anonymous messages ever since they asked me to interview for bishop." I recited each one verbatim.

"You never told us."

"No, Mom, we didn't," Kim said. "We thought it might be a practical joke at first. But they kept coming and sounded more and more threatening."

"What makes you think your father sent them? Surely he wouldn't do anything to upset you." Christina had a way of always seeing the good side of things, except about her own health. On that subject, she could find more ailments than a diagnostician.

"I didn't think he did, at first. In fact," I said, "I confronted someone else. His reaction made it clear he didn't do it. Then we thought maybe Brenda did it. She could have found out our schedule from you and fit the message to the event."

"Tell me Sweetie, what makes you think Brenda didn't do it?" Iver had been standing behind the dining room table ever since we came in.

"We asked her when she confessed all her other faults and tricks. We just came from Palm Springs. And please don't call me 'Sweetie.'"

"I suppose she denied she sent them?" Iver liked to ask ambiguous questions.

"She said you did, Dad. She told us you bragged about it. And we believe her."

Iver moved farther into the corner behind the table. "I sent them because he's so uppity and should never have even thought about running for bishop. I was just joking around."

Before I could say anything, Kim and her mother blurted it out together. "Uppity!"

"Yes, uppity. You know we shouldn't have bishops who aren't…"

"Aren't what? White like you?" I asked.

"I didn't say that."

"You've always talked like anyone but a Dane is inferior." Kim had him backing up.

"No, just people with color in their skin. It's in the Bible. The Ishmaelites. I've always said race is about genetics. It's like the seeds in your father's garden. If you plant good ones, you get good plants. If there's something wrong with the seed, Jon…"

"Daddy, did you ever think someone from another race might enrich you? Danes don't have a corner on the market of everything that's good."

"Enrich? You call Liberian blood enriching? Good fruit can't come from a poor plant."

I decided to ignore his abuse of the Bible to prove his point. "I guess you've never loved anyone who's not white." I knew I'd never felt loved by him.

"It's not the same. I can have affection for my horse, but I don't marry it or elect it bishop."

I'd had it. "We're done here, Iver. You've insulted me and my family enough for one day."

"Just remember," Kim said, "if we do have a child some day, you can forget about getting to see her. Ever!"

I'd never seen Iver look so shocked. Christina held out her arms. "Now, Kimmie, don't say something you don't mean. Come give me a hug."

"No hugs. Not now. Not until Dad apologizes and promises never to do anything like that again." Kim struck her "hands on hips" pose with "the look" that withered mature trees. Christina backed off, and Iver stayed behind the dining room table.

"You have no right coming into my house and scaring your mother this way, Kimberly Yvonne Sondergaard. As for never seeing my grandchild, you've certainly done nothing to produce one."

"Iver!" Christina looked as shocked as Iver had when Kim gave him the ultimatum.

"Let's stay on the topic, Iver." I moved across from him with the table between us. "Are you going to do the right thing and apologize for sending the messages or not?"

"I don't see why I should."

"Then we'll do the right thing. We forgive you. We expect you'll never pull a stunt like that again. And if you want to be welcome at our table, you'd better work on your racism." Kim delivered the message as if she were telling him what we had for lunch. We'd figured he wouldn't admit it, or if he did, there'd be no apology. We didn't want to carry the poison of hate around so we'd agreed to forgive him and move on.

"Call me next week, Mom. Maybe we can have lunch." We walked out as fast as we'd come in, leaving Iver cowering behind the table with a confused expression on his face. Kim and I had never confronted him with such power. We didn't know what he'd do about it, but we felt relieved to let go of the messages and the meanness of the messenger.

\*      \*      \*      \*

Dean Davidson's threats ended in a whimper. When I had insisted on seeing the pictures, and Beverly had confronted him with his lies, he figured out he loved his wife more than messing around with the neighbors or threatening a bishop. I shared the substance of his threats without names when I met with the president of the Executive Board, and hoped we'd hear no more about it.

My meeting with Dr. Jergens vacillated between tearful regrets and strategic planning for the future. She understood my deep feelings about transparency, but questioned the need for a full revelation.

"The diocese loves you, Jon. I see marvelous leadership gifts in you, mixed with a down to earth humanity everyone trusts. If we make this public, some will call for your resignation."

"I'm prepared to offer it."

"No!" As chair of the board, she faced the dilemma between supporting me and carrying out her responsibilities. "I want this to go away."

"I've known since the phone call came from the nominating committee that I needed to confess."

"You give me no choice but to call a special meeting. I hate this, Jon, but I'll do it."

Back at my office, I decided to call Peter to tell him to expect the Executive Board meeting. I didn't plan to reveal him as the confidant who knew my secret, and I wanted him to know that. I also hoped he'd agree not to break our confidential pact.

"Sorry, Jon, he's taking care of the grandchildren this afternoon. He loves to do it and they love him. He's so good with them. If only..." Peter's wife sounded like she wanted more than she could have.

"If only?"

"If only he'd be as nice to you as he is to his grandson, maybe we'd start having tail gate parties again."

"He and I have some issues." I didn't want to hurt her feelings, or tell her more than she needed to hear. "Besides, I'm an Angel fan now."

"I don't blame you. The Padres are suffering. So is Peter. Even though his father's dead, he still feels his wrath. He was a tyrant at home, you know."

I hadn't realized Peter and I had difficult fathers in common. "No, I didn't. I knew him as a scholarly bishop."

"I've said too much. I'll ask Pete to call you when he gets home."

*       *       *       *

I'd lost track of Larry Poulson since he'd resigned from the roster. He'd left San Diego, but didn't leave a forwarding address. Ginger had moved to Arizona and filed for divorce. Evidently, Larry kept her on his "notify in case of emergency" list, and Ginger kept me on hers. When she called, her voice sounded more like a grieving widow than an angry ex-wife.

"Larry has—a few hours to live. We're at Cedar Sinai—in L.A."

She met us in the lobby, eyes red, wadded tissue passing from fist to fist. "I meant to call you sooner, but I kept thinking he'd be okay. I wouldn't be here now except the doc called and played on my sympathy."

"What's the doctor say?"

"He's got pneumonia. Complications from AIDS. Had it for years and I didn't know. He probably got it from one of those prostitutes he'd been visiting—never did see a doctor. He tried to apologize, but it's too late." Her tears and outstretched arms demanded a long hug. Kim took over while I walked the painful path into his room. On the way, I jotted down a note to call the victims so they'd get tested.

Larry smiled his old smile and waved. "Hey ol' buddy. Whatcha doin', slummin'?" The oxygen tubes in his nose and the intravenous in his arm couldn't slow down his attempt at humor. When we first met in seminary, every time I'd wandered into his room, he'd ask the same question about "slumming"—something about his unworthiness to receive a visit from an upper classman. We'd become buddies, drank beer and ate pizza in preference to studying at the library, and talked about life and death. But not about AIDS. And not about our own deaths. Until now. I leaned over to give him a hug, but he started coughing.

"Gotta do—cough—something—before I die."

"Save your strength, Larry." The coughing subsided.

"I gotta tell you something." He hesitated a long time. "I hated your guts for dragging me in front of the committee. I wanted to get you…" He started coughing again.

"I didn't feel good about doing it, either." My memories of carefree seminary days made saying good-bye all the more difficult. Friends didn't abandon one another just because one delivered discipline, while the other received it.

"I forgive you, Jon." He grabbed my hand and held it like a vise until he had no more energy. The more he released, the stronger I squeezed.

"And I forgive you, Larry." Forgiveness didn't depend on approving of what he'd done.

"Anoint me?"

He closed his eyes while I whispered the words from Scripture and dipped my finger in the water glass next to his bed. "In baptism, you were sealed with the Holy Spirit and marked with the cross of Christ forever." I traced a damp cross on his forehead repeating the ancient formula of commendation for the dying: "Into your hands, O merciful God, we commend your servant, Larry. Receive him into the arms of your mercy, into the blessed rest of everlasting peace."

His chest heaved a deep sigh, and his eyes opened. "No funeral, Jon. Just tell the church I didn't die because God punished me. I died because I made stupid choices."

I took his hand and whispered, "Our Father in heaven, hallowed be your name…" He interrupted me before I finished saying, "…as we forgive those who sin against us."

"Tell Ginger I never stopped loving her." Every word sapped his energy, but his voice sounded tranquil. "Now go. God's lying here beside me. You've done what I needed."

I backed away, watching his eyes close. His breathing slowed as he relaxed into that mystical state somewhere between life and death. We sat with Ginger on the impersonal hospital benches, waiting for the inevitable. A long loud beep of the monitor interrupted our stuttering attempts at conversation. The nurse ran to his side, took his pulse, and honored his request for no heroic measures. He didn't want a funeral, but he deserved some recognition, so I put it on the diocesan web site.

> Larry Poulson died of pneumonia Saturday, October 26 at Cedar Sinai Hospital, Los Angeles, at the age of forty-five. Ordained in 1979, he served congregations in Sacramento and San Diego. A popular preacher and teacher, his wit and creativity endeared him to many parishioners. Like so many of us, Larry's life limped along rocky paths at times, and he asked me to say his death came, not from God's wrath, but from his own bad choices. He spent his last few months making amends with those he'd wronged, trusting God's gracious forgiveness. His ex-wife, Ginger, and two younger brothers, Sean and Barry, survive him. May he rest in peace.

# CHAPTER 24

▼

Larry's painful death helped me keep my perspective. My career might die, but my wife and I looked forward to many good years together. When I left for the Executive Board meeting, I felt the strong encouragement of Kim's embrace. She repeated our mantra, "Don't forget to breathe," and waved me on my way to the meeting that might send us out to unexplored possibilities.

Peter Bloch glanced at me when I came in, and then at the others in the Conference Room. He had returned my call, but made no promises about breaking confidentiality. "It depends on how things go," he'd said. Peter always wore black for formal occasions, even, I suspected, black shorts and socks. I hadn't ever checked. That day, he showed up in an impressive gray suit and red clergy shirt. I didn't want to think about the blood-red symbolism.

Presiding Bishop Clemente and twelve men and women elected by the diocese gathered around the table to decide my fate as bishop. Peter had one vote like everyone else, but his voice carried considerable weight. I noticed his eyes darting from one placid Monet print to the other, as if to fill them with thorn bushes.

His glance fastened on Albert Magnusson, his outspoken ally. From my interview onward, Mr. Magnusson made no secret of his animosity toward me, while Peter vacillated between his passive-aggressive "yes, but's" and his direct attacks.

Seated in swivel chairs around the conference table, the members of the Executive Board shuffled their papers. They looked uneasy, with good reason. They'd received a confidential packet containing my confession, and instructions about their authority to ask for my resignation, to censure or suspend me, or do nothing.

Dr. Jergens opened with Ephesians, chapter four: "…Lead a life worthy of the calling to which you have been called…bearing one another in love…maintain the unity of the Spirit." She prayed for guidance, clarity, and calm conversation, somehow working in the message from Jesus to the legalists, "Let those without sin cast the first stone." I knew she'd be fair, balancing good order with compassion. She turned to me and asked, "Bishop Larsen, will you please read your letter aloud to all of us?"

I shuddered inside, but called up all the dignity and calm I could muster.

Dear Members of the Executive Board,

In considering Bishop Clemente's request to visit Liberia on behalf of the Lutheran Church—North America, I concluded I could not accept until I confessed an old deception. When he heard my confession, we agreed you, the Executive Board, must hear it, too.

The facts are these: In May of 1989, I spent a month of my sabbatical in Liberia. During that time, I fell in love with the country and with a woman not my wife. Despite our commitment to remain chaste, we made love the night before I left. Since I returned, there has been no other contact.

You may remember I confessed during my candidacy speech to having some "clutter" in my spiritual closet, but gave no specifics. Thirteen years ago, I confessed the specifics to my spiritual mentor, and to a trusted confidant. I did not, however, confess to the bishop.

I have received absolution from my wife and the spiritual mentor, and advice from my confidant. I discussed it with him last spring, prior to accepting nomination, after which I made the choice not to explicitly reveal the nature of my transgression.

I have lived with the agonizing consequences ever since, and cannot live with the secret any longer. I regret the pain I am causing the diocese, and am prepared to abide by whatever decision you make.

With deep regret,

Bishop Jonathan Larsen

I put the letter back in my notebook, and looked around at the somber faces. "I feel what the Psalmist wrote about when he said, 'My heart is weighed down within me.' The secret I've kept is something like the famous 'elephant in the living room,' which must be faced." Other than my own breathing, I heard no other sound in the room when I paused for a sip of water. Several board members shifted in their chairs.

"I confess to God and to you, and ask your forgiveness. You are the ones who must decide the consequences when a pastor, a bishop, violates a trust." Mr.

Magnusson coughed and reached for water. Each board member stared either at the printed pages or at Peter. No one looked at me, except Mr. Magnusson who twirled his hand in a circle, signaling me to keep going, as if he were in charge. "When I considered the nomination this spring, I decided my private confessions and attempts to be responsible to the persons involved were sufficient. I accepted the nomination, confident I wouldn't be elected, because—I expected Peter Bloch to become bishop."

Peter's face turned crimson at the mention of his name. I took a deep breath and continued. "During the months after election, my guilt deepened when I dealt with the sexual misconduct hearings, and my conscience wouldn't let me rest. I felt tarnished, and decided I couldn't keep quiet any longer. For the diocese to carry out the vision and mission I have in mind, we'll need enormous trust and energy. I can't ask you to do that while I hold onto this secret. Now you know. I'm sorry to place this burden on you."

Dr. Jergens tapped the gavel three times and the questions started with Peter. "Did your confidant advise you to tell the bishop thirteen years ago, and to tell the nominating committee last spring?"

"Yes, he did." I felt relieved Peter did not seem inclined to tell the others what we both knew. Before he could continue, questions came from all directions.

"What about the victim of your misconduct?"

"Neither Margrethe nor I saw ourselves as victims."

"You know as ordained clergy, you're an authority figure even if you're off duty and out of town, don't you?"

"Of course."

"Do you know if she ever married?"

My head started pounding "No, I haven't heard from her."

"Did you try to contact her family?"

"No. Her parents had been killed in a rebel raid near Phebe Hospital in 1990."

"Do you know if she's still alive?"

Each question felt like surgery without anesthetic. "No, I don't know. She lived in constant danger. Why do you ask?"

"If we could find her, we could ask her to testify, even by e-mail."

I paused, hating the thought of telling them about the note buried deep in my briefcase. Sharing such intimate words seemed outrageous. Still, if I believed in transparency, I had to let them know about it. "All I have is the note she wrote me before I left."

"Would you read it to us?"

"With great reluctance."

"Please. We need to hear from her somehow."

I opened my notebook, stalling for time, wanting my anger to subside before I read. My hands trembled as I unfolded the yellowed paper. I hated invading her privacy, but I hated my deception even more, so I read to them.

> My dearest Jonathan,
>
> Tomorrow, when we kiss good-bye at the airport, it will be as if you are returning to a far off planet. I cannot travel with you, or contact you through space, and I cannot ever expect to see or hear from you again. So it must be. You know I wish otherwise, but we have chosen to live within our duties, even if we have broken vows and violated values. Forgive me for inviting you into my life so deeply, for welcoming your love of me, for ignoring your holy vows. The mystical bonding seemed beyond our control. Never blame yourself. Do not carry guilt with you. Go in the certainty of my love, my respect, and yes, even my wishing you happiness with Kim. Remember your gifts for ministry in the church. Nurture them, and never regret our love.
>
> Margrethe

Silence. Then, a soft voice from the far end of the table said, "You are blessed to know such love. I see no victims here."

Mr. Magnusson jerked his head toward the speaker. "There's no such thing as victimless misconduct. His lover in Liberia and his wife are both victims." He turned to me. "By your deception, you've made the church a victim. By your confession, you open the wound for all to see and feel."

"I understand, and seek your forgiveness."

A young Hispanic woman spoke up. "I have no problem forgiving you for deceiving the board, but what about all the people who have come to love and trust you as bishop? I can't speak for them." They began to talk among themselves as if I didn't exist.

"Suppose we keep this confidential. He hasn't broken any civil law. The victims in the misconduct have all forgiven him. We'll make a real mess of things if we make this public."

"But the confidentiality might be broken. If the word gets out, then we're all guilty of a 'cover-up.'"

"A confidential censure is the prerogative of this Board, in consultation with the Presiding Bishop." Dr. Jergens looked at Bishop Clemente, who nodded in agreement.

Peter stood up. "Under church law, yes. But we can't withhold this information, even in the sanctity of the confessional. The people have a right to choose whether or not they want to forgive."

Dr. Jergens turned toward me. "Are you prepared to resign to avoid…"

"Yes. However, if I resign without explanation, rumors will fly, making matters worse for the diocese. I would rather the Executive Board make a decision. I'll agree to it and we can tell everybody what I've told you."

Dr. Jergens turned to Bishop Clemente. "Didn't you say Bishop Larsen is the best one to represent you during this critical period in Liberia?" Again, he nodded in agreement without speaking. I offered my own answer.

"I feel a deep responsibility to the people of Liberia. I know my visit would encourage them, and I'd bring back powerful stories to stimulate us. But would it be wise?"

A tall man stood up to speak. "I don't say much in these meetings—but I gotta say this. We've got a great bishop here—who made a mistake a lotta years ago. He asked for forgiveness. Let's say *Gesundheit* and get on with doing our jobs back home."

Before Mr. Magnusson or Peter could say anything, a woman from Honolulu raised her hand. "I'd like to say something. Scripture and experience teach us we've all sinned and fall short of the glory of God. Martin Luther taught that we're both sinners and saints, at the same time. So, nobody's perfect. Besides, we know not all rules are equal. We don't put people in jail for adultery, but we do for molesting children. And, when someone asks for forgiveness, we give it. Our bishop is a repentant sinner. He didn't break the law. He's humble. I can't see how we can ask for his resignation for what he did so long ago."

The room fell silent, vacuumed of energy. I stood up to excuse myself. "If you have any more questions, I'll respond. Otherwise, I'll be in my office."

No one said a word. Peter grew red-faced and popped a pill into his mouth. Mr. Magnusson started pacing. Dr. Jergens rapped her gavel again.

My brain boiled over with concern for Margrethe, for the church in Liberia— and a dozen things I wish I'd said to the board. A sense of calm crept into my mind, though, and my body relaxed. I settled back into my office chair knowing I'd done the right thing. Transparency. Dad would have been proud of that part.

I heard loud voices from the Conference Room, but didn't recognize whose, or what they said. I called Kim. "I should know something pretty soon. And you know Margrethe is behind us, never to bother us again."

Our marriage bond had deepened to a level beyond passion and romance, though we still managed to get away now and then for excursions into the sensual realms of succulent food and uninhibited sexual stimulation. The pressures of our careers and the strains within our families stretched our resilience, but the counseling made us stronger.

A many-stranded cable kept us connected through the emotional struggle over revealing my deception, and the recurring presence of Margrethe's ghost. Trust, commitment, and honest talk wove together with good humor, fighting fair, and intense battles on the tennis court. A confident faith in God's grace encased the strands of the cable like a protective coating.

"Yeah, I know she's no threat," Kim said. But I wonder what'll happen if you meet her in Liberia."

"If I go. We'll talk when I get home. I want to check my e-mail first." As I hung up the phone, I opened my laptop.

# CHAPTER 25

▼

I jostled the mouse and glanced at the subject lines and sender list. Henry Madison's subject line read, "You're a good man, Jon" and Kim had typed her usual "Don't forget to breathe." The third, from the Lutheran Church in Liberia, mystified me. Why would the bishop write such a subject line? "Mom said you're a kind and good man." I froze.

> Dear Bishop Larsen,
>
> I'm living with Bishop Hosea for now, and he said you're coming to visit him. My mother told me to contact you if anything bad happened. She's dead. Can you help me?
>
> Anna Margrethe Christiansen, age 12

"She's dead." Who's dead? It can't be. Margrethe! I slumped onto my desk, releasing all the pent up tension from the last six months. My shoulders shook—tears streamed onto my arms—my throat uttered sounds I didn't recognize as human. Sacks of guilt I'd dragged behind my bent body for so long emptied into the growing pool of salty water on my desk. Molten vats of rage at whomever caused her death boiled over into the emptiness of my office. Agony for what we never had—never could have—roared through my system, nailing every nerve ending to my bones.

The wrenching shudders of my grief quivered to a stop, as the reservoir of tears registered empty. The clock said a half-hour had passed. I looked at the screen, and once more swallowed the message staring back at me in huge bold letters. "She's dead." I blinked, and the letters returned to normal size, but the pain in my skeleton didn't diminish the least bit.

"Anna Margrethe Christiansen." The name couldn't be coincidental. Margrethe must have a daughter. "Age 12." If Margrethe got pregnant when I left in June, the baby would be born in—I counted on my fingers—February. Twelve years. But she took "the pill" because of the doctor.

*"Think how beautiful our children would be, if…" Her body nestled beside mine, leg over leg, fingers entwined. "But—it's not to be." She sighed and kissed me with a tenderness as delicate as the rose petals decorating our bed.*

Does Anna know her father? Lloyd what's his name—or am I the father? If Anna knew, wouldn't she say so?

"A kind and good man." Margrethe had called me that. The shuddering started all over. The twinge in my chest morphed into the same body ache I felt when I left Margrethe at the airport thirteen years ago: the "pummeled by George Foremen" feeling. Waves of tears from a new source broke over my face. My back bent under the weight of the message, head falling once more into my crossed arms on the desk. The back of my head pounded with the rapid beat of my heart. The drumming erupted with the essence of the message: Margrethe is dead. Her daughter—maybe my daughter—needs me.

*"One last kiss before we go to sleep. Tomorrow you fly away and we'll never speak again. Until we die. Somehow, let me know if you die, Jonathan. Tell someone to let me know." We clung to the kiss as if death's angel could be driven away by its length and passion.*

*"I may die, but our love will always live," she whispered.*

Margrethe lived in constant danger, ignoring her own safety to bring healing to the little ones wherever she could find them—in the jungle, the villages, the city. Revolutionaries roamed the trails and streets. Government troops didn't stop shooting just because children needed treatment. Margrethe must have been killed doing her job. I didn't know that, but it made sense. I wanted to know everything. Death demands details, even if they don't change a thing.

✳    ✳    ✳    ✳

I hadn't heard the knock. "Bishop Jon? We're ready to report."

"It doesn't matter."

"What doesn't matter?" Bishop Clemente moved toward me, staring at my tear stained face.

I blurted it out without thinking. "Margrethe's dead."

"What? How do you know?"

My sobs interrupted my answer. "Her daughter e-mailed me." The words didn't want to come out. "She might—she might be—my daughter."

The presiding bishop sat quietly for a moment. "That changes things."

"A lot of things." Somehow, over the next few minutes, I told him what needed to be said. "I must turn down your offer. I'll go to Liberia on my own. I've got to go find out if she's my daughter. When I get back, I'll do whatever you've decided."

"They've decided to postpone action and to keep it confidential. We wanted you to carry out the Liberian mission."

"I can't." The sobs diminished. I used a dozen tissues to blow my nose. "I can't represent you when…"

I opened my briefcase. "I can't use this ticket you gave me."

"Please, use it. Reimburse the church if things don't work out."

"I can't serve the church when I'm…" I packed up my briefcase like a man possessed. "I'll call Dr. Jergens tomorrow to work out details." He stood there in disbelief as I strode out the door.

*     *     *     *

I called Brother David from the car.

"Hi Jonathan, how'd it go?

"Confidential censure and…" My voice cracked and my body shuddered.

"What's happening to you?"

"E-mail…" Crying turned to coughing.

"Breathe, Jonathan." My breath came and went in short bursts beyond my control. "Breathe deep," he soothed.

His voice slowed my involuntary shuddering, and I said, "Okay. I'm okay."

"Tell me who you are."

"I'm still bishop. And maybe a father."

"They found you a child to adopt?" Ironic he should put it that way.

"No. I mean, I got an e-mail from a twelve year old girl in Liberia."

"She wants you to adopt her? How did she…"

"No, no. She doesn't know we're trying to adopt. Her mother wrote her a letter." The shuddering started again. "Before she died." He calmed me again, and I told him what I knew and what I feared. We prayed on the phone, his consolation connecting me to the subterranean river of strength God provides.

"Call me after you've talked with Kim. We can get together this afternoon if you want."

Somehow, I'd find a way to tell Kim. "A funny thing happened from my visit to Liberia, dear. A daughter was born. And her mother's dead." I'd lost my mind. Telling Kim about Anna didn't feel any easier than telling her about sleeping with Margrethe.

"You know how we've been wanting to adopt someone who needs us? Guess what?" No, she'd be shocked by whatever I said; I needed to find a cushion.

As I drove through the neighborhood, I waved to the kids playing outside—all white, clean, and overweight. How would a twelve-year-old Liberian, no doubt undernourished, fit into this community?

*     *     *     *

When Kim met me at the door with a big kiss, I almost lost it again. "Come on outside. I've got wine and cheese ready."

I wanted to head for the Sacred Space and lose myself in prayer, but I needed to face her. "Thanks, hon'."

"I want to hear all about it. What'd they decide?"

"Postponed action."

"Are you still going to Liberia?"

I swirled the deep red Cabernet and breathed as deep as I dared. "Yes. And Margrethe's dead."

"I know. You and I buried her in therapy, and now the Executive Board buried her, too."

"Yes, and she's buried in Liberia, too."

"What?"

"I got a very unusual e-mail right before I left the office."

"Another threat? Surely Dad wouldn't...I mean after..."

"No, this one is different. It has me..." A wave of nausea passed through me, and my head felt light. I grabbed the chair arms to steady myself.

"Jon, you're scaring me. What did it say?"

The wave passed, and I took the printout from my brief case and handed it to her.

As she read, her face turned more and more white. "Oh God, Jon. Margrethe's dead and has a daughter."

"Yeah." I choked on the one response I could muster. I reached across the table, but she ignored the gesture. After a silence that seemed as long as one of my sermons, she threw her wine glass into the garden, splashing red liquid over the landscape. "I've cried through three miscarriages. I've filled out a hundred forms and waited years for adoption. I've prayed every day for a child—someone who needs us—someone we can love. And this is God's answer?" She stomped into the house.

I sat alone in the Sacred Space, wanting to hold Kim, telling her we'd get through this somehow. I knew she needed time alone. So did I. Grieving the loss of someone I hadn't seen for years felt strange. Why such emptiness in my soul? Because I'd kept her close despite my denial? Because all the angst about interviewing for bishop roused the slumbering giant? Dead! "Oh God, receive her into the tender mercies of your loving arms."

One of the benefits of staying married to the same person for twenty years is knowing when to let go and when to hug. She deserved time and space to think it through. I didn't know how she'd do it, but something in me said she'd want Anna as her daughter.

*     *     *     *

An hour later, Kim strode across the yard to my hideaway, carrying a new half-filled glass. She held it high toward the sun, as if toasting the cosmos. "If that's the best you can do, God, I guess I'd better take it. I sure as hell haven't been able to do it on my own."

I didn't debate her theology or try to reassure her. I felt a need, though, to give her an out. "She might not be my daughter."

"Shush! God's not playing a trick on us. We need to go and bring her home."

"Okay…" Her mothering instinct overpowered my rationalizations. I'd never understand how she zipped so fast from anger to acceptance to determination.

"I went in and sat on the floor and thought about all our plans for a baby. The crib and mobiles and frilly little yellow curtains look perfect. But not for Anna. So I went in the guest room and sat on the bed. It's not bad, but the room needs paint and new curtains."

"You want to hire someone to come in to redecorate?"

"Absolutely."

"We aren't even sure she'll coming back with me."

"Us. I'm going with you."

"But it's dangerous. And I have just one…"

"Then we'll get two. And a third for coming back. We'll use the farewell gift from the congregation."

"But we were going to Princeville." I knew she had everything figured out.

"We'll do that, too, some day. She's coming. And I want things to be right. I'll call the maintenance guys at school. They work after hours, and…"

Her damp eyes sparkled with excitement, yet her body relaxed. The slanting sun headed for its resting place, and the breeze whispered a subtle reassurance. Kim brought me confidence, despite the fear hovering in my heart as I looked for the travel agent's number. It took some doing, but she came up with the tickets, taking us through cities I didn't know existed.

I typed a request to Bishop Hosea asking if both of us could come, and then composed a reply to Anna's e-mail, hoping the messages would get through. Kim looked over my shoulder. "Be sure to say we can't wait to meet her."

Dear Anna,

We will do whatever we can to help you when we arrive in Monrovia Wednesday afternoon. Bishop Hosea has the schedule. We can't wait to meet you.

Jonathan and Kimberly Larsen

*     *     *     *

I hadn't missed a Sunday of preaching since I took office. Anniversaries, installations, and dedications gave me opportunities to proclaim the good news and show the congregations and pastors they belonged to something bigger than their local turf. On the first day of my "vacation," I looked forward to sitting in the pew beside my wife.

We decided to drive to Malibu for worship at the chapel, where we'd shed so many tears in May when the miscarriage claimed the tiny bundle of cells we'd named Stephen. When we responded to the celebrant's invitation to "pray aloud for anyone you want to remember before God's altar," I overheard Kim's first prayer, expecting to hear "for Stephen" or maybe "for Ginger." Instead, she breathed: "for Anna Margrethe Christiansen—Jensen."

I worried that Kim had transferred her passion for a child toward someone we didn't even know. Anna asked for help, not to be carried off to California with strangers. Still, Kim's enthusiasm and intense commitment to helping Anna inoculated me with hope.

"Maybe Anna would like to visit us if she doesn't want to live with us." Something about me needed to lower Kim's expectations.

"Oh, she'll come home with us, all right. She needs us as much as we want her."

After worship, Brother David hugged us and invited us to stay for lunch. "We can take ours out on the deck and have some private time."

Our tears flowed while we shared the loss of Larry, the news about Anna, and the meeting with the Executive Board. As always, his calm demeanor and the ocean view helped us relax and see through the haze to what needed to happen next.

By the time we drove in our driveway, the answering machine had collected half a dozen calls. Brent and Andrea gloated about their tickets for the World Series. Peter Bloch wondered where we were and why we weren't answering the phone. The others came from various family members. I didn't feel up to talking to anyone, so I clicked on the television, hoping to catch some of the Angel-Giant game, wanting to avoid Peter and ease my grief over Margrethe's death.

I couldn't concentrate, even on the World Series, so I called Dr. Jergens and discussed our plans. She told me the board agreed to postpone action, and several wanted me to know their sadness about the little girl's loss of her mother. Since I'd planned to be gone for two weeks anyway, I'd made arrangements for Teresa and Shirlee to cover the office. We agreed I'd e-mail from Liberia when I knew more, and she'd wait to re-convene the board when we returned. I told her I'd bring back a full report on the conditions in Liberia even if I couldn't go as Bishop Clemente's official representative.

Kim walked in, assuming I'd been talking to Peter. "What'd ol' purity pants want now?"

"I haven't called him yet. That was Dr. Jergens. Pete's next."

Peter jumped right on the subject. "I want you to know I voted for the postponement. Mag abstained. I talked with him afterward, and we'll abide by the board's wishes to keep it confidential. All of this could have been avoided if…"

"It's done."

"The board doesn't want to lose you, Jon, and some aren't sure we've got enough evidence to hang you. If this girl turns out to be your daughter, though, you're going to have a lot more explaining to do."

# CHAPTER 26

▼

As the plane descended and banked over Monrovia, the turmoil below hid in the long distance shadows cast by the late afternoon sun. Stretching in three directions, the lush jungle blanketed the poverty, hunger and displacement of thousands. Violent skirmishes between revolutionaries and government forces had poured red blood on the ground beneath the leafy green canopy.

"I wish I hadn't come." Kim looked at me with eyes so sad I blinked back tears. "It's not fair to Anna. She'll feel pressure." We talked through the descent, bouncing on the rough runway toward the terminal. "She makes the choice," I said. Kim looked more resigned than confident. I felt the same.

I shivered with a combination of distress over the devastating conflicts, and the anticipation of re-connecting with the exotic land I'd come to love in 1989. Landing at Robertsfield resurrected memories too painful to savor. The rainy season suggested a country full of tears, in an atmosphere of fear and instability. Plodding through security checks and customs took over an hour.

Bishop Jacob Hosea stood in the dripping rain, extending his arms out wide in welcome, looking as if he were nailed to a cross—a grim reminder of his country's suffering. Armed guards greeted us along with the bishop, showing us the power of terrorism everywhere. Passports and luggage in hand, the bishop led us to his car for the thirty-mile ride to the Lutheran compound in Monrovia.

"Sorry about the last minute changes. You're very gracious to invite both of us to your home. A hotel would have been fine."

He looked chagrined. "Hotels aren't safe."

I first met Jacob Hosea when he spent a year in California studying at our seminary in Berkeley. I wondered if my age showed like his: hair graying, eyes bloodshot, furrows in his forehead. Still, he stood tall and proud, shoulders back, carrying the confidence of one who knew God's Spirit sustained him. Since his election, he'd faced one crisis after another, from personal survival to the decimation of the congregations by disease and dispersal by the armed conflicts.

After years of re-building hospitals, churches, and homes after the 1997 elections, the cycle needed to start again. Looting, vandalism, and torching gutted the beauty and usefulness of many compounds. Several of the forty congregations were weakened, and re-building awaited precious resources from sister churches around the world, and some measure of peace in the land.

The city I'd learned to love while walking with Margrethe through its parks, looked desolate and damned, holes in the street forcing the driver to pick his way along. Dozens of buildings sat neglected, some boarded up, some empty shells. Except for those belonging to the government, most others needed paint and repairs. The rain washed the streets clean, but trash mounded on many sidewalks because of no regular pick up.

*Late in the afternoon, before the opera, we sat on our favorite park bench overlooking the harbor. The chattering parrots above us in the ironwood tree drowned out the distant sound of tug boats and anchor chains. I held her hand as gently as I would a baby bird, and swallowed my heart that somehow had made its way up into my throat. The words struggled their way past the lump. "I can't help myself. I've fallen in love with you, Margrethe."*

The stench of rotting garbage awakened more than nausea in me. Worrying about my career seemed meaningless when I saw the squalor and devastation. On my first visit to Liberia, life seemed exotic, if a little uncertain politically. I'd committed an act of adultery when I'd fallen in love with a woman not my wife and a country I could never claim as mine.

"You are brave to speak for peace and justice, Bishop. The Lutheran congregations in America respect you more than you know."

"I'll show you more than you'll want to remember in the next few days, Bishop Larsen. I'm afraid you'll have to spend your time in the compound, Mrs. Larsen. White people have been targeted by thugs this past week, and our government has warned all foreigners to stay indoors at night, and not to travel inland."

"I understand," Kim said. "It'll give me more time to get to know your wife and Anna." She had a way of finding the rainbow.

He paused to exhale what must have been grief over his church and the violence, and turned to me. "There were no reports of skirmishes today, so I'm hoping we can drive up to Grbanga tomorrow—at least as far as roads will take us. Then, we'll walk."

"Will we see Anna tonight, Bishop?" Kim's eagerness mirrored my own.

"Of course. She's been asking a lot of questions."

"I know Bishop Clemente told you about what happened here in 1989. I'm sorry to have caused you so much pain." My apprehension grew as we entered the city, and ripples of grief ran up my spine.

"Yes, he told me, and it does hurt when someone violates a covenant. I'm sure you two have spent many hours trying to repair the damage to your marriage." We nodded and squeezed one another's hand, recalling the anguish. "It's not mine to judge. You're here to help Anna and to bring back our story to the United States. Neither will be easy tasks."

Surrounded by walls, the Lutheran headquarters provided some measure of protection. Parts of it had been damaged or destroyed more than once and joined the rest of the city in lacking reliable utilities such as water, electricity and sewers. Telephone and mail service functioned spasmodically. The pain of this proud land radiated through me. I needed time to grieve for it and for Margrethe, but couldn't, because I needed to be strong for Anna and Kim.

*          *          *          *

She looked more like Margrethe than I thought possible for a twelve year old. Her long legs and slender body quivered, and she dipped her head toward us, eyes penetrating whatever barriers of unfamiliarity separated us—blue eyes. Yes, definitely, blue eyes, and long black hair. Anna extended her hand, much as her mother had done the first time we met.

"Welcome to Liberia. I hope you had a pleasant journey." Margrethe's child spoke with her same English clarity and elegance. Dressed in black shorts and a white polo shirt with some kind of logo I didn't recognize, she seemed tall for twelve, but thin as I expected. I wanted to embrace her, but, like Kim, shook her outstretched hand and smiled. "This is my mother's brother, Timothy, from London, and Mrs. Hosea," Anna said, showing us her best manners.

"Please, call me Dorothy." The bishop's wife looked frail, but her face radiated a sincere welcome.

The tension in the room crackled as four sets of sad eyes set deep in their black faces peered into ours. They no doubt wondered why Margrethe had told Anna to contact this American bishop if she needed help. Maybe they already knew why.

The bishop and Dorothy excused themselves to take our luggage to a cottage. Uncle Timothy broke the awkward silence that hung between us in their absence. "Margrethe and baby Anna came to live with my wife and me in London soon after the Christmas Eve revolution started in 1989. My father and mother, Ben and Edie—you know them through your grandmother, I believe—stayed here in Liberia. They were…" His voice trailed off and his eyes bored a hole in the ceiling. "They were killed in a raid on the Lutheran mission compound where they lived."

I interrupted Timothy to say how sorry I felt, and how much they had taught us about Liberia when we were in college. Timothy nodded and took a deep breath.

"Margrethe and I wanted to bring Anna for their funeral, but the war wouldn't allow us to travel. Years later, when Charles Taylor was elected president, things seemed to settle down, so when Margrethe finished her residency, she and Anna moved back to Monrovia to help fill the intense need for doctors."

*"I'd love to finish medical school and do a residency in pediatrics. Maybe after you leave, I'll look into it." She floated like an angel among the children in her ward, touching the head of one, rubbing the back of another. Their smiles at her touch proved that healing wasn't just about pills and surgeries.*

I still didn't know how Margrethe died, or if I were Anna's father. I couldn't help but stare at her, wanting to ask a million questions.

"So, when Mom was killed in the…" Anna read the dismay on our faces, stopping mid-sentence to ask, "You didn't know how she died?"

Kim touched my hand, rubbing from fingers to wrist, soothing the best way she knew how. The death of my father and grandmother had touched that deep place in the bones where emptiness dwells. So did Margrethe's.

"No, we…"

Kim finished what I couldn't. "We assumed from your message she either died of a disease or…When did it happen?"

Uncle Timothy glanced at Anna, whose swollen eyes appeared ready to flow with tears. "A month ago," he said. "I had a difficult time obtaining permission to enter the country. Bishop Hosea persuaded an official…"

"How did it happen?" I blurted out the question before I thought of Anna's feelings.

Timothy explained "She'd gone to Phebe Hospital several times to help train some medical assistants and to perform surgeries. Back in May, government security forces attacked the hospital. Senseless! The whole staff evacuated to the Catholic Hospital. About a month ago, she went back to help re-stock and repair the hospital and see patients. One night, while she walked to her cottage, shots—another staff member saw her fall. They couldn't revive her."

"We had a funeral last week in the cemetery where Grandmother and Grandfather are buried." Anna looked like she didn't want to talk about it any more.

*"This is where I grew up, Jon. I learned the catechism and how to play soccer here, and had my first kiss behind that tree when I was fifteen." A few small cottages were scattered around the edges of the jungle. Parrots squawked in a huge tree that shaded the largest bungalow. A weathered white school and church sat in a clearing with a small cemetery to one side. "Someday, I'll be buried here in the family plot."*

"Anna, Timothy, we are so sorry about your loss." Kim said words I felt, but couldn't manage to push through the closure in my throat. I nodded and leaned forward, about to move closer to them. Anna's question stopped me.

"I've been wondering why my mother told me to contact you if I needed help. Can you tell me?" I looked at Kim and cleared my throat. How could I tell Anna a doctor blackmailed her mother into bed with him before I met her? Or that an American pastor—me—made love to her mother when we weren't married.

Timothy came to my rescue. "I think we need to tell him about the lock box." He stepped to a table where a small gray metal box sat open. "Margrethe left this with Bishop Hosea with instructions to unlock it if she died, not before."

"That's where I got the letter that said to contact you. There's a big brown envelope with your name on it, and these medical reports we don't understand." My hand trembled as I took them from Anna.

*"I'll keep a diary, Jon, and every Valentine's Day, I'll think of you. Will you keep one, too?"*

*"Of course. I've already started. As for Valentine's Day, I'll always face Monrovia and blow you a kiss."*

I hadn't, of course, except for a few times. I felt too guilty. After awhile, I forgot. Not the love, but the ritual. With the news of her death, all my work of building boundaries around Margrethe had collapsed. I struggled to keep from leaving the room.

Kim asked Anna to show her our cottage so she could change clothes before we ate. I knew her real reason involved giving me time to open the brown envelope without anyone around. Timothy started to go with them, but I asked him to stay for a minute.

"Timothy, what do you know about Anna's father?"

"Just what Margrethe told me. He's a doctor in India. His name is…"

"Lloyd Shebenay?"

"Yes. Did you meet him where you were here?"

I explained the doctor took a sabbatical during that time, looking for a position in India, because he feared a civil war here. I scanned the paper and held it up. "Do you know what these medical reports mean?"

"No, Anna and I just glanced at them, and we haven't shown anything to Bishop Hosea."

At dinner, we enjoyed animated conversation with Anna about her school and soccer team, the part she hoped to land in a play, and the solo she planned to sing in church on Sunday. I noticed Anna asked a lot of questions when we told her about playing tennis in high school and college. She told us she didn't play much, because there were no courts at her school, but she loved to bang balls against a wall, pretending to be Serena Williams.

The hours passed quickly while Jacob told stories about his visits to congregations, and some of the hopes he had for peace. When the clock struck ten, he said, "You're tired from your long journey. Sleep as long as you like."

At our cottage, I fought to stay in control of the urge to break loose in rage and anguish about Margrethe's senseless death. Kim kissed me goodnight, picked up the envelope from the dresser, and said, "Read it Jon. You're dying to know what she went through. It's the one way you'll break free from her."

*        *        *        *

Opening the brown package meant unsealing a grave. Margrethe's words, buried inside, deserved my respect. The generators stopped running at ten, so I lit the two candles beside the chair, and slid my finger under the seal. I pulled out a tablet of lined yellow paper with a round coffee cup stain at the top of the cardboard backing. Running my fingers up and down the tablet felt the way I remembered touching Margrethe's face. When I turned it over, my breath caught, and my eyes blinked without my trying.

Dearest Jonathan,

I'm writing this in hopes you will never read it. I promised never to be in contact, but to have someone let you know if I died. By now, you know I haven't broken my first promise, and the second must have happened despite my love for life, and for you.

May 27—I kissed you good-bye today. Wanted to fly away with you. What's right? That you go home to K? Yes. That I stay here and care for orphans? Yes. That we fell in love. Oh, yes! How many rights make a wrong?

Her words entered my eyes with the same elegance and accent as her speech massaged my eardrums when we first met. Her training in London and the formality of her speech integrated the compassion and sensitivity delivered at birth in the genes.

May 30—I can tell you a wrong that's very wrong: L! He forced himself on me tonight. Back from India. He threatened—again—about telling I'd stolen drugs. I told him to go to hell with his lies.

What looked like an old tearstain separated May 30 from the next entry. My anger at the doctor pushed me to stand and pace awhile before I could continue reading.

May 31—I cried myself to sleep last night. This morning, I remembered our lovemaking—how tender you were—how loved I felt. L's a pig. I told him I'd report him for rape if he ever touched me again. My job's not worth enduring another touch from his sticky claws.
June 27—Already a month has passed since your departure. L's leaving next month for New Delhi. He's kept his distance at the hospital, but I'll be relieved to have him out of sight.
July 6—Missed my period this month.

I could hear a soft "damn" under her breath. Margrethe seldom swore, and never so others could hear unless her lips touched my ear lobe—then I alone heard. Soft as the sound, the feeling beneath growled like a tigress protecting her cubs. I imagined her squinting eyes and clenched teeth, grinding out the words.

July 10—I hunted up a couple of home test kits. Both say I'm pregnant. God, I hope it's not L's. Can I manage an infant? Oh, Jon, I hope it's yours. But can I keep something so important from you?
July 29—Told L today. He demanded a blood test to prove "it." It? If I'm pregnant, the cells growing inside me are more than an "it."
July 30—L sneaked me the lab test proving I'm pregnant. He said we might as well have sex, since no more "damage" could be done. I told him to go to…

She no doubt crossed her arms the way she did when something made her upset, cocked her head to the left, always the left, pursed her lips, and spit it at him. I saw her take on the administrator one day when he told her she couldn't keep treating three orphans because they needed room for adults. Scorched earth!

> August 3—Rumbles about revolution. Neighbors killing neighbors. Stupid! New life in my womb, dying children in my ward. Three more today.
> August 8—I still wake up wishing you were here. I must tell my parents. L is leaving soon. I'm getting his blood type from the files so I can compare when my baby's born.
> August 11—Told momma and daddy last night. Momma cried. Daddy grilled me. Who's the father? Is it Jonathan? How could I let it happen? Before I could say much, he told me to get out of his house.
> August 13—Momma called, asking if I planned to abort the baby? No! Maybe adoption. Daddy's demanding I leave Monrovia.
> August 27—Do you miss me like I miss you? How I wish I could contact you, but we promised. Daddy wrote me a note telling me I'm no longer his daughter. I wrote back and said he'd always be my father, and not to think you're to blame. I don't want your life messed up. Besides, I don't know for sure.

I wondered how Ben could deny his own daughter. Wait. I'd denied her for thirteen years. I had an excuse, of course, but I should have been there.

> September 15—Mr. "Adults First" Administrator asked today if I'm pregnant. I asked if it mattered. He replied not if I can do my job. I informed him I'd need a fortnight free in February. He said he'd see.
> October 27—I've counted sixty-three children dead here since the year began. Most of them from malnutrition. How many are lying in the jungle? How I wish we could jump in the jeep together and go searching.
> November 27—I imagine you celebrated Thanksgiving this month—hope you're still thankful we met. I am, but…The administrator transferred me to the up-river villages today: Phebe Hospital. Remember our visit there? I'm grateful to get away from the wagging tongues and daddy's hostility. I'll miss momma.

Of course, I remembered our visit. How could I not? I started talking back to the diary. "You grew up there, became a kissable young woman there. Our return trip tightened love's grip on us both. By the time we'd lived through the love story in the opera, we no longer made moral choices." I remembered how we'd melted into one another's bodies.

December 23—I wrote out a Christmas list today. One thing on it. You. Well, a healthy baby, too. I'm feeling like an elephant. Delivered three babies today. Wish mine were ready.

I stopped, eyes watering from the candle smoke and the painful pleasure of reading her letter. The next pages would have to wait. I slipped into bed. Kim patted my arm and mumbled her love when I kissed her cheek.

# CHAPTER 27

▼

Kim stayed with Anna and Dorothy, while Jacob, Timothy and I spent the day visiting pastors and people trying to keep their congregations together. From the very beginning of Liberia's formation as a democratic nation, violence, bloodshed, disease and malnutrition decimated the villages.

The bishop talked as the driver picked his way around potholes in the streets. "The current president, Charles Taylor, is a descendant of the former American slaves who helped establish our nation. He studied in America in the 1970's, then returned to Liberia to work as a government bureaucrat under President Samuel Doe."

"Didn't Doe bring about a coup to get himself into office?"

"Yes. It's not unusual here."

He told me Taylor, accused of embezzlement, fled to Boston where they arrested him on an extradition warrant. "He sawed his way out of a prison cell and dropped to the ground using bed sheets. I thought that only happened in American movies."

"How did he get back to Liberia?"

"Through Libya. He trained with Sierra Leoneans, and helped form a militia to unseat Doe. The Revolutionary United Front began with a small invasion on Christmas Eve, 1989, and then for the next seven years, warlords battled one another, shattering the nation."

"Is that when so many left for England and America?"

"And many other countries, too. Margrethe and Anna made it out. Ben and Edith didn't." His voice dropped, as he stared into the windshield.

"Didn't the United States help put down the violence?" I should have known, but after Ben and Edie's deaths, I hadn't paid attention to what little news the media carried about Liberia.

"No. They let us handle it ourselves. We couldn't. Then what you called Desert Storm came along and we disappeared from your country's radar. The war here lasted seven years. Sometime in the spring of 1996, the fighting slowed enough to let West African peacekeepers restore peace to Monrovia. In 1997, Liberia elected a democratic government."

"Charles Taylor, president?"

"Exactly. Because of his drive to unseat Doe, over 200,000 Liberians died, and about half became homeless. Many of those who left the country took their expertise with them. With all our great natural resources and diamonds, we should have a strong economy, but the fighting…" His voice drifted off, looking out the window at the government buildings we passed. Warlords still attacked now and then, and many wanted them to overthrow President Taylor because of his corruption.

*       *       *       *

While Kim and Anna hit tennis balls against the back wall, I unfolded the note Anna gave me from her mother. She told us she'd read it a hundred times. The creases in the notepaper matched the ones in my forehead.

> Dear Anna,
>
> I wish you didn't have to see this, because it means I am no longer alive. Death is no stranger to you. Since we've come back to Liberia, we've seen too much of it.
>
> When you asked me about your father, I told you the truth, but not all of it. I loved a man who went far away, never to return. I promised I'd never tell anyone about our love. He doesn't know about you, but if he finds out, I know he'll love you.
>
> By now, you have found two other envelopes in the lock box. One is a medical report. The other is a letter to Jonathan Larsen who visited our country many years ago. He is a kind a good man. If you are in big trouble, and need his help, ask the bishop to help you. Last I knew, he was a Lutheran pastor in California.
>
> I love you more than I can say. Always remember, as long as stars still shine, God is with us, and my love for you lives. Love, Mama

I held the letter close to my heart, numb with grief. When I blinked clear of the watery film, I examined the medical reports. I recognized one as Anna's DNA. The initials L.S. appeared on the other form, and the blood type, "AB Neg." Scribbled in Margrethe's handwriting were the year, and words that sent a blow to my kidneys: "no match."

How could I have doubted? A DNA test would be more proof, but I already knew. I picked up the tablet, wanting more from the mother of—of my daughter?

> January 13—I'm in the Monrovia Hospital now. The revolution started near the border on Christmas Eve. I wrote a story for the hospital newsletter about what happened to me. It's very long, so don't fall asleep reading it, dear one.

I started pacing around the room, hungry to hear something besides a letter. She told me writing didn't come easy for her, but she yearned to keep a kind of journal to teach future generations how it felt to live and serve in the 1990's. She started the story in a place I'd seen, and the image added to her words.

As Long As The Stars Still Shine

> I sank into the rocker outside my cottage door, exhausted from a day full of children with malnourished bodies and frightened faces. Delivering four babies brought joy; losing one opened tear ducts. My compassion and determination grew as I watched our people, our dear children, struggle against poverty and a cycle of violent revolutions.
>
> "It's Christmas Eve, Margrethe. Come have chicken and rice with us before worship." With no energy left to gather vegetables from the garden or fruit from the trees, I welcomed the invitation from Rachel Donay.
>
> I ate with gusto, and laughed with the children as they opened their gifts, but inside, I agonized for the baby boy who'd died at sunset on the way to the hospital. His mother shed a pool of tears, soaking my uniform. Later, I shed my own tears over the boy who should have been saved.
>
> Rumors of revolution swept through villages and churches as we all prepared to celebrate the birth of Jesus. The pastors here, like those around the country, gathered the faithful to listen and reflect, pray and sing. We moved to the beat of the music, bending and stretching as we sang, sounding like the angels in the hills outside Bethlehem. While revolutionaries plotted violence, we gathered to hear Luke's story of God's supreme gift—the Prince of Peace.

I thought about all the Christmases our congregation had gathered at Anaheim Hills, praying for peace in the world, basking in the glow of our comfortable church. I had thought about Margrethe some times, but had no idea where she was.

As midnight approached, the jungle's night noises mingled with creaks from the wicker rocker. A rustling noise startled me out of my Christmas reverie. Sumon, whom I'd treated for sores weeks before, came for me. His wife, Anna Ruth, couldn't come to the hospital because the contractions were too painful, so he asked me to come to her.

I knew the risks. Revolutionaries. Dark Trails. And my baby. I shouldn't travel, but my heart couldn't refuse a mother-to-be. Besides, this was my first request to help someone away from the hospital. I told Sumon I'd ask Doctor Donay to borrow the jeep, but he said the trails were too narrow, so he'd brought a horse for me to ride while he ran alongside.

I hurried into the cottage to pick up a lantern, much the way Felicity Baron, the beloved "Grandma" of the 1940's, did in her day. She'd delivered dozens of babies in the villages, and adopted many of them when their mothers died.

Sumon led the way behind the cottage where I discovered the horse had no saddle. I didn't know how I'd get on, but Sumon made a stool with his hands and boosted me up. Imagine the picture: me with my big tummy holding a lantern and medical bag trying to grab the mane to hang on.

I chuckled in spite of myself, and started pacing. I felt the danger, and didn't want her to go. Then I realized even if I'd been there, she would have gone. Duty called.

The distance seemed farther than the miles. Pregnant women should not bounce around on horseback, if for no other reason than a complaining bladder. We arrived as a cloud moved away from the moon, and from the star chasing the bright round ball. I couldn't help but think about the Wise Men following a star to find the young Jesus.

Anna Ruth praised God I arrived in time to help her. I told her to push, and before we knew it, a whimper, and then the wail of a newborn filled the hut, joining the laughter and tears. "It's a boy! What will you name him?"

Without hesitation, she smiled through the tears, and said, "Emmanuel."

Anna Ruth had learned its meaning from the Bible lady before her baptism: God with us.

Sumon wanted to accompany me back, but I told him to stay and tend to Anna Ruth and Emmanuel. I rode slowly, avoiding the bounces, and feeling weary satisfaction from doing what I felt born to do. A few minutes before Christmas Day dawned, the bright moon moved toward the horizon, providing less and less light. As I rode farther into the jungle, it completely disappeared into the canopy of tall trees.

Muffled men's voices startled me in the darkness. Blowing out the lantern's flame, I eased the horse to a stop, patting his neck, whispering to quiet him. I heard rustling along the trail ahead, and knew I'd never avoid them with no room to turn the horse around to run for it.

Even though I knew she survived this ordeal, my breath came in short bursts, shallow and tense. I stopped pacing, staring at the story.

"Horse on the trail," I called out, hoping I didn't sound as frightened as I felt. My skin grew tiny bumps as two men emerged from the trees. They carried guns, and wore belts filled with bullets.

"Wha' you doin' here, fat woman?" The tall one shook his menacing automatic rifle at me. "Ge' down. I wan' th' horse."

"I delivered a baby. I need the horse to get home."

"Ge'down!" Louder this time, with the rifle pointing at my head.

I struggled with the medical bag, and dropped the lantern as I slipped down the side of the horse to the ground. I lost my balance, tipping toward one of the soldiers, when the butt of his gun finished the fall. I didn't want to give them the satisfaction of crying out in pain, until I felt the gun butt slam against my side. I screamed, and turned my back to protect my baby as best I could. The soldier pounded me on the shoulders once, twice, and again.

Oh dear God! How could they do that to her? Why are humans so cruel? What makes us treat one another with such hate? Sick! Sick! Sick!

"Shoot th' bitch."

"No. The villagers mi' hear and fi' us." The last thing I remember is the searing pain of something hitting me on the skull. Sumon told me later they must have dragged me off the trail and left me for dead.

He said the revolutionaries invaded the village, killing as they went, setting fire to the huts. When he heard the shots and screaming, he grabbed the baby and helped his Anna Ruth to her feet so they could run. They circled around to the trail toward Phebe Hospital. He struggled his way through the darkness, when he stumbled over something. He recognized my lantern and then searched along the trail until he found me. Anna Ruth said he carried me like a large child all the way, stopping now and then to listen for soldiers.

I am so grateful they got me to the hospital where Dr. Donay diagnosed me with a severe concussion and broken ribs, but the baby seemed to be normal. When I woke up, I remember a terrible headache, and sharp stabs in my side when I tried to move.

They arranged for all the patients to be moved because of the threats. I bumped along in a jeep to Monrovia, worried about the baby growing in my womb. I'm not sure which hurt more, the beating or the ride with broken ribs. I passed out several times, so I missed the worst.

A week later, the Monrovia Hospital administrator walked into my room with a letter in his hand. "It's from the bishop and the Phebe Hospital Administrator. You've won the Felicity Baron Citation for Compassion. It says, 'As long as there are nurses like you, our country will survive.' You saved a young mother's life on Christmas Eve, and you deserve this award."

I felt honored, but embarrassed. I told them then I didn't know how soon, but I'd be back on duty as fast as possible. Then I preached a one-sentence sermon. "No matter what the violent ones do, some of us will work for healing and peace as long as the stars still shine."

I couldn't begin to understand the agony and hardship she must have felt. I hurried back to the entries.

January 20—My headache is almost gone. The doctor said the blow could have killed me. My ribs are healing, but I can't laugh or turn over. Wish you were here to scratch my back. And a few million other reasons.

January 22—Momma came to see me today. The administrator called them immediately after I arrived in Monrovia, but Daddy didn't tell Momma. Since the revolution started, she volunteers here once a week. How she missed seeing me here, I'll never know. She found out when a nurse told her I seemed better. We cried a lot. She said she'd get the family who saved me into Monrovia somehow.

February 14—I'm so excited. She's exquisite. Four hours old and already singing. Sort of. I won't give you all the gory details, but giving birth is not all breathing and pushing. It's a lot of screaming and jabbing pains, too. Doctor Donald says I had an easy birth. I offered to swap duties with him next time. What a feeling to have her at my breast. Love personified. Momma came again. I named my baby, "Anna Margrethe Christiansen." Anna for the prophetess who saw the baby Jesus in the temple on his eighth day, and another important Anna—the new mother who helped save me.

February 17—Daddy came to the hospital today with tickets to London for Anna and me. He said Liberia is too dangerous. I asked him if I was his daughter again. When he held Anna, he said he'd think about it.

The writing stopped. I wiped my eyes, wishing with my whole being I'd been there. The emptiness in my stomach felt like a combination of guilt and loss. I turned blank pages, one after another, and then discovered more writing toward the back of the tablet.

February 16, 1998—Anna and I came back to Liberia yesterday. We lived in London with my brother, Timothy and his family, but always, I wanted to come home. Three months after we left in 1990, my parents were killed. They visited a village one Sunday morning to worship, planning to help repair the damage the revolutionaries had done. They got caught in an ambush on the way back to Monrovia. I still have some of their letters. After awhile, Daddy admitted I'm more important than moral rules. We couldn't get back into the country to bury them, but the bishop had a service.

February 17—There is so much to tell you about medical school and my new position as pediatrician at the Monrovia Hospital. The country is re-building after the revolutionary leader got himself elected president. One of our Lutheran leaders is working in the government, hoping to keep peace and justice walking together. Anna is adjusting. In London, I talked about Liberia all the time so she'd know where she belonged. By the way, I gave Anna a tennis racquet for her birthday. I didn't tell her I hoped she'd play against you some day, but I do.

December 25—Eight years ago, the revolution started and I almost died. Now, Anna is happy in school, I have a wonderful (but busy!) job, and life seems almost normal. Three men asked me for dates the past month, but there is no room in my heart for anyone but you.

March 2002—I had Anna's blood typed, and ran a DNA test. I've put the results in the back of the tablet. It would be meaningless except to you, if you have a test, too. The other lab report tells you L's not the father. So, you can assume…

I talked to her again. "Yes, Margrethe, I assume I'm the father. I'm overwhelmed. I abandoned you to have my baby alone. And nearly be killed. You were in London and I didn't know. You should have called me. Written. Anything to let me know I had a daughter. I would have helped. I would have…" What would I have done? I decided to finish reading, and then do what needed doing.

April 2002—I never seem to have the energy to write, even to you, my dear Jonathan. I leave tomorrow for Phebe Hospital to spend time training some new nurses. The rumors of another revolution rouse memories of what we heard in 1989. I pray we can find peace, but…Because I never know if I'll return, I'm sealing this tablet in an envelope the way I'd post a letter to you. I'm not breaking my promise to never contact you. I'm just letting you know my love never died even if I do. All my love, M.

No more words. Just more blank pages. I put the tablet back into its envelope, licked what glue remained on the torn seal, and folded the clasp closed. As my fingers worked the seal against the envelope, I thought of the dozens of times I tossed dirt on caskets as a pastor. "Dust to dust…" The envelope would remain sealed until Anna needed to know.

# CHAPTER 28

▼

I thought I'd worked through the guilt in therapy, confession, and prayer. Re-sealing the envelope on Margrethe's story unsealed the container of guilt that had never been completely emptied. Reading her letters re-filled it to overflowing.

After a restless night, Kim turned to me with swollen eyes. "I can't believe I have a daughter. I mean, she's not, but…"

She knew in her heart I was Anna's father. I did, too. "It's bittersweet."

"Yeah." The last two tissues in the pack from the plane disappeared into the wastebasket, and she rolled into my arms. My guilt and anxiety dissipated, at least for a little while, in tender kisses and gentle caresses. I couldn't tell Kim yet about my strenuous guilt over abandoning Margrethe. Sometimes, it's better to give feelings a rest before sharing them.

At breakfast, Anna looked from one to another, and then leaned closer to her uncle. "Have you thought about how you can help me, Bishop Larsen? I mean, about getting me out of the country?"

"I want very much to help you, Anna."

"They tell me it's not safe for me to stay. They make girls like me into prostitutes." We learned her wisdom came at a high price when she told us about three of her young friends who had been tortured, raped, and left for dead.

Timothy explained that many children were sold as slaves, especially girls. The government couldn't stop the slave traders so instead, they shut down all children from leaving legally. But that's not all. The government won't let me take her back home because I'm not her parent or legal guardian."

"Then we'll have to find another way to make sure you're safe, Anna." Kim spoke with confidence I didn't feel in myself.

"I have some more checking to do, Anna, and we'll talk more about this another time." I didn't know the odds of getting a DNA test in Monrovia under the present conditions. I asked Bishop Hosea if we could take a walk.

As we left, I noticed Kim doing her best to comfort Anna. She wiped her tears and pat, patted her. My own eyes dampened when I saw Anna lean into Kim, receiving what I knew Kim wanted so much to give: a mother's love, even if it could never be Margrethe's love.

*     *     *     *

The minute I'd first seen Anna, I knew I couldn't leave her in this dangerous country. Kim and I wanted to be her parents, and a DNA test would prove my fatherhood. I needed to be a good father to her and a faithful husband to Kim. They meant more to me than all the purple shirts and pectoral crosses in the world. I joined Bishop Hosea in his office and closed the door.

"I've read her diary. I'm almost certain Anna is my daughter."

The bishop stared at me, not with judgment so much as disappointment. "You thought she could be someone else's?"

"Yes. A doctor had forced himself on her several times before I arrived. He went away for a while and came back after I left. Margrethe did a blood test and he is not a match with Anna."

"What will you do?"

"First, I want you to hear my confession."

"Is that customary in America? To have private confession?"

"Not very often. I've confessed as part of worship every Sunday. I've confessed to my spiritual mentor back home. But I have wronged you and the church here, and I hope you'll hear my confession."

I knelt beside his desk, laying my head on the top while he stood behind me with his hands on my shoulders. "Speak to me," he said.

"I confess that I have sinned again God and against the Lutheran Church in Liberia. I did not mean to fall in love with Margrethe, but that gives me no excuse. I did not plan to lie with her in bed, but that gives me no excuse. I have violated your trust, and that of all those who showed such wonderful hospitality to me when I was here. I plead for your forgiveness and place myself in your hands." I closed with part of Psalm 51. "Create in me a clean heart, O God, and renew a right spirit within me. Cast me not away from your presence, and take not your Holy Sprit from me."

Bishop Hosea pressed his strong hands against my shoulders, and spoke with a choked voice. "God is merciful and blesses you. By the command of our Lord Jesus Christ, I declare unto you the entire forgiveness of all your sins, in the name of the Father, and of the Son, and of the Holy Spirit. May you walk in the light from this day forward. Amen."

I stood up slowly and received his embrace, trembling at the power of God's love through this servant of love. "I know we don't require penance in the Lutheran church, Bishop, but I want to use every ounce of my strength to bring hope to the people we visit, and carry back to America the message of your people."

"I pray you will, Jonathan. We'll leave soon for places who need your uplifting words."

\*     \*     \*     \*

Two days and visits to six outlying churches passed before Bishop Hosea learned about a doctor who might help us. We caught up with him between patients at the hospital. "I don't know when I'll have time to do it. The hospital keeps me busy day and night."

"We understand, Doctor, and we wouldn't ask if it weren't important. Perhaps you can recommend a laboratory. If you could just send a written authorization with us." The bishop's voice sounded calm, but I could see his hands flexing as he talked.

"No, forgeries are too common. I must go in person. My schedule…"

I held back from grabbing him by the lapels of his white coat, but I couldn't keep quiet any longer. "Imagine your daughter living here, and you wanting to help her escape an orphanage, and probably getting raped, maybe even—"

"My daughter was raped and killed two months ago." The doctor's strained voice hinted at deep pain.

We stood there, shocked. "I'm so sorry…" The bishop and I said it together. I added, "If this is too painful—"

"No. I don't have time for my own pain. Too many people are dying. My God, Bishop, can't the church do something about making peace?"

"We're trying, Doctor. Even now, one of my pastors is meeting with the government officials about a cease-fire. You know how complicated it is. But we have one simple request. Can you help us get this man's daughter out of the country before she, too…"

"I'll take the test to the laboratory on Sunday, not before." We felt some relief until he added, "I might have the results in a couple of weeks."

"We can't wait a couple of weeks." Bishop Hosea's voice became stern, then more conciliatory as he explained our predicament and how difficult it would be to change plane reservations, and reminded the doctor of our holy mission to help Anna leave the country.

After a half hour of denials and rejections, the doctor said, "I'll do my best."

I reached into my pocket where I'd stored the report I'd found in the back of Margrethe's tablet. "Here. They did this DNA test on Anna in March."

He checked the report and smiled. "This laboratory is one of the few still operating. I'll take it there on my way to the hospital Sunday morning. I'll tell them to rush."

"Thank you, Doctor. You're helping save Anna's life."

*      *      *      *

While Kim entertained Anna, or more the other way around, the bishop took Timothy and me on one last tour of a school and church struggling to feed and clothe displaced people. Refugees poured into Monrovia. Hunger, disease, wounds, and homelessness demanded more resources than the churches or government could muster. Private international agencies had pulled most of their workers from the northern area because of the danger to their lives. I shot several rolls of film and filled a notebook to help me make a report to the church back home.

On Sunday, we worshipped with the bishop in a church outside Monrovia. He based his sermon on the text from Matthew where Peter asks Jesus if he must forgive seven times. Jesus replies, "Seventy times seven." In other words, an infinite number. The bishop followed his own advice. The solo for which Anna had practiced so hard touched me to my core and left me limp.

The sermon and a simple lunch after worship fortified me for facing the implications of the DNA test.

*      *      *      *

The bishop drove in silence while I fingered the potent package from the laboratory. "Aren't you going to open it?" I'd been treating it like a newborn baby, looking at it from all angles, stroking it, and turning it over in my hands. The bishop's words startled me, and I tore open the report. I growled when the sheet inside stuck on the corner of the torn envelope. I ripped one corner pulling out the form—nothing fancy—just one typewritten sentence with an official stamp on the signature. I read it aloud as we drove.

"The DNA of Anna Margrethe Christiansen and Jonathan Soren Larsen demonstrate a parent/child relationship." Adrenalin pumped through my system. I shook my head in relief and breathed the words I'd yearned to say.

"She's my daughter."

"Truly." The bishop beamed. "Sometimes God gives us new opportunities to do the right thing."

We found Anna and her uncle sitting by the table talking with Kim about London. "It's a marvelous city. If I can't live here, I'd love to go there," Anna said. Kim looked worried, then turned to me. When I nodded, she smiled as if she knew what the report said.

"I need to talk with you alone for a few minutes, Anna."

"Why not use the chapel? It's private there, and if you listen, you might even hear the angels whisper to you." The bishop knew how much I wanted to say the right words.

"Coming Anna?" Her brow furrowed as she looked from her uncle to me and back, and then crossed her arms, just like Margrethe used to do when she dealt with the crusty hospital administrator. She didn't budge.

Timothy said, "Go with him, Anna. He has something important to tell you."

She scraped her chair back from the table, and followed me toward the small white chapel in the courtyard. A rough wooden cross sat on top of the chapel's peaked roof, surrounded by multi-colored birds chattering away in the drizzle—not angels, exactly, but encouraging sounds. Inside, we sat facing one another in front of a small wooden table used for the altar, feeling the sacredness of the space. Her eyes wandered around the room, avoiding mine.

"I'm going to be direct with you, Anna, because you deserve the truth without any..."

"You're my father, aren't you?" Her eyes opened wider than I'd seen them, and her voice quivered. "Aren't you?"

"What makes you think I am?"

"That piece of paper. And because Momma told me to contact you if I needed help—if she died."

"What else?"

"The minute I saw you, I had a sick feeling in my stomach, like I hated you."

My stomach ached, too, but not with hate. "Do you know why?"

"No, but that night when I prayed, I told God you abandoned us." Pacing now, she looked like Margrethe when she first told me about the doctor who blackmailed her into bed. Three steps, pivot, three steps, pivot. Her glare tore a hole in my chest. "How could you rape my mother?"

"I didn't rape your mother."

"You did too. You must have. You're just like the men here. They rape and run." In her world, babies and rape went together. The men who made women and girls pregnant never became fathers, just rapists. She started crying and ran out of the chapel.

"Anna. Come back…" Gone. I'd lost her. Pain sucked all my energy and smashed my hopes. I felt like Margrethe and I were saying good-bye all over again.

Kim found me in the chapel, my head in my hands. "What happened?"

"She hates me."

"No, Jon, she's just scared."

"She thinks I raped her mother."

Kim wrapped her arms around me, and patted my shoulders. "Give her some time. You know what happens when I get upset."

"Yeah, you get over it in an hour. But she's made up her mind to hate me. I don't know if I can convince her I didn't…"

"Maybe if you showed her the diary?"

"I'd planned to wait, but…" We found Anna in the courtyard, and held out the envelope.

"I don't want to read anything." She took it and threw it against a tree.

"It's your mother's diary. Maybe if you read some of it—not everything is what it seems."

"I can see what happened. I hate you and I hate America. You'll never get me to go there." She stormed into the house, leaving Kim and me with open mouths.

Kim started pacing. "She hates you Jon. And now I think I hate you, too. You never should have come to Liberia. You most certainly never should have slept with Anna's mother. I want to go home. Alone!"

# CHAPTER 29

▼

The enclosed courtyard resonated with angry words. Kim's exodus left me in the silent space without anyone to face except myself. My abdomen felt like a huge barrel echoing with accusations. My brain pounded like an air hammer breaking up cement. My heart's spasm signaled how far I'd fallen into despair.

How long I sat by the tree, staring at the diary on the ground, I don't know. Head in my hands, back bent, I felt like death had visited every cell of my body. A gentle touch on my shoulder brought my aching head up to see who dared to interrupt my grief and self-loathing.

"God is near." The bishop's voice sounded hollow, distant, and distorted. My mind filtered out the hope he must have been offering. It reminded me of the phrase I'd used too many times in my ministry. "Near? God took off and hid away beyond the sun the day I left Margrethe behind. God near? God's so ashamed of me I can't begin to tell you."

"Let's walk." I don't remember what we said, which may have been little, in words. His arm around my shoulder and his soft breathing said more than words. In my darkest moment, afraid of losing my wife, my daughter, and probably my career, a pastor comforted me. He temporarily set aside the fact that hundreds of Liberians died each day from violence or hunger or disease. He put on hold his agony over the medical centers and schools destroyed by civil strife. He closed his eyes, for the moment, to the abuse of children like Anna. For me. To walk and listen and comfort me.

In our movement, God's Spirit filled the emptiness within, and flowed into my legs and arms. The muscles in my neck relaxed and the vise around my head released. Slowly. Not completely. Enough to know I'd live.

"You're God's presence for me. I don't know how to thank you."

"Be God's presence to others, Jonathan. That's what we're called to do."

"Yes. And maybe—maybe I should stay here for the rest of my life."

"You feel like you belong here."

"I know how to build and repair things. I'm a decent gardener. And now and then, if the churches needed a preacher…"

"And what does the diocese in California need?"

"They don't need a divorced bishop with an out of wedlock daughter who wants nothing to do with him."

The bishop put strong hands on each side of my upper arms, turning me to face him. "You can trust God to be working in Kim and Anna, too. Give them a little time. They both feel overwhelmed. Timothy is with Anna. Dorothy is with Kim. No one is alone."

"I hope so, but I don't know…"

"Trust God. Dig deep into all you've learned in your life so far. Hang on to what you value most."

My darkness began turning to dawn, not yet to sunrise, as we walked together without words.

We returned to find Kim in the kitchen helping Dorothy prepare the evening meal. They reminded me of Kim and my mother in Solvang, talking and laughing as they cooked. Kim looked at me and smiled, a glimmer of hope.

"Let me do that, Kim," Bishop Hosea said. "Dorothy seldom lets me help her cook. You and Jonathan have things to talk about."

In the empty courtyard, an evening breeze had blown away whatever angry words and tears still littered the ground. Kim turned to me beside the tree. "I didn't mean…" She put her arms around my neck and kissed me in a way that said more than any words. We stood there, holding one another, the warmth of a lifetime of love flowing between us.

"I've given you too much grief…"

"Hush, Jon. With all our praying and all those hours of counseling, we've learned to trust. Even when it feels terrible. We belong together. And somehow, we'll find a way to help Anna feel it, too."

"She's so young. Been through so much trauma."

We went in to eat. Dorothy told us Timothy and Anna went to an old friend's house. "They'll be back late. Tomorrow will be a new day, you'll see."

*     *     *     *

My hope for bonding as father and daughter rested in the contents of one brown envelope. DNA might prove our physical connection, but I wanted a deeper one, a soul connection. The diary told a story Anna needed to hear. I put it in her room before we went to bed.

The next morning, she came to breakfast carrying the brown envelope. "Can we talk about this?"

"You two go along," Kim said. "I'll help Dorothy finish in the kitchen."

I followed Anna into the courtyard, and stood there shifting my weight, hoping she didn't notice. After what seemed forever, she fumbled with the packet of paper. No sounds except an occasional sniffle. "You didn't rape her?"

"No. We loved one another. We even talked about marriage, but I had to go home"

"Why didn't you come back?"

"Because your mother and I agreed…"

"How could you do that if you loved one another?"

"Because we thought God wanted us to do the right thing. And, Kim and I…"

"You fell in love with my mother when you were married. Did you tell Kim when you got home?"

"Eventually. And we've spent a lot of time re-building our love."

More pacing. I tried to keep calm, but my heart started racing. Every question made me feel like the emperor with no clothes. "Kim seems like a good person. How could you betray her?"

"Your mother and I didn't plan to fall in love. But the first minute we met, something special happened—like we were soul mates."

"My mother told me that once—that my father and she were soul mates"

"She did?" I hadn't read that in her letters.

"Were you? Soul mates?"

"Do you know what a soul mate is?"

"She told me a soul mate is someone who makes your toes wiggle." I laughed. Anna smiled and melted the icy distance between us.

"And your tummy turn summersaults," I said.

"Yes, she told me that, too." Anna stopped pacing, not twelve inches from me. I almost whispered the rest.

"The last night I spent with your mother, she told me I made her toes wiggle. I told her she made my tummy turn summersaults. We decided we were soul mates."

"She said something about mysticalism or something, too."

"Mystical connection?"

"Something like that."

"Soul mates have something that starts with tingling toes, but it goes a lot deeper, to a place where words can't explain. For us, it felt like we'd loved one another all our lives."

"I don't think I understand all that yet."

"You don't need to. Some day."

"So you couldn't help it? You just fell in love?" I reached out and lifted her limp hand from where it hung by her side. I closed my two large ones around her small one, and smiled.

"Right. We couldn't help it. And because we couldn't, you were born."

"You never knew about me?"

"Not until your e-mail."

"Momma never wrote you?"

"Just what you've read." She put her other hand on top of mine. Tears rolled down four cheeks at once.

"I'm your daughter, for certain?"

"Yes, Anna, and I love you. You make my tummy tumble."

She looked up at me with something between sadness and a smile. "My toes aren't wiggling, but my heart sure is."

"Then we'd better hug, if it's okay with you." She nodded, so I wrapped my arms around her shoulders, resting my cheek on the top of her head. She wound her long thin arms around my middle, and lay her damp cheek against my chest. "We have so much to talk about, Anna. This isn't easy for any of us."

"Will I have to call Kim, 'Mother'?"

"No, but we'll need to talk about things like that. She already thinks you're special."

"Is she jealous? She must be. You have a daughter from another woman."

Anna seemed far more mature than I'd imagined. Margrethe did a marvelous job of helping her grow up. "Whatever Kim feels, we'll be able to talk about it. It took awhile, but she forgave me for falling in love with your mother."

"My mother told me God loves me just the way I am so I don't have to be perfect. I just do the best I can."

"Your mother was a wise woman. Maybe Kim and I can be that way, too."

She stepped back from the embrace and put on her "brave" face. "I want to call you 'Daddy' if that's alright."

"You can call me whatever you like." My chest rose, breathing in the wonder of someone calling me "Daddy." I knew we still had miles to go before we'd rest easy with this new bond, but we'd made it over a huge mountain. "Want to go see the others?"

"Not yet. Hold me a little longer. I've never had a father before."

\*　　　\*　　　\*　　　\*

Anna and I joined the others in the living room. She sat beside her uncle. "Are you going to take me away from Uncle Timothy?" I'd assumed if she accepted me as her father, she'd want to live with us. Not necessarily.

Kim reached out to touch Anna's hand. "We won't do anything you don't want. But we'd love to have you come to live with us." All the conversations we'd had since the e-mail arrived pointed to one thing: Kim wanted Anna for our daughter. Her mothering instincts overpowered any qualms she held about what Margrethe and I had done to create a child.

"Uncle Timothy and Aunt Maryjean have been my family almost all my life. I can't leave them. I don't want to go to America. Except…"

"Except what, Anna?" Kim asked with a catch in her voice.

"Except they won't let me leave with him."

I felt a cable of disappointment tighten around my chest. Kim wiped a tear away, smiling and patting Anna's hand. Kim could heal almost anything with her pat, pat, patting. I needed a million pats to relieve the growing despair. My daughter. I wanted to hold her and provide for her every need. But she didn't want to go home with us.

"We'll work things out, Anna. Don't worry. We'll always be your family." Timothy pulled her close, touching her cheek with the tenderness of a father. After breakfast, they went to their rooms, and Kim and I wandered into the courtyard. The humidity and heat of the day already made it uncomfortable.

"She's so mature, so beautiful, so not mine." Kim had carried the conversation during breakfast, drawing out Anna and Timothy and their disappointment about another separation. She seemed in control of the feelings I knew must be bubbling inside, and inspired me to do the same.

We'd heard Anna's wavering between wanting to stay, yet knowing the dangers; between wanting to see Disneyland, but preferring London. We'd reassured her we loved her and wanted the best, wherever it took her.

"She's not mine either—yet. We share the same genes, but…"

"I want to love her like my own. I want to forget what you did with her mother, but…" She collapsed into my arms, sobbing and limp. Somehow, even with all the pain, our bond deepened.

"I know. And I wish it were easier, but we knew it wouldn't be. We did the right thing in coming, and somehow, the right thing will happen tomorrow."

"I hope so, Jon, but we're asking her to give up the family and country she knows."

# CHAPTER 30

▼

Whether Anna would eventually live in London or Anaheim Hills—or even in Liberia—remained to be seen. She'd agreed to go home with us—for a while—and decide later about staying. Anna went with Dorothy and Kim to pick flowers from the garden.

Timothy and Bishop Hosea agreed to go with me to deal with the visa, "You've treated me with kindness beyond belief. I don't know how to say thank you for all you've done," I said.

The bishop shook his head. "Just go home and tell the story of what's happening here. Your people will respond. Food and medicine will come for our church. That's my reward. In an imperfect world, the imperfect do their best, and that's enough."

The government official protested, took the DNA report, left the room, returned, grumbled some more and then stamped her visa. Twenty hours before our plane left, everything fell into place. Except for Anna's feelings.

"I don't want to leave. I want to stay where Mamma died. I want to visit her grave and help take care of the sick children like she did. I want..."

The bishop, Kim, Anna and I sat around the kitchen table looking off into the tense space. I wanted to talk about what might happen when we got to America, but felt glad she talked about her mother.

Bishop Hosea's wisdom moved us from uneasy silence to hesitant conversation. "You must always say whatever you're feeling about your mother, Anna. You are going through a difficult time."

She smiled and said, "And next you'll say 'God is near.'"

We laughed. "I always do, don't I," the bishop said.

"Is there any way you two could stay here for awhile?" She looked from Kim to me and back again.

"I talked with Bishop Hosea about that yesterday. I told him I'm pretty good at hammering and painting, and know a lot about making gardens grow."

"Do you know about pawpaws and plaintain?" Anna's eyes brightened.

"Yes, I know you eat a lot of them." I noticed Anna tried not to laugh. "I could learn how to grow them, and I already know about sweet potatoes and a dozen kinds of lettuce and…"

"And I could teach music and cooking and…" Kim wanted to be part of the fun going on.

"I'd love to help re-build some churches and schools. And Kim will tell you about my experiments with new seeds in the garden. But…" I hesitated.

The bishop laughed. "Wouldn't that be fun? I know you must return to America for a while, of course. Anna deserves to see Disneyland, after all. But you know there will always be work for both of you here, and Anna can teach you more about Liberia than you can imagine, I'm sure."

By evening, Anna seemed to accept the idea of leaving with us, and began to ask questions about the beach and mountains, and was Los Angeles the same size as London, and did we have soccer in America, and did we get any television shows from England. We answered, "Yes," to everything and told her about our schools and churches and children her age in our neighborhood.

When she awoke the next day, Anna stood straight as a tree, drawing on her mother's instructions and London upbringing, took a deep breath, and said, "I'm ready to give it a go."

Kim took Anna's hand. "I can't replace your mother, or your aunt. But I will love you with all my heart, and keep you safe so some day you can get the training you need to come back to do what your mother did."

\*          \*          \*          \*

On the flight home, Anna and I talked about her mother while Kim dozed. I told her to ask questions about anything she didn't understand. She touched a delicate nerve. "Why didn't you and my mother use protection?"

Anna knew how to zero in on the basics. "We made a mistake, Anna. But that mistake turned into the beautiful and bright young lady sitting beside me."

Kim woke up and asked what I thought the Executive Board would do.

"I don't know. The church will do what it will do. Whatever comes, I know one thing for sure."

"What's that?" they asked together.

"I know I love you both. Nothing is more important to me."

"Will you lose your job because of me?" Anna looked worried.

"If I lose my job, it's because of me, not you. You haven't done anything but bring us a whole lot of joy. And if I do lose my job, we'll be okay. I can find work."

"But Bishop Hosea said Bishop Clemente said you were the best new bishop in the Lutheran church."

"Thank you, Anna. I love my calling as bishop. And I love you and Kim even more. God won't leave us without something important to do."

I didn't worry about the future. I could find work in the corporate world or better, in a non-profit advocacy agency for a while. Based on Bishop Hosea's invitation, Kim and I could always resign, sell the house and go back to Liberia.

What made the most sense to the three of us, decided somewhere over Colorado, involved the annual Leadership Conference. I'd already written my opening sermon focused on global mission, and now I had a beautiful daughter who wanted to "tell those guys" how they could help the church re-build in her home country. We'd announce whatever the Executive Board had decided at that time.

Whatever might happen, we'd made our decision. All our bold failing produced at least one wonderful outcome. For the first time in years, I felt clean and good, forgiven and free, and—transparent. I still didn't know for sure how to describe the term, but one thing came clear. Deceiving Kim and the church stood at the opposite end of whatever transparency meant.

\*       \*       \*       \*

We landed and sailed through customs without a problem. As we walked down the airport hallway, Kim started singing. "Jesus loves the little children…"

"I know that song." Anna joined in. "…All the children of the world, red and yellow, black and brown…" I tried, but my swollen throat kept most of the words from coming out.

I wondered if my e-mails had gone through. When we turned the corner to the baggage claim area, I had my answer. Kim interrupted her happy song. "Look, there's Janelle and Michelle and Mom and Dad and—why he's got a 'Welcome Granddaughter' balloon." A crowd of family and friends held up a dozen red and white balloons and a huge welcome sign. After the initial rush of excitement, I noticed they were wearing Angel tee-shirts with "2002 World

Champions" blazoned on their chests, and rally monkeys on their heads. When they saw us, several of them started beating their thunder sticks.

Anna held on to my arm, and looked up, eyes sparkling. "All this for us? I think I'm going to like it here."

"My Gosh," Kim said, "the Angels won the World Series. A miracle." Anna looked puzzled. "I'll explain later."

I stood there with my mouth open. "Amazing. The Angels win, and so do we. After all our failures." I looked around and saw Annette Jergens and Peter Bloch standing off to one side. When she saw Anna, Dr. Jergen's sober face broke into a huge smile. Peter Bloch blustered, pulled out his cell phone, and strode away.

# AFTERWORD

▼ ————————

Novel discussion groups grow in number each day. If you're not part of one, gather some friends and use any of these questions, or others, to start the discussion.

1.  With whom do you most identify in the book? Why?

2.  Who bothers you in the book? Why?

3.  What does "transparency" mean to you?

4.  Is transparency one of your values? What are some of your other values?

5.  What has happened to you because you kept a secret? Good things? Bad things?

6.  What do you believe about racism? Sexism? Where did you get your beliefs?

7.  What do you believe about the role of homosexual persons in society? Church?

8.  What have you found helpful to keep relationships vibrant?

9.  What losses have you suffered? What have you found helpful when you're sad?

10. If you could do one thing to make this a better world, what would it be?

# RESOURCES:

| | |
|---|---|
| Author, A.E. Nielsen | www.aenielsen.com |
| Alcoholics Anonymous | www.alcoholics-anonymous.org |
| Current News: search "Liberia" | www.reuters.com and |
| | www.allafrica.com/liberia |
| Fair Trade Coffee | www.fairtradefederation.com |
| LaLeche for breast-feeding mothers | www.lalecheleague.org |
| Lutheran World Relief: a reliable organization for information and for transmitting contributions for assistance to Liberia and other places | www.lwr.org |
| Lutheran World Federation for information about Lutheranism throughout the world | www.lutheranworld.org |
| Marriage Education Inventories | www.lifeinnovations.com |
| Marriage Education Resources | www.smartmarriages.com |
| Opera *Turandot* Synopsis | www.metopera. org/synopses/turandot.html |
| PFLAG—Parents, friends, and families of gay, lesbian, bi-sexual and transgendered persons: an organization for support, information and advocacy | www.pflag.org |
| Postpartum Support International | www.postpartum.net |

## Books about the Lutheran Church in Liberia:

*Payne, Bishop Roland J., *A Miracle of God's Grace*—A History of the Lutheran Church in Liberia (2000)

*Schmalenberger, Dr. Jerry, *Liberian Song* (1987), contact jlschmalen@aol.com

*Stull (now Schaffer), Betty, *A Trip to Liberia December 1988*—A journey in words and sketches, available from gpbgmb@aol.com

0-595-28802-2

Printed in the United States
1483500004B/215

9 780595 288021